THE
FALLEN
HERO

HERO IN PARADISE SERIES

BONZAI MOON

BonzaiMoon Books LLC
Houston, Texas
www.bonzaimoonbooks.com

Angel Vane has been entertaining readers with her brand of crime thrillers for women. Now you can get one of her novellas for FREE, you just need to go to the link and tell her where to send it:

GET MY FREE SHORT STORY NOW
https://BookHip.com/PJQDTT

Prologue

He inhaled deeply as the harpist began to play Pachelbel's Canon in D. As the sun sank below the horizon, the soft plucking swelled over the sound of the waves crashing onto the beach. A hidden gem enclave, Miami's Mid-beach provided an idyllic setting for the wedding. The day he would stand before God and his family and vow to love, honor and cherish the woman who'd changed his life completely.

Between the narrow expanse of dense foliage surrounding the boardwalk, the love of his life emerged.

Mena Nix.

Barefoot, she stepped down tentatively on the sand. Arm looped casually in her father's, she blessed him with the most brilliant smile. His heart skipped a beat. Dozens of their closest friends and family stood between the rows of white folding chairs. Cameras flashed as she passed down the aisle.

Mena was breathtaking. The white strapless gown clung to her svelte curves. From the moment he met her, he'd known he would never be the same. His only desire was to make her happier than she ever thought was imaginable.

Mena's eyes locked onto his as he gave a nod to her father, Caleb Olivier. Caleb gave a low grunt as he stepped away from his only daughter. Mena pressed her soft hands within his. Her eyes danced with excitement and pure unadulterated love. A love he probably didn't deserve.

The minister's words faded in his ears as he mouthed "I love you" to her. Mena giggled slightly, then blew him a kiss before responding softly, "I love you more."

Few men were lucky enough to find their soulmate. The one woman who gave life a new perspective and direction, a reason to be the best man he could be. He was lucky to have found Mena. Lucky that she saw the good in him and loved him in return. He vowed right then and there that he would never take her for granted. She was the most important person in the world to him. He would spend every minute of every day making sure she knew it.

"... do you take Mena to be your wife? Do you promise to love, honor, cherish, and protect her, forsaking all others, and holding only unto her forevermore?" The minister's words jolted him from his thoughts.

He squeezed her hands. "I do."

"Mena, do you take—"

A knock tapped lightly on the door.

Dr. Michael Marsh reached absently across the desk for his mouse and pressed pause on the video playing on the laptop. He stole one last glance at Mena. The camera focused on her beautiful face, caught in a slight smile as she stared back at him. She would look at him that way again. He would make sure of it.

Closing the laptop, Michael called out, "Come in."

His assistant poked her head in his office. "Sorry to disturb you, Dr. Marsh, but your two o'clock appointment is here early. Should I send him in or ask him to wait?"

Michael gestured for her to send him in.

She nodded, then disappeared for a moment before reappearing with a man behind her. "Dr. Tufa, please go inside. Dr. Marsh is expecting you."

Grabbing the laptop, Michael slipped the bronze key from the pocket of his white lab coat and unlocked the bottom drawer of his desk. Resting the laptop on top of the wedding photo album, he closed the drawer and pulled against the handle to check that the automatic locking device had triggered.

Dropping the key back in his pocket, he looked up as Dr. Tufa entered, closing the door behind him. Michael leaned back in his chair, appraising the man as he strode across the room with an air of confidence and defiant swagger. A demeanor not unlike his own. Guess it came with the M.D.

Michael had researched the Ethiopian doctor. Dr. Tufa could single-handedly pave the way for an expansion of Michael's human clinical trials with one generous donation.

Michael stood, reaching an arm across the desk to shake Dr. Tufa's hand. "Good to finally meet you in person."

"Likewise," Dr. Tufa responded, cool and distant.

Michael said, "I'm surprised at your interest in my research. It's not in your field of expertise, Dr. Tufa."

Dr. Tufa raised an eyebrow, a slight challenge in his gaze. "I've read the articles on your breakthrough protocols in several medical journals. Embryonic stem cells are the hallmark of the work you are doing. Isn't that correct?"

Embryonic stem cells were more than the hallmark, they were the single most important aspect of his work. Without the stem cells, his protocol wouldn't exist. But stem cell therapies still garnered scrutiny. Regulation of obtaining and using stem cells was Draconian and excessive, stymieing his ability to expand his human clinical trials to more patients.

Moving to the Rakestraw Blake Center in the Aerie Islands had solved half of his problems. The governmental oversight of medical advancements in the tiny island nation was liberal and relaxed, allowing cutting edge medical breakthroughs to flourish.

Now he just needed more financial backers to procure a continuous source of stem cells for his research.

"Yes, that is correct," Michael said.

"My family owns the largest portfolio of cryobanks in the world. We specialize in the storage of embryos for hundreds of thousands of couples desperately trying to have children. We also recognize that many couples will be burdened with the decision of what to do with excess embryos. While destruction is always an option, we counsel couples on alternative methods that exist. And we go the extra step to provide rewards to those who choose these alternative methods," Dr. Tufa explained.

"You give the couples a financial incentive to allow their unused embryos to be ..."

"Used in a manner to benefit human medical science in whatever way we see fit," Dr. Tufa said. "Which could prove lucrative, if we were to partner with you by providing embryonic stem cells for your trials."

Mind racing, Michael kept a calm expression on his face. Could he trust Dr. Tufa's offer? If something seemed too good to be true, it usually was, but this wasn't an opportunity Michael could afford to drag his feet on. What did he have to lose? "That's quite a generous offer."

Dr. Tufa held up a hand. "It's a strategic potential business transaction. You've only had one successful patient, is that correct?"

"He was a miraculous first case. After only three months on the protocol, he emerged from the coma with no loss of muscle function or memory. I monitor his progress monthly and have noted no adverse effects."

Michael thought about the former PC-5 gangster, Beaujean Ali. The man had barely survived the hit put on him by another faction of the gang, languishing in a coma for years. A revolving door of specialists had tried to do what Michael's protocol had done in a fraction of the time. But Michael feared that Ali was an outlier. He needed to test more patients to determine a more typical outcome.

"Any other patients?"

"A Navy SEAL who also suffered physical trauma and has been in a coma for about four years."

A crease rose on Dr. Tufa's forehead. "I didn't realize your work was limited to patients in comas from physical trauma."

"It isn't," Michael insisted. "Comas induced from physical traumas are more complex and difficult to treat. Other causes should respond even faster."

"And you've tested this?"

"Not yet," Michael reluctantly admitted. Twisting the band of his wedding ring around his finger, he fought the urge to curse under his breath.

"Would you be open to incorporating patients in comas from other causes into the clinical trials?"

"Of course, I would," Michael dropped his hands into his lap, waiting, hoping that Dr. Tufa would commit to sourcing the embryonic stem cells for his protocol.

"Then I would be happy to support your work, Dr. Marsh," Dr. Tufa said, rising from his chair. "I will have my assistant send you the paperwork to sign."

Michael rose and stepped closer to Dr. Tufa. "This is all upside for me, but what's in it for you, Dr. Tufa? What do you want in return for your generosity?"

Michael had no intention of sharing the credit for years of painstaking research with anyone. When his protocol was proved to be a success, the world would know only one doctor had been the brains behind it all.

"The ability to add patients to your clinical trials," Dr. Tufa responded, straightening the monogrammed cuff of his expensive white shirt. The diamond cuff link sparkled under the harsh florescent lights. "With ... *no* ... questions asked. Do we have a deal?"

Chapter One

Julian squeezed his eyes shut, rubbing his face as he took a deep breath. This was harder than he'd thought it would be. Harder than he ever expected, but he had to keep talking. Get it all out so he could move past the disappointment and the pain of being rejected by the woman he loved more than his own life.

It was the only way he could get their relationship back on track.

"She started to cry, and they weren't tears of joy, you know," Julian said, resting his hands on his lap as he leaned back in the worn cushioned chair. "I kept thinking, what the fuck is happening? This wasn't how it was supposed to go. But then, Mena had never minced words about marriage. She wasn't ready and yet, after everything we went through in Kenya ..."

Julian paused as an old man passed by, holding the hand of a small child. His soothing words explained why the kid's mommy still needed to be in this place. Pale blue walls enclosed the room, lit with halogen lighting. A window at each end let in a moderate amount of sunlight through the wide blinds.

Julian shook his head. "I did the only thing I could do to protect us both. I closed my hand around the ring and just pulled her into my arms. I never let her say the words. It would have fucking crushed everything in me to hear her say no. The next day, I returned the ring to the jeweler. We haven't talked about it since."

Julian glanced at the row of monitors lining the side of the hospital bed. Jagged lines jumped and zigzagged across the screen. A discordant melody of intermittent beeping increased, then slowed.

Years had passed since he'd last seen his best friend, Broman Garrison. Getting the courage to visit Broman was easier now that he was in the Aerie Islands. Broman had been accepted into a coveted experimental clinical trial at the Rakestraw Blake Center. Broman's wife, Dawn, had sold her Jacksonville home. She lived in a small bungalow in St. Basil with her adopted son, Elliott, and made the trek out to the RBC several times a week.

Picking at a string on his jogging pants, Julian continued, "I don't know what this means for our relationship, but I can't ... I won't walk away from Mena. I don't want to go back to being that guy I was before she was in my life. Man, I don't understand how you did it. How you just walked away from Sunny when you loved her so much. I get it. She lied to you. She didn't want you to know that she'd hooked up with your best friend before she met you. Hell, I didn't want you to know either because I saw how in love you were with her. Sometimes, I look back and wished I'd lied to you too. Pretended like I'd never met her before. Would that have made things better? Who knows? Anyway, I saw her when we moved to Nairobi. She's made a great life for herself, runs this top-notch private executive security firm. I worked with them for a while, which helped when Mena was kidnapped. But that's a story for another day. Don't want to pile too much on you in one visit. I'll tell you all about that and running into Tubeec Hirad next time."

Julian leaned back in his chair. Whatever treatment Broman was receiving here, Julian could already tell a difference. Four years ago, after undergoing dozens of surgeries, Broman had been thin and frail, a shadow of his former self.

Looking at him now, he was much the same as he'd been before the ambush in Central Sulawesi. He'd gained weight and appeared muscular and strong, ready to take on the world again, if he could just open his eyes.

Julian would give anything to have his best friend back. The Broman he grew up knowing and loving like a brother had to still be in there somewhere.

Glancing at his watch, Julian couldn't believe he'd been here talking to Broman for almost an hour. The room was still and quiet.

The chair legs scraped against the tile floor as Julian moved closer to the bed. He stared at Broman for a long moment. His dreadlocks had been cut off, hair trimmed to a low fade. Dawn would catch hell from Broman if he woke up and saw his beloved locks gone.

If he woke up.

When he woke up.

Julian would have to decide whether to be honest about what happened in Central Sulawesi. Could he tell his best friend that he alone was the reason four SEALs had died? That he was the reason Broman had lost four years of his life?

As much as he thought he'd moved past that horrible moment, the guilt lingered. It wasn't just that he'd led El Mago's rebels to their base. It was how he'd taken the time to corrupt the evidence of his actions on that laptop before checking on his team. That haunted him the most.

SEALs knew that every mission could be their last.

But one of their own leading them to slaughter and covering up the crime wasn't in any SEAL playbook.

"I hope you'll be able to forgive me," Julian said, then pushed away from the bed.

"Friend of Broman's?" A male voice wafted from behind him.

Julian turned and faced the Black man wearing the signature crisp white lab coat of doctors at the Rakestraw Blake Center. He was a bit shorter than Julian, with deep brown skin and hazel eyes. "Yeah. Are you his doctor? The hotshot from New York City?"

"Hotshot? Hadn't heard that one before. Miracle worker is what they usually call me."

"Is that right?" Julian frowned.

"Seriously, I just do what I can to help people in need." The doctor shrugged, then laughed, extending his hand. "I'm Mike."

Julian shook it. "Dr. Mike."

"How about just Mike." Slipping his stethoscope around his neck, the doctor glanced down at the clipboard, then back at Julian. "Glad to see he's getting some more visitors other than his wife. He can hear you, so keep coming and talking to him."

"You sure about that?" Julian asked.

"It's a big topic of debate, but I've seen too much evidence to support it in my career. Take the first patient I had on this protocol, for instance. One of the nurses took a liking to him and told him stories about her struggles with dating and the like. When he woke up, he asked for her by name and gave her some advice about her love life. He didn't really understand why he felt compelled to, but I know it's because he heard her talking to him all that time."

Julian looked away, studying the webbed pattern in the marble floor tiles. "Is the protocol working for Broman? He looks a lot better than the last time I saw him."

"Everything is slower with Broman than my first patient, but I suspect Broman is presenting a more typical trajectory that can be expected for the average patient who'd receive the protocol. The first patient came out of the coma after three months of treatment," Mike explained.

"Why did your first patient responded quicker to the treatment? Any theories? Anything we can do to speed up the process?"

"Many times, it's about what's driving the patient internally," Mike said.

"What got the other patient to wake up faster?"

"I'm not one to gossip, but it's more than an educated guess that he woke up to get revenge on the man who put him in the coma."

Chapter Two

"You don't look so confident anymore," Mena said, easing into the plush chair.

Nash Iverson scratched absently at his temple as he stared out the window. He'd been optimistic when she'd hired him a few weeks ago to represent her in the divorce from Michael. Mena was grateful to find an attorney on the islands that was also licensed to practice law in Florida. It was a good sign, or so she had thought.

"The ruling was upheld," said Nash, shaking his head. "Despite my efforts to explain why you shouldn't need to divorce your husband, the judge confirmed the earlier decision. Your marriage to Michael is valid."

"How can he get away this? It doesn't make in sense."

"No, it doesn't. Your husband is very well connected. I've never seen a precedent like this before that would trap you in a marriage with a man that was, for all intent and purposes, a polygamist. Yet, he has two judges willing to side with him."

"You think he paid them off?"

"He had to have done something to get this outcome," Nash leaned over the desk toward Mena. "The ruling is bizarre, to say the least."

"What's my next move then? How do I get out of this marriage?" Mena raised a shaky hand to her throbbing hand.

"One of you has to be a resident of Florida for at least six months before you can file for divorce. Michael moved to New York almost a year ago. You haven't lived in the States for four years."

"To be free of Michael, I need to move back to Florida? Pause the life I have here. Walk away from my career, my ..." Mena took a deep breath. She couldn't let Julian find out about this. Not when their relationship was already on shaky ground since she didn't answer his marriage proposal.

"Florida is a no fault state. He'd have a hard time finding a legitimate reason to contest the divorce. You could be free in six months. It's not that long of a time period," Nash explained.

"If Michael doesn't do something else to manipulate a judge or create some stall tactic, right?"

"Right."

Mena's cell phone rang. Reaching into her purse, she glanced at the screen. It was Julian.

"Nash, I have to go. But please check and see if there are any other options that don't involve me moving from St. Basil," Mena said.

"I'm sorry. There are no other options, Mena. You have to move back to Florida." Nash held the door open for her.

Resigned to the truth she hadn't wanted to accept, Mena rushed out of the Iverson Law Office and answered the phone.

"Where are you?" Curiosity simmered in Julian's smooth baritone.

"I should ask you the same thing." Mena secured the cell phone between her ear and shoulder. Julian had left the condo early this morning while she was still sleeping. Instead of waking up in his arms, she'd been alone. Panic had gripped her for a moment as guilt washed over her. Two months had passed, and she still hadn't explained to Julian why she'd freaked out when he proposed to her. Why she couldn't marry him. She'd thought that was going to be the end of their relationship, but he'd surprised her once again. Everything had returned to normal almost immediately. Julian kept being the amazing man she loved, and she kept being the woman who was lying to him.

"You skipped breakfast, I see," Julian said, laughing slightly under his breath.

Mena stepped inside the elevator within the Heritage Center and pressed the button for the third floor, where the Office of the District Attorney was housed. "What does breakfast have to do with why you left me this morning without saying goodbye?"

The elevator door closed, and she leaned against the wall, waiting for his explanation.

"I left the note on the milk carton, so you'd see it when you ate your cocoa puffs," Julian said.

"So, if I had indulged in my normal sugar laden breakfast, I would have found out exactly where my man had disappeared to. That's what you're saying?"

"I like that."

"You like what?" Mena stepped forward as the elevator door opened.

"You said, 'my man.' I am yours, completely forever. You know that right?"

Heat flushed against Mena's cheeks. Would he still say that if he knew he came home every night to a married woman? "Yeah, I know."

"Good. I'm in the Aerie Islands. Broman's treatment starts at nine each morning, so I wanted to get here before then to see him," Julian explained.

Mena heard the soft rustling of waves crashing in the background. "I'm glad you finally visited him. How was it?"

"Hard as hell and easier than I expected. This treatment protocol has him looking healthier than ever. For a minute, I thought he'd wake up and want to go dirtboarding," Julian said.

"One day the two of you will do that again," Mena said. The clinical trial was supposed to be groundbreaking and Broman had a good chance of waking up within the next year.

"Ferry is here. I have to go through security," Julian said, then paused. "Where did you say you were?"

"I didn't," Mena teased as she strolled down the wide hallway toward the door at the end of the hall.

"Keeping secrets from me?" Julian asked, a playful hint in his tone.

His words were like daggers to Mena. She inhaled sharply. "Of course not. The D.A.'s assistant called this morning. I need to sign off on the release of my medical records for the trial. Then I'm headed to work."

"Well, don't stay too late. I have a surprise for you tonight. Try to get home by seven if you can," Julian said.

"What kind of surprise?"

"You'll see tonight."

Mena slipped the cell phone into her purse. Reaching for the door, she stepped inside and bumped into a man exiting the District Attorney's Office.

"I am so sorry," Mena said, bracing herself against him to stop from toppling over. She glanced up into the man's face. "Norman? Norman … Gale?"

"Mena Nix, we meet again but under less than ideal circumstances this time. How is your Fellowship at the Tribal Museum going?" Norman asked.

Regaining her balance, Mena hid her surprise that he remembered her. She followed him into the hallway. When she'd introduced herself to Norman at the fundraiser for Kenyan President Thairu months ago, he'd been less than cordial. Finding out they both had worked for Priscilla Dumay had made him aloof. Now he seemed more willing to talk.

Mena responded, "I decided to end it early." She spared him details of the kidnapping she endured with Wangari Irungu.

"Africa isn't for everybody. I found the climate too oppressive to live there full time. That's why I took another position at Wangari's new Museum for African Art in Amsterdam instead. Living near the red-light district was just an added perk." Norman smirked. "Where are you working now?"

Mena avoided his gaze, staring at the pale pink polish on her freshly manicured nails. This was the last question she wanted to answer, but why should she keep it a secret? She didn't need to be ashamed of the choice she'd made. "I'm back at the Genesis Gallery. It has a new owner now. Things are going extremely well."

"How brave of you to go back to the scene of the crimes. I suppose you'll be testifying against Priscilla tomorrow."

"Yes, I am. Are you a witness for the prosecution, too?"

"Well, I damn sure wouldn't be a witness for that bitch. I never wanted to set foot back on this God-forsaken island, but I was subpoenaed," Norman admitted.

"Why? You were long gone by the time any of this came to light—"

"I was the first one to bring it to light. I found a pregnant woman in the basement of the Genesis Gallery the year I was fired. I'm guessing only a few months before Priscilla hired you to take my place," Norman said.

"Wait a minute. Are you saying that you knew what she was doing? All this time?" Mena asked.

"No, I had no clue Priscilla was selling genetically modified babies to infertile couples. But I knew that there was a kidnapped woman desperate to escape from the Genesis Gallery. I found her and tried to get her to go to the police. She refused and disappeared, but I told the cops what I'd seen anyway," Norman said.

"What happened when you told the cops?"

"What do you think happened? The cops found nothing. I looked like a fool. Priscilla made me pay for telling what she was really doing at the Genesis Gallery. I had to move to Africa to get a gallery to hire me again. Priscilla made sure of that," Norman explained.

"Well, I'm glad you're here. Your testimony will help strengthen the case against Priscilla," Mena said.

Norman scoffed. "I doubt that. The D.A.'s case is not strong. He's running out of witnesses. Another surrogate was found dead the other day."

"Are you serious? That's what? Four now?"

"Try six. A couple of suicides, but there seems to be a pattern of cardiac arrest that's developing in the others. Of course, the autopsies reveal nothing that points to Priscilla's involvement. But think about it. She's the one with the most to gain."

"Not many surrogates left." That was an enormous blow to the case against Dumay.

"One of the assistant D.A.'s told me that the three surrogates willing to testify are getting antsy," Norman explained. "That leaves your testimony and mine. But it's our word against hers. I have no proof she was behind anything and I'm guessing you don't either."

"The jury has to see that all of us can't be wrong. We have no reason to lie," Mena insisted, though she was worried. A year ago, the case had seemed airtight and now things had taken a one-hundred-eighty-degree turn.

"All she needs is reasonable doubt. With only three of the surrogates testifying, it's going to be a lot easier for her to pull off than any of us imagined."

"You think she'll be acquitted," Mena said, bothered by Norman's perspective. As much as she didn't want to agree with him, she could see how it could happen.

"I do, and when it happens, you and I better watch our backs. She'll be coming after us even harder than before."

Chapter Three

Mena crossed the open lobby of the executive level of the Genesis Gallery. The soft tapping of her heels on the glossy floor echoed through the space. The traditional decor routed in island colonialism had been erased, replaced by modern twenty-first century sleek design with accents of Caribbean culture. For someone who had very little experience in art, Mena had marveled at Beaujean Ali's progressive vision for the museum. The entire staff was inundated with his drive to relaunch the gallery to focus not just on historical art pieces, but to showcase contemporary ethnographic art. Being part of the change had made leaving behind the Fellowship at the Tribal Museum easier.

Rounding the corner, Mena passed by Irving Bond's former office that now had her name emblazoned on the outside and made a beeline for the office of Omar Johnson, the new museum director and her best friend. She slipped through the narrow open of the partially closed door and plopped down in one of the cool turquoise chairs in front of his desk.

"No, ma'am. I don't have time for you right now," Omar said, raising a finger in the air and wagging it at Mena. "You roll into work three hours late and you're already up here trying to distract me."

Mena pressed a hand against her chest, feigning surprise. "I would never try to distract you from your work. But every brilliant museum director needs to take a mini break to grab lunch. And how did you know I was late, anyway?"

"Our boss was on the rampage looking for you and you weren't in your workshop. I heard security giving him an update when you finally arrived," Omar said. "You in trouble, boo."

Mena frowned. "Any idea why he wanted to see me?"

"Nope, and I don't even have time to speculate. Beaujean moved up the opening of Quark's permanent exhibit by two weeks. I'm about to lose my mind trying to make sure we'll be ready," Omar complained.

"Brilliant move, if you ask me. Coincides with the ten-year anniversary of Quark's signature piece that catapulted him onto the art scene," Mena said. *The Coward and the Cow* was still one of the most impressive works of Caribbean inspired neo-expressionism paintings, taking the torch from greats like Basquiat.

"Ain't he brilliant? And sexy, too. Don't tell Charlie I said that. He's already sensitive about me working so close with Beaujean," Omar said.

"Come on, I don't want to eat lunch by myself," Mena whined, twirling a strand of her dark hair between her fingers. "I need your advice on how to make things right between me and Julian. He says he's planning some kind of surprise for me tonight."

Omar slammed his pencil onto the desk and leaned toward her. "This is the only advice you need. Even though you didn't give that man an answer to his marriage proposal, despite the fact that you love him more than anybody on this planet, which I still don't understand, he stood by you. He didn't make demands or pressure you. That's the kind of man you keep, especially since he's rich now. Stop worrying. You don't need to do anything to keep a man that refuses to lose you. Now get out of here."

Mena stifled a smile. She knew Omar would make her feel better. "Fine. I'll get Regina to go to lunch with me."

"Do not bother her. She's triple checking inventory of Quark's pieces for the exhibit, and I need that done in the next two hours."

"Both of you suck," Mena said as she left his office. Glancing toward Regina's desk, she saw her other best friend with her head down pouring over numerous spreadsheets. Mena would have to grab lunch from the Genesis Grill and eat alone again.

Ten minutes later, she arrived at the lush entrance to the restaurant located adjacent to the gallery. The gate was adorned with hibiscus bushes with blooming flowers in bold yellows, magentas and pinks. The restaurant had always been one of her favorite places on the property. Another perk introduced by the new boss: employees ate at all gallery restaurants for free. He was even building two more casual dining options for the average tourist who visited the campus.

Mena waived at the hostess and skirted around a group of severe looking men overdressed in business suits during the heat of midday. A quick glance at the posted sign near the private dining enclaves explained it—Area Reserved for North American Neurology Conference Speakers and Panelists. Mena headed to the right, toward the bar, and away from the growing crowd of doctors and hospital administrators filing into the restaurant.

Leaning against the bar, she lifted a menu from the edge and perused the section for the daily specials.

"Salmon croquettes were always one of your favorites. I hear the chef's version is divine. Probably still won't hold a candle to your mom's though."

The hairs on the nape of Mena's neck stood on end. Dread slithered down her spine.

North American Neurology Conference.

Neurology.

No.

This could not be happening.

Chapter Four

"It's good to see you," Michael said, sliding onto the barstool next to her. Handsome as ever, Dr. Michael Marsh's bright hazel eyes danced as he looked at her. "I knew you worked at the gallery, but never thought I'd be lucky enough to run into you while I was on the island."

It had been two months since Michael had crushed her with the devastating news that they were still married. She'd hoped he'd lied or been mistaken. A few weeks later, the lawyer she'd hired confirmed she was still legally Mrs. Michael Marsh. Her attempts to get Michael to sign divorce papers had been met with staunch resistance. He wanted to convince her to give him another chance, even though she'd made it clear that there was no future for them. Not now. Not ever. But here he was in St. Basil, her home with Julian.

"How long are you here?" Mena pushed the words from her lips. She wouldn't make a scene. She had to keep her cool or become the fodder for museum employee gossip by the end of the day.

"Another week or so. I'm on the committee for the conference that starts next week. We're here early to make sure everything will go smoothly. Record attendance this year. I think it's because of this gorgeous location. Have a drink with me." Michael beckoned for the bartender. "Bishop's X.O. dark rum straight and a glass of pinot noir for the lady."

A flush of heat warmed Mena's neck. Their signature order from years ago, bar hopping in Miami and along South Beach. How many times had they shared these drinks with each other in the past? Too many to count.

"Forgive me for being nostalgic, but I couldn't help myself," Michael said.

The bartender sat the tumbler in front of him and then turned and slid the wine glass toward Mena. She would need the liquid courage sitting in front of her to endure a trip down memory lane. Tipping her glass toward Michael, she took a sip as a hint of a smile played on his lips.

"Guess it's too much to hope you've come to your senses and will sign off on the divorce papers while you're on the island," Mena said, turning towards Michael.

"Just like it's too much to hope that you've told your new boyfriend that you're a married woman." Michael gulped the rum in one motion, then rested the glass on the bar.

"You're delaying the inevitable," Mena said.

"So are you. Tell me. Why haven't you moved back to Florida? Six months isn't a long time, and with it being a no-fault state, I'd be hard pressed to come up with ways to contest the divorce. You could be a free woman in that short time. For some reason, though, you haven't done that. Can't help but get hope from—"

"Six months? If you agree to sign the papers, I can get our divorce processed right here in St. Basil in six hours," Mena said. "Why should I disrupt my entire life just to be free of you?"

"I'm not trying to disrupt your life. I'm sorry for everything I put you through," Michael said. He raised a single finger, and the bartender rushed over to refill his glass of rum.

"It doesn't matter anymore," Mena said, annoyed. Michael had some nerve to show up on the island where she lived and try to force her to listen to his apology. Saying sorry wouldn't change everything that happened between them. How he destroyed her faith in love and her trust in men. She only got both back when she'd met Julian and realized what real unconditional love was.

"It does to me. I still remember the red strapless dress you wore when we first met. When you came up to the bar, I would have sworn you were one of the models prepping to walk the runway on the beach that night. We laughed. We talked for hours."

"I thought you were a kind bartender taking pity on the girl whose purse had been stolen in the crowd," Mena said, remembering the night like it was yesterday.

"I didn't let you think that for long. The truth came out when ... I'd gotten you safely back to your apartment," Michael said, a slyness in his gaze.

The truth had come out the morning after they'd had sex in her apartment. Mena hadn't been able to resist the charismatic bartender, his chivalry, the late night conversation on the beach as the sun rose over the ocean or the blistering sexual attraction building between them. The neurologist subbing in as a bartender for his friend. Back then, it seemed like the perfect beginning for some romantic comedy.

A romantic comedy that turned tragic. If she could go back in time, she would never have allowed him to walk her home that night. How her life could have been changed if she'd just made a different choice.

"We were perfect back then and we could be again. The next morning, when I held you in my arms and you told me why honesty was so important to you, something in me broke. Everything you felt about how you were conceived. That changed me."

Mena's teenage years had been rocked by learning her father was an award-winning journalist who cheated on his wife during a month-long whirl-wind romance with her mother. Her mother had been devastated when she'd learned the truth and had left the island. Months later, her mother realized she was pregnant. At sixteen, Mena finally learned the truth. From that moment, she refused to tolerate liars or cheaters in any of her relationships.

"It didn't change you enough. You still duped me into the same situation. Being lied to and manipulated by a married man just like my mother," Mena said, gulping more of the wine. "I shared everything with you, Michael, and all you did was lie to me over and over again."

"That's what I've been trying to get you to understand. When you told me about your mom, I knew my situation. I was wrong for having multiple wives at the same time. But there was no way I was letting you walk out of my life. I needed to see you again. To be with you. You were my future," Michael said, his eyes pleading. "By the time we were on our third date, I had put everything in place. If Courtney hadn't been a lunatic, I would have been divorced, free to be with the most amazing woman I'd ever met."

Cringing, Mena reached for the wine glass. It was empty. Setting it back on the bar, she tried to ignore the earnestness in Michael's words. She couldn't forget that he was a master manipulator, twisting the truth to fit the story he wanted others to believe.

Mena said, "Maybe things would have been different if you'd told me back then you were married or separated or something. But you didn't."

"I never wanted to lose you. You and I had the commitment, the love, the family that I'd always wanted. The kind that is worth risking everything to keep and to hold on to. You have to understand why I can't just let you go without a fight," Michael said.

"My love is not something you can win in a fight, Michael. You never had a stable family, not once in your entire life growing up."

Bouncing from foster home to foster home, he'd fallen in love with families repeatedly, but never had the chance to stay with any of them for very long. Mena felt sorry for what Michael had to endure during his childhood. But that didn't excuse the lies he'd told her.

Mena continued, "So, when you were an adult, you made sure you always had a backup family and a backup to the backup by marrying multiple women. You were determined to never lose your family again—"

"Until I met you," Michael said.

Mena shook her head. "You let me believe that I was free to fall in love with you, when I wasn't. You knew you were married to three other women while I was falling in love with you. That wasn't fair to me."

"Now, I guess you're the one not being fair," Michael said, resting an elbow on the bar as he stared at her.

"What does that mean?"

"To Julian Montgomery." Michael spat the name as if it was something foul in his mouth.

Mena recoiled, his words slamming into her. She inhaled sharply.

"Funny how the situations can turn. You are lying to someone you say you love. You're no different from me. We are the same, Mena. I can't give up on you and you want to know why? Because there was a time when you were head-over-heels in love with *me*. You swore to love *me* in good times and bad, but now you look at me with contempt and can't forgive me. When Julian learns the truth about you, that you are still married and you didn't tell him, his feelings will change too. He won't forgive you either."

Pushing against the bar, Mena slid off the bar stool and stood.

Michael's hand gripped her forearm, pulling her back toward him.

Mena snatched her arm from his grasp. "Don't touch me."

"And when he leaves you, I'll be here waiting to love you like you were meant to be loved."

"I don't want you or your love."

Michael's arm slithered around her waist. His hot breath burned against her face as he pressed against her.

"Love can make people do things they wouldn't normally do," Michael whispered in her ear, then pressed his lips against the side of her head. "We will never be over."

Mena writhed within his grasp, struggling to get free. "Let go of me."

A command, forceful and intense, came from behind her. "You heard the lady. Let her go."

Chapter Five

Hand trembling, Mena struggled to calm herself as she pressed a finger against the biometric lock on the door and entered the Conservators Workshop. The cluttered desks of her team of four conservators had been left in disarray when they went to lunch. She was grateful none of them had returned yet, giving her at least a few moments of peace to collect her thoughts after the run-in with Michael.

"You forgot your lunch."

Mena flinched. "I didn't order lunch."

"Really? Well, here's a salad, anyway. Can't have my Head Conservator lacking energy to get her work done." Beaujean Ali, the new owner of the Genesis Gallery, dropped the to-go container onto her desk, then crossed his arms over his chest.

Uneasy, Mena struggled with what to say. After moments of uncomfortable silence, Mena said, "Thank you for stepping in back there."

Beaujean took a long look at her. Too long of a look. Mena grew tense and uncomfortable under the scrutiny.

"What was that about?" asked Beaujean.

Mena swallowed and took a deep breath. "My past coming back to haunt me. That guy knows things that could hurt someone I love, and I'm not sure what to do about it."

She wasn't sure why she'd just revealed something so personal to her new boss. Something about his tone warned her that lying or trying to evade his question wouldn't be in her best interest.

"How about some simple advice."

Mena was quiet, relieved that he didn't ask any more probing questions about Michael.

"Secrets hurt the most when you find them out from someone else instead of the person you love. If that guy knows something about you that's as bad as I'm guessing it is, then you need to be the one to tell it. All of it. Leaving nothing out. Then let the chips fall. The results might surprise you."

"Pretty wise advice from an art gallery owner," Mena whispered, slumping down into a nearby chair. It was advice she wasn't ready to take. Deep down, she truly believed she could convince Michael to sign the divorce papers and end her marriage without Julian ever finding out. If she'd just contacted an attorney back then and officially filed for an annulment, maybe she wouldn't be in this mess right now.

"Learn from my mistakes. Things could be very different for me if I hadn't lied to the woman I loved. Different for her too," Beaujean said. A dark sadness settled on him, likely from the pain of whatever memories he was reliving. Mena wondered what secrets haunted her new boss. Could they be worse than her own?

Beaujean continued, "You know, I found out a lot about you in the HR records. Can't help but wonder if the incident at the Genesis Grill was related to the terrible things you experienced while working here before."

"What things?" Mena asked.

"Apparently there was a pregnant woman who showed up at the gallery late one night. She held a gun to your head and took you hostage. Then you delivered her baby on the side of the road," Beaujean said.

"Who knew my HR file was that accurate." Mena couldn't hide the sarcasm in her voice. Back then, she'd trusted Priscilla to keep those details from being known by the rest of the staff. She guessed she shouldn't be surprised that they were all documented in her personnel records. Those events felt like a lifetime ago.

"Whatever happened to the pregnant woman and the baby?"

"Priscilla Dumay sent a hit man to murder her," Mena deadpanned.

"Sorry, I shouldn't have been so blunt. I'm sure you've heard about Priscilla's crimes, how she sold genetically altered babies to infertile couples."

Beaujean nodded. "She used surrogates to give birth to the babies."

"Unwilling surrogates. All the women who gave birth to babies had been kidnapped by Zak Webber on Priscilla's orders," Mena explained.

"Even the woman who held the gun on you?" Beaujean asked.

"Ella and two other surrogates were held hostage in the basement of the gallery. That night, she'd been desperate to escape and get her freedom back. After she gave birth, she left the baby behind. I'm guessing it's because he wasn't her biological child. Some kind of way, Zak found her and killed her before she could tell the cops what was going on," Mena said.

Beaujean stepped away from the desk and walked toward the window. "That's tragic."

"It's one of the reasons I'm so committed to testifying against Priscilla tomorrow. She has to pay for her crimes. She can't terrorize and kill people and get away with it."

"She won't," Beaujean said, then turned to face Mena. "Tell me about Uma Fischer, your former assistant. Where is she now?"

"I don't know," Mena stammered, confused by Beaujean's abrupt change in subject. "You realize she worked with the former Director of the gallery to replace stolen art with forgeries."

"I also heard she tried to get a job at a few other galleries and museums and no one would give her a second chance," Beaujean said.

"You want to hire her back at the gallery? She wasn't even that great of a conservator," Mena said.

"I believe in second chances," Beaujean said. "Find her. Let her know she's welcome to come back if she's interested."

"I don't think that's a good idea," Mena said.

"I didn't ask you what you thought. I asked you to find her and give her the offer."

Bristling, Mena nodded. "I'll see what I can do."

Chapter Six

Wind rushed through the open accordion doors leading out to the balcony that traversed the entire length of the living room of Penthouse Suite A. The warm breeze wafted across Julian's face as he leaned over the wrought iron carved railing. He gazed at the hypnotic, deep blue Caribbean waters stretching far into the distance. The low hum of carefree partygoers wafted up from seven floors below, the beginning of revelry as the sun began to set.

Harmony Towers was at the apex of the upscale St. Basil Entertainment District, where Bishop Avenue and King Street intersected. Lined with ritzy shops, trendy clubs and the best restaurants, it was the premier location to live on the island. Julian had snagged the prime real estate in Harmony Towers after a month's long bidding war between him and three other potential buyers. He'd overpaid for the penthouse, but he didn't regret it.

It was a place for him and Mena to call home. A way for him to show the woman he loved how committed he was to their relationship, even in the wake of her meltdown over his marriage proposal. The multi-million dollar pay out for saving Wangari Irungu's life was more than enough to fund the new lifestyle he shared with Mena.

Julian leaned back, glancing inside the living room at the clock mounted on the wall. A twenty-two thousand dollar addition to the decor purchased on a whim after seeing Mena's face light up as they perused the stores on King Street. It was half-past eight and Mena still wasn't home.

Tomorrow, they'd face Priscilla Dumay head-on, testifying in her trial. But tonight, he wanted to give Mena an escape to relax her and take her mind off everything. A subtle chasm still existed between them, almost two months after his proposal, despite all his efforts to reassure her. She wasn't ready to get married. He knew it was tearing her up inside to let him down. In her mind, she thought he'd end their relationship because she didn't want to be a wife again. Each day, in little ways, he could feel her seeking assurances that he wasn't going to walk out on her. It damn near broke his heart.

Her divorce wasn't a subject she'd opened up to him about. At first, he didn't care about the details. He didn't want to think about her committing to be some other man's devoted wife before friends, family and God. The thought of it left a sour taste in his mouth.

Now, he wanted to know why. What had happened between her and her first husband that turned her so completely off the institution of holy matrimony?

And why couldn't his love for her, the unconditional love they shared, get her past that pain?

She knew his darkest secret. The mistake he'd made that could land him in prison for the rest of his life. Opening up to her had been the hardest decision he'd ever made. No one else knew what he'd done. He was blessed that she saw past the arrogance and selfishness of his actions and still believed in him. She still loved him, despite his flaws.

Didn't she know that she could trust him with her past?

Or was he pushing for access to a past that would do nothing but harm them in the future?

He wasn't sure, but he was going to try again to eliminate the undercurrent of strain and tension that his marriage proposal had created. He didn't regret telling her that he wanted nothing more than to be her husband. But marriage never was and would never be a deal breaker for him.

Tonight, he would make it clear that he loved Mena no matter what. Living the rest of his life with her, on whatever terms she was comfortable with, was the only thing he needed.

The door shut behind him.

Julian glanced over his shoulders as Mena stood in the center of the foyer.

She stepped out of her strappy sandals and wiggled her toes in the rose petals that covered the floor. Placing her purse on the kitchen island, she headed toward the dining table, adorned with fine china place settings. A bouquet of purple and red roses rested in the center. Mena ran her fingers along the edge of the table, her face illuminated by the cascading candles burning brightly on towering tiered stands. She finally looked toward him.

"All this for me?" Mena asked.

"You're worth it," Julian said, walking into the chilled air of the penthouse.

Julian pulled her into a tight embrace, kissing her hair softly. "Chef Gilbert Farrell has prepared all your favorites."

"A celebrity chef has made our dinner?"

"Only the best for you. I'll text him and the food will be up here in twenty minutes," Julian said.

"Not yet," Mena said. She gripped his hand and placed it on her bare thigh. Guiding his hand beneath her pencil skirt, Julian allowed his fingers to slide across her skin until his palm rested against her mound. Slipping his fingers beneath her thong, he felt the hot moistness. His cock twitched in anticipation of what was to come.

Mena pressed her body against his. "I need you to take care of me first. Can you do that?"

Julian fondled her as his head leaned toward her mouth. Mena's lips met his with a blistering kiss that stoked every fire burning within him. His cock threatened to burst through his sweatpants, but he held himself in check. Tonight wasn't about a quick fuck. No, he was going to take his time and savor every single moment. Her body was his to explore and tantalize and lose himself in completely.

He trailed his hands along the length of her. The undulating curves of her hips, her tight ass and soft thighs. Fingering the button on the back of her pencil skirt, he freed her of the garment, pushing it down to the floor. Mena slipped her jacket off and pulled her silk shell over her head, flinging it over to the couch. She stood before him in her lacy underwear with no barriers between them.

He slid a finger over the turquoise lace that complimented her deep brown skin, mesmerized by her ample breasts threatening to spill out of her sexy bra. A little more force against the fabric and he'd freed the girls from their constraint. Dipping his head low, his tongue stroked one nipple and then the other, moving between the two as Mena moaned. Her hands laced within his hair as she held his face in place. The heady scent of sandalwood and orange wafting from her was driving him wild with desire. He plunged one breast into his mouth, sucking hard as he gripped her ass. Their bodies grinded against each other until his manhood was almost strangled within his pants.

Mena sensed his growing need and released his cock, her hand stroking the shaft as he devoured her other breast. As her moans grew in intensity, his dick grew harder until his mind was completely consumed with being inside of her. Easing her body down onto the pillows crowding sofa, he gripped the edge of her thong and eased the skimpy fabric down to the floor. Mena spread her legs, giving him an amazing view. For a split second, he debated whether to taste her before making love to her. His cock won the battle. He thrust inside her. The warm slick wetness welcomed his entry as he began slow methodical strokes, building the friction between them.

A moan caught in Mena's throat. "Julian."

Julian glanced up at the dazed passion burning in her eyes.

"Don't torture me like this," Mena whispered as her breathing increased in intensity.

Julian gripped Mena's hands, pushing her arms above her head as he pulsed faster and harder. Their bodies pounded against each other. Mena cried out with each thrust, her body accepting all of him within her. Jolts of ecstasy blazed through him as her warmth tightened around him. Pleasure increased like waves crashing onto the shore, one after the other, as he lost himself in the sensations shuddering through his body. His eyes locked on her beautiful face as their damp bodies pressed against each other.

Mena gave him a smile that damn near took his breath away. He turned it up a notch as he rocked harder and faster. He was so close to plunging over the edge, ready to explode from every touch. With every stroke, he rose his hips higher, plunging deeper into her. His name slipped from her mouth as her body writhed and shook with intense passion. The pure intense pleasure on her face made him come hard and fast.

Mena went limp below him, a soft sheen of sweat coating her skin as he slipped his arms around her.

"Best ... surprise ... ever." Mena ran her hand through a pile of the rose petals and flung them in the air. The flowers fluttered around them, landing on their skin as they lay still on the sofa.

"You're the best thing that ever happened to me, you know that, don't you?" Julian said, tightening his arms around Mena.

"Don't say that," Mena whispered into his neck as she wrapped her arms around his chest.

"It's true. I ..." Julian hesitated, hoping he was doing the right thing. "I understand why you turned down my marriage proposal. It was too soon. I get that now. I'm sorry for putting you in that situation."

Mena grew stiff in his arms. Was she holding her breath?

Julian stared at the Caribbean motif commissioned by a local artist on the ceiling. He could feel the tug-of-war going on within Mena as her body rested next to his. "Marriage isn't a deal breaker for me. All I want is to be with you forever."

"That's what I want too, I was just ..."

Julian was quiet, waiting for Mena to continue.

"Afraid to tell you that I couldn't. Not yet. I don't want to lose you."

"That's never going to happen," Julian shifted onto an elbow and stared directly into Mena's eyes. He saw her worry and shame. She still thought her aversion to marriage could break them apart. "Never, Mena. I love you too much to ever spend another day without you."

"You might not always feel that way," Mena said. She tried to pull away, but Julian held her firm in his grasp.

"You're wrong. Nothing can change how I feel about you."

Mena rested her head against his chest. "There are no guarantees, Julian. That's one thing that life has taught me."

Her sober words hung in the air between them. Was that what happened with her ex-husband? Had the bastard stopped loving her? Maybe even left her for another woman? Anger welled within him, but Julian couldn't be upset. If the asshole hadn't hurt Mena, then Julian never would have had this chance with her.

"You trust me?" Julian asked.

"With my life."

"How about with your heart?" For the first time, he got a glimpse at how deep the scars of Mena's failed marriage were. She thought she'd had a forever love before, and it turned out to be a disaster. Now, she was wary of trusting in that kind of love again.

Mena propped her head on her hands and stared at him.

He was willing to wait all night for her answer, but thankfully she didn't make him wait that long.

"I trust you with my heart the most."

Chapter Seven

"What are you thinking about?" Julian asked, taking a finger to smooth out the wrinkle from the frown creasing her forehead.

"Like maybe we should have thought twice about walking to the court-house," Mena said, laughing under her breath. The ten-block trek along palm-tree-lined sidewalks from Harmony Towers to the Governmental Promenade under normal conditions would have been a breeze for both of them. But this morning, the heat was uncharacteristically sweltering. Humidity clung to her skin, suffocating her pores as sweat beaded along her hairline.

"Come on," Julian teased. "This from the woman who spent days in the Kenyan desert?"

"Don't remind me," Mena said, glumly. The last thing she needed was another reminder of how her former mentor and boss, Priscilla Dumay, had been the mastermind behind another attack on Mena's life. Between the stress of being a witness at the trial and knowing that Michael was on the island, her nerves were fried. Even the sexual distractions, of which there were more than enough glorious moments to count, hadn't been able to push her worries far from her mind.

A quick check of the North American Neurology Conference website showed Dr. Michael Marsh as a prominent lecturer and panelist in many of today's sessions. With the conference being held an hour away at the five-star Blue Moon Resort, the likelihood that Michael would show up at the trial and make a scene with Julian was unlikely. Still, him being on the island was a huge risk. She didn't want Julian to learn the truth before she was ready.

You need to be the one to tell it. All of it. Leaving nothing out. Then let the chips fall.

She couldn't bring herself to follow Beaujean Ali's advice. Not yet. Last night when Julian explained that marriage wasn't a deal breaker as long as they were together, that would have been a perfect time to reveal the truth. Julian insisted that nothing would make him stop loving her. He would forgive her for keeping the secret and help her get the divorce from Michael, wouldn't he?

When Julian learns the truth about you, that you are still married and you didn't tell him, his feelings will change too. He won't forgive you either.

Trepidation clawed at Mena's chest as she stood on wobbly legs. Lying to Julian about being married wasn't just bad. It was probably the worst thing she could have ever done, and Michael was right. Julian wouldn't understand why she didn't tell him immediately when she found out she was still married. With each passing day, coming clean got harder and harder. Mena didn't want to blow up her relationship because of a stupid, legal loophole that made her still the wife of Michael Marsh. She had to find a way out of this. With Michael on the island, she could get the divorce without Julian ever finding out. She had to keep Michael away from Julian and convince him to drop this ridiculous notion that he could ever get her back.

Julian slipped an arm around her and lifted her in the air, spinning her around.

Startled, Mena squealed, infected with a fit of laughter from his impromptu display of affection. Passersby stopped to gawk, and a few clapped their hands at the sight.

"Alright, put me down. You pulled me out of my funk," Mena said, pushing all thoughts of Michael Marsh and the marriage she was trapped in from her mind.

"That was easy," Julian said with a sexy grin. Slowly placing her feet back on the ground. Mena leaned into his embrace and rested her head on the tailored suit covering his muscular chest. "Forget what Norman Gale told you about the surrogates and the importance of our testimonies. All we need to do is tell the truth on the stand. It's up to the D.A. to prove that Dumay is guilty."

"And if he isn't able to?" Mena asked. The thought of Priscilla going free was enough to make her skin crawl.

"There are other ways to make sure—" Julian paused.

Mena turned to look at what had caught Julian's attention. The historic Georgian architecture that housed the criminal courts stood between a canopy of massive mahogany trees. Circular box hedges surrounded a marble fountain near the entrance to the building. Sitting on a stone bench nearby, Detective Kendrick Caillouet was engaged in what looked like a flirtatious conversation with a woman.

"You didn't tell me Kendrick was dating anyone," Mena said, turning back toward Julian.

"He's not," Julian said, slipping his hand in hers as he pulled her toward Kendrick and the mystery woman. "Let's go find out who she is."

"We shouldn't interrupt," Mena warned, not wanting to ruin any chance the detective might have of jump starting his perpetually dead love life.

"Trust me. There's no way Kendrick is going to seal the deal if we don't get over there and help him out. He's bound to nice his way out of a love connection," Julian joked.

"That's mean," Mena whispered, falling into step next to Julian as they stopped a few feet away from Kendrick and the woman.

"Well, look here, the star witnesses have arrived. Happy Friday, my friend," Kendrick said, patting Julian on the arm before turning to Mena. "Looking lovely as always, Mena. How are you?"

"Ready to get all of this over with," Mena said, leaning into Julian's arms.

"Star witnesses?" the woman asked, tilting her head toward Kendrick.

"These are my friends, Julian Montgomery and Mena Nix. They are also two of the D.A.'s witnesses in the Priscilla Dumay trial," Kendrick explained to her, then made introductions. "This is Stella Young. She works at the courthouse."

"As a court reporter ... covering the trial of Priscilla Dumay," Stella added with a sheepish, apologetic look.

"Nice to meet you, Stella," Mena said, regarding the demure woman. She was petite and pretty, but in an almost forgettable way. Dressed in a conservative, plain tan suit that almost matched her skin tone, her only striking feature was the long column of straight, cinnamon brown hair that cascaded down her back.

"Guess we'll be seeing a lot of you today. Are you ready for the trial of the year?" asked Julian.

"Never in a million years did I think anything this salacious would happen in St. Basil. Being assigned to the most high-profile case in our courts is surreal. I thought this kind of stuff only happened in St. Killian." Stella said, taking a handkerchief out of her purse and dabbing it against her neck. "The Palmchat Gazette has people here, of course, but the number of international reporters covering the case is staggering. At least cameras won't be allowed inside the courtroom."

"I hadn't even thought about reporters being inside, listening to my testimony," Mena admitted.

Mena cringed at having to dodge intrepid reporters trying to get a sound-bite for the evening news. The last thing she needed was for Michael to see her on television or read about her testimony in the news, although she supposed that was inevitable. Keeping him far away from Julian was her only priority until his conference ended and he went back to NYC.

Mena frowned and looked ahead, noticing for the first time that Kendrick and Julian had stepped away, onto the emerald manicured lawn. The conversation between them looked intense.

Stella noticed as well. "Looks like the boys don't want us to hear what they're saying. Want to get out of this heat?"

Mena gave another quick glance to Julian, then glanced down at the sweat stains starting to show through her shirt. "Let's go. They'll catch up with us later."

"You know, when you think about it, the jury really has the toughest job in the trial. There are so many people who don't believe the allegations against Priscilla Dumay," Stella said.

Mena bristled at the islanders who'd given statements in the news supporting and defending Priscilla, refusing to believe she could do something as horrible as kidnap women and force them to be surrogates. Even with the mountain of evidence against Prissy, many on the island still revered her.

Stella continued, "It sounds too far-fetched and crazy. This is the woman who brought an internationally renowned gallery to the island, finally helping us to step out of the shadows of St. Killian and St. Cera. Was she really worse than the PC-5?" Stella fell into step next to Mena as they ascended the steps to the courthouse.

"Trust me, she is. I've been kidnapped on her orders multiple times with the wounds to prove it," Mena said, sliding her hand over the scar from the gunshot wound to her arm. She and Stella joined the growing crowd of people in line to go through security.

"I must sound so insensitive right now. Gossiping about all of this when you lived it. I'm sorry," Stella said.

Mena waved away her concern. Stella expressed what many were thinking. Mena just hoped the testimony at the trial would be enough to convict Priscilla.

Reaching the door, Mena stepped inside the air-conditioned courthouse. Stella hadn't been lying when she said Prissy's trial was getting a lot of attention. Journalists and other onlookers swarmed the hallway outside the courtroom beyond the security checkpoint.

Anxiety flooded Mena. She needed a distraction. "How long have you known Kendrick?"

Stella blushed. "Don't get me started about the detective. He's such a sweet man, but completely clueless."

"What do you mean?" Mena rested her bag on the rolling conveyor that inched toward the x-ray screening machine.

"We run into each other almost weekly at this food truck that we both love and always have good conversation. That's been happening for almost six, seven months now. I flirt and try to show him I'm interested, but he still hasn't asked me out. The more I get to know him, the more I realize that he's a friendly guy ... to everybody. I was reading more into it than there was. Still, I wouldn't mind if he asked me out," Stella said, sliding her bag onto the belt behind Mena's.

"Kendrick believes that good guys finish last in matters of the heart. He may not be trying anymore," Mena explained.

"Julian seems like a good guy and he got you. Why can't Kendrick see that as proof that it's possible?" Stella asked.

Mena scrunched her face. "I wouldn't say that Julian falls into the typical good guy category. Not that he isn't amazing. He truly is. But he's a bit of a magnet for danger. He doesn't back down in life or death situations.

He goes on the offensive and faces them head on. A real badass, military type."

"Is that what attracted you to him?" Stella asked.

"Actually, no. It was his gentleness that did it. He has this silly side to his personality that counters all the toughness. He cares deeply and protects the ones he loves fiercely. But in the end, he just gets me, and I get him. When you have that, it's hard to not fall in love," Mena said. She slipped her bracelet from her arm and placed it into the holding bucket and watched as it disappeared into the machine.

"That bracelet is stunning. Let me guess, a gift from Julian?"

Mena nodded. "He can be a bit of a romantic. Each year on our anniversary, he's going to give me another charm for it."

Wistful, Stella said, "It's been so long since a man has done anything nice for me. I haven't been on a date in years. I probably wouldn't even know what to do if Kendrick asked me out."

"He just needs a little nudge," Mena said, winking at Stella.

An alarm buzzed in the air. Mena glanced to the right and watched as a security guard held up her purse.

The guard yelled, "Who's bag is this?"

Mena stepped toward the security agent. "That's mine."

"I need to check inside," the security agent explained, giving her a suspicious look.

Stella grabbed her purse from the belt and stood next to Mena. "I'm sure it's nothing. Surprised they didn't flag my bag for a search. I'm diabetic and I have my case of insulin and syringes inside."

"Guess they must have gotten distracted by whatever it is they think I was stupid enough to smuggle in here," Mena said, agitated as she grabbed her bracelet from the bin and placed it back on her wrist.

"What's going on?" Kendrick asked, walking toward them from the hallway.

"You creating trouble?" Julian rested his chin against the top of her head.

"My purse is being searched. How did the two of you get in before us?" Mena asked, growing worried as the guard shifted her purse to a back table, dumped everything out, and picked over the contents.

"If the two of you hadn't left us behind, you would've gone through the V.I.P. entrance with me and Julian and avoided all of this," Kendrick taunted.

The security guard turned to Mena and waved a metal fingernail file toward her. "Looks like this was the culprit. You're good to go."

The guard stepped away from the table and resumed his post, reviewing the monitors of the other bags being x-rayed. Mena rolled her eyes as she approached the surface littered with the contents of her purse. How nice of him to put things back like they were.

Mena reached for her purse, then smiled as Julian gathered her items and slipped them back inside.

"Ready?" Julian asked.

"Just a minute. There's one thing I need to do first," Mena said. She walked over to Stella and Kendrick. "I'm going to need a drink after today's testimony. How about we meet up at King Street Lounge afterwards for some drinks ... you know, the four of us?"

Kendrick gave her a knowing glance but didn't resist. "Sounds good to me. You up for that Stella?"

Stella smiled brightly. "I'm in."

Chapter Eight

Mena stepped inside the courtroom, her eyes drawn to the twelve faces staring back at her from the dark cherry, wood-paneled jury box. She licked her dry lips and stifled a cough as she eased down the aisle and sat in the row of chairs behind the prosecutor table.

Liam Bishop, District Attorney for the Commonwealth of St. Basil, glanced over his shoulder as they entered. One of the three heirs to the famed Bishop family known for the wildly popular Felipe beer and luxury brand of Bishop's rums, he had chosen a job in the community instead of working for the family's business. Liam's face registered only mild interest before returning his attention to the judge, sitting high above them in the center of the back wall of the courtroom. The name plate read Judge Diana Carter. Light brown skin and hair with more gray than black, the judge studied a set of papers, her glasses balanced at the tip of her nose.

As Julian sat next to Mena, she peered around him to see Priscilla Dumay for the first time in almost a year. Sitting next to her attorneys, Priscilla was dressed in a simple white sheath dress and flat shoes. Her dark hair was straight, tucked behind her ears, making her look much younger and ... innocent.

Prissy had always been a master at controlling the narrative about her life. Mena hoped the jury would see through her lies. Prissy wanted the world to believe that she was helping women who'd been violated and gotten pregnant in other facilities. The truth was, Prissy had orchestrated the surrogates' pain. She had kidnapped and kept them from their loved ones, all so she could produce genetically modified babies to sell to infertile couples.

At least the two massive correctional officers seemed oblivious to her manipulation. Dressed in dark gray uniforms, they stood near the end of the defense table. Each officer rested a hand on the large weapon in his holster. If Priscilla made one wrong move, Mena had no doubt that the officers would make her regret it.

Over the next few hours, Mena was riveted by the opening arguments. Despite her concern over Norman Gale's warnings, Liam Bishop's solid opening statement had left the defense reeling. Priscilla's attorney, Camille Reichland, had done her best to weave a story of lies to counter the District Attorney, but the jury's faces had registered skepticism. As the opening statements drew to a close, Mena and Julian exchanged a hopeful look.

The judge spoke, "At this time, the Commonwealth may call its first witness."

Liam Bishop stood and said, "The Commonwealth will call Julian Montgomery, your Honor."

Julian rose. Mena squeezed his hand, then watched as he approached the witness stand. He was sworn in and then over the next forty-five minutes, Liam Bishop questioned Julian about every crime he'd observed that was ordered by Priscilla. Julian was confident and decisive in his responses, emanating truth and honesty.

"That's all I have for this witness judge," Liam said. He walked back to his table and sat down.

"Ms. Reichland," Judge Carter said. "Your witness."

Camille Reichland stood and said, "You recounted a very detailed, tall-tale of interactions with Priscilla Dumay from the month of February of last year." She chuckled, then added. "One worthy of a novel or some kind of television movie."

Liam interrupted. "Objection, argumentative and speculative, Judge. Counsel should not add interpretation of witness' testimony."

"Objection sustained."

Ms. Reichland tipped her head to Liam, then turned back toward Julian. "Are you aware that Priscilla Dumay denies ever seeing you at her medical facility on her private island? And that Quentin Tufa denies being at the same facility last February?"

Julian leaned back in his chair. "Yes. It doesn't matter, they are both lying—"

Ms. Reichland interrupted, "Your honor." She raised her hands in the air as if Julian had done something wrong.

Judge carter responded, "Mr. Montgomery, you are to answer only the questions being posed to you and refrain from adding extra commentary that does not pertain to your response. The jury is directed to strike anything beyond Mr. Montgomery's answers of yes to both questions."

Ms. Reichland continued, "Mr. Montgomery, the police spoke to all the people on the island that day in February and none of them remembered seeing you there, except Mena Nix, who you are dating. Now, tell me, did you happen to video record or tape via audio, perhaps on your cell phone, these conversations you claimed to have had with Priscilla Dumay on that day?"

If looks could kill, the one Julian was giving Ms. Reichland would send her straight to the morgue.

Julian responded, "No."

Ms. Reichland said, "Basically, you expect the jury to just take your word that you were at Ms. Dumay's medical facility and had these conversations with her. That she invited you in and was gracious enough to give you a tour of some women you claim were kidnapped before locking you in a basement with Mena Nix. But you have no proof of those claims."

Liam interrupted, "Objection, your honor. Mr. Montgomery has already answered the question."

"Move on, Ms. Reichland," Judge Carter said.

"Mr. Montgomery, why do you believe that Priscilla Dumay tried to kill you?" Ms. Reichland asked.

"Because she told me she was releasing carbon monoxide into the mansion to kill Mena and me. She also said that she was going to detonate explosives around the mansion once she and the staff were safely away from the island to cover up her crimes."

Ms. Reichland pivoted and approached the defense table, grabbing a couple of sheets of paper, then handed them to the Judge.

"Your Honor, I have here as an exhibit, the Official Investigative Report of Genesis Clinic by the Palmchat Islands Bureau of Fire and Arson Investigations," Ms. Reichland said, handing one copy to her. She then held out the other toward Julian. Julian didn't budge as he stared at the paper.

"Mr. Montgomery, would you please read the conclusion from the report?"

"Dangerous levels of carbon monoxide present at the site. Inconclusive on whether the explosion was accidental or a result of foul play," Julian said.

Ms. Reichland smiled at the jury, then continued, "Thank you, sir. Now, you testified earlier that you used Zak Webber's cell phone to talk to Ms. Dumay and claim to have learned that Mena Nix was being held against her will by my client. How did you know you were calling Ms. Dumay on Zak's phone?"

Julian rolled his eyes, sighing loudly before responding. "I scrolled through the contacts list until I saw her name."

"Was the name in the contacts list Priscilla Dumay?"

Julian frowned, hesitated as he sat up straighter. "Well ... no."

"What was the name in the contacts list that you dialed?"

"Boss Lady," Julian said.

"Did the person on the line introduce herself as Priscilla Dumay?"

"No."

"How often had you interacted with Priscilla Dumay as a member of the staff of her security team at the Genesis Gallery?"

"I didn't," Julian snapped.

Mena shook her head. This was not good. Camille Reichland was twisting Julian's whole testimony and making it seem less credible. Liam needed to do something. Now.

Ms. Reichland, unable to hide her shock. She glanced at the jury, then back at Julian. "You didn't? Are you saying you—wait? Did you ever interact with Priscilla Dumay while you worked as a security guard at the Genesis Gallery?"

"No, I did not," Julian admitted.

"So you assumed that the person on the other line was Priscilla Dumay, but you really don't know who you were talking to, do you?"

"Objection!" Liam thundered.

"Withdrawn," Ms. Reichland said. "Why did you decide to work at the Genesis Gallery after being unemployed for three years?"

Julian took a deep breath. Mena could tell he was perturbed and maybe even worried by the turn his testimony was taking.

"I was trying to find Ella Sapphire," Julian said. "Ella called her sister and told her that someone was holding her against her will and she was afraid the person would kill her."

"Now in that call, did Ella identify the gender of the person she believed was going to kill her?"

Julian looked away. "Yes, but she really didn't know the truth—"

"What gender did she reference?" Ms. Reichland asked.

"Male," Julian said. "But she didn't know it was Priscilla Dumay who told Zak Webber to murder her—"

"Mr. Montgomery," Ms. Reichland interrupted, "Zak Webber confessed to killing Ella in a crime of passion and to kidnapping Mena Nix. When Mr. Webber was sentenced to twenty years for those crimes, he made it clear he had acted on his own. Why do you believe my client told Zak Webber to kill Ella Sapphire?"

"Dumay told me herself," Julian spat the words.

"When did my client tell you that?"

"When I was at her medical facility on the island she owns," Julian replied.

"This is the same medical facility where neither my client nor any of the staff recalled your presence. Is that correct, Mr. Montgomery?"

"The cops found me bleeding out on that island, so that's proof I was there," Julian said.

"But not proof that you had any discussions with my client, isn't that correct?"

"This is ridiculous," Julian threw his hands in the air.

"No, your testimony is ridiculous—"

Liam stood and shouted, "Your honor!"

"Ms. Reichland," the judge said, a warning in her tone.

"Withdrawn," said Ms. Reichland. Turning her back on Julian, she walked back toward the defense table. "No further questions."

Chapter Nine

Yanking at the tie choking his neck, Julian stepped down from the witness stand and crossed the courtroom. Priscilla Dumay sat at the defense table with a demure, pensive expression, no doubt pleased with the way his testimony had ended. Her leg, crossed underneath the table, swung back and forth playfully.

This was all a game to that bitch.

A game he wouldn't let her win.

Justice didn't always come through a court of law.

Stopping at the row of chairs where Mena sat, Julian allowed the tension to ease from his muscles. The urge to punch a wall had dissipated with one glance from the woman he loved. Mena looked strong and determined, but her hands fidgeted with her charm bracelet, spinning it around and around her wrist. She was trying hard to be brave, trying to reassure him that he hadn't fucked up on the stand. But they both knew the truth. Now she had to go up there with extra pressure to make things right, and that was his fault. He hated putting her in this position.

Slumping down into the chair next to hers, Julian leaned against her.

"You okay?" Mena asked.

Before he could answer or even give her a word of support, Liam Bishop announced, "The Commonwealth calls Mena Nix, your Honor."

"Don't worry, you're going to be great," Julian whispered in Mena's ear. He draped an arm across her body, forcing her to stop and look at him. He saw the trepidation in her eyes.

Mena bit her bottom lip as she gripped his hands.

"I love you," Julian said, summoning as much strength as he could to give to Mena before she headed up to the witness stand.

"I love you," Mena said, then stood.

Liam made quick work of her testimony, wrapping his questions after only about twenty minutes. He seemed to be pleased with how it had gone and gave a sly smirk toward Dumay's attorney before returning to his seat. The looks on the faces of the jury members said it all. They were horrified by what Mena had been through. Many of them wouldn't even look at Dumay, who had been conferring with her attorneys frequently during Mena's testimony.

"Ms. Reichland," Judge Carter said, giving the defense a chance to cross-examine Mena.

Camille Reichland approached Mena. "I'm very sorry that Zak Webber attacked and kidnapped you, that must have been a horrible experience. Unfortunately, I need to take you back to that day to ask a few more questions."

Mena grew ashen, her eyes darting away from the attorney to find Julian's. Julian felt his stomach drop as he tried to figure out where Dumay's attorney was going with this question.

"Ms. Nix, After Zak grabbed you, what did he do next?"

Mena said, "He kidnapped me."

Reichland's voice grew low and comforting, dripping with fake concern. "Are you aware that there was a surveillance camera in the elevator, Ms. Nix?"

"I didn't know it at the time, but yes, I found out later."

"The video of what happened to you in that elevator is quite disturbing and heartbreaking. Can you please tell the court exactly what Zak Webber did to you after he pushed you into the elevator and before he injected you with the syringe?"

Mena's head dropped as she gazed into her lap.

The muscles in Julian's neck grew tight, pinching with pain as he maneuvered to the edge of his seat. Why did she stop looking at him? What the hell had happened after Zak took her? Why hadn't he ever asked her to talk about that night? And if he had, would she have? Julian knew the answer, and he didn't like it.

"He pinned me against the back of the elevator."

Reichland's voice was louder when she asked, "Did Zak Webber sexually assault you?"

Mena rubbed a finger against her temple. "He tried to, but I fought him and he stopped."

"What did he do to you?"

Mena exhaled a shaky breath. "He ripped my shirt and grabbed one of my breasts with his hand. He licked and sucked on my neck as he shoved his other hand into my pants and ... groped me. He tried to kiss me, but I pushed him away. I clenched my hands into fists and just kept hitting him until he finally stopped."

Seething blind rage roared through Julian. That motherfucker Zak Webber had put his disgusting hands on Mena. He'd tried to rape her. Mena had never told him what she'd gone through the night Zak Webber kidnapped her.

"But that wasn't enough to help you get away, was it? What did he do after that?" Reichland asked.

"He got really angry. He cursed and grabbed me and forced me down to the floor. When the elevator door opened, I tried to get up and run, but he was too strong. That's when I saw the syringe in his hand." Mena stared into the distance as if seeing her memories playing out in front of her.

Julian squeezed the edge of his chair. If Zak Webber wasn't in Tiverton, he would hunt the bastard down and make him regret ever laying a hand on Mena. Was that why she never told him what happened? Was she afraid that he would take matters into his own hands and kill Zak for hurting her? He should have made sure Zak Webber died the night he realized he'd kidnapped Mena. The bastard didn't deserve to live.

"And what did he do with the syringe?"

"He stuck it in the back of my neck," Mena said, then reached a hand behind her head. "Here, near the base."

"What happened after that?"

"I got really dizzy. Drowsy, disoriented."

"Did you pass out, Ms. Nix?"

"Yes," Mena said.

Reichland asked, "What is the next thing you remember after passing out?"

Mena rubbed her arms. "Being cold and in a room with bars. I was trying to wake up ... but, I ... I ..."

Julian's heart ached for Mena as she struggled through her torment on the stand. Leaning forward, he stood, but felt Kendrick's firm hand behind him, forcing him back down. He couldn't make a scene and disrupt the testimony. That wouldn't be good for the trial or for Mena. Watching her in agony was about to kill him.

"Ms. Nix, do you need a moment to collect your thoughts?" Judge Carter asked. "Ms. Nix?"

Mena still wouldn't look at him.

Come on, baby. Julian needed her to trust in him and just look his way. He loved her with every part of him, and he would do anything to help her through this.

"No, your Honor. I'm okay. I can go on," Mena said after several seconds had passed.

"Ms. Nix, I have handed you what's been marked for identification as Exhibit No. 19 and it is being projected onto the screen for the jury to see. Please tell us what this is and read to us what is on the document."

"These are my medical records from after the mansion exploded," Mena said, her voice wavering. "Patient suffered a concussion and confusion from the effects of the following sedatives found in high concentration within her blood ... I'm not sure I can pronounce these right."

"That's okay, Ms. Nix. How many sedatives are listed there?"

"Six."

"Quite a lot of drugs still present in your body after going through that ordeal. I'm amazed at how well you can remember what happened back then. After you found yourself in the cold room with the bars, what happened?" Reichland asked.

"I remember Julian ... umm ... Julian Montgomery. He was in the room with me, on the other side of the bars. I thought I was dreaming, but he was really there," Mena responded. "He found a way to open the bars and get me out. But we were still trapped in the room. Priscilla locked us inside and there was carbon monoxide in the air—"

"How do you know that Priscilla Dumay locked you in the room?"

Mena looked startled from the interruption, confused by the question. "Julian told me she led him down there and locked him inside with me—"

"Did you see or hear Priscilla Dumay yourself, Ms. Nix?"

Mena stammered, "Well, I ..."

"Isn't it true that every criminal claim you've made against Priscilla Dumay is based on information told to you by Julian Montgomery, and not because you witnessed Priscilla Dumay committing any crime yourself? You were too doped up by Zak Webber to realize what was happening to you, isn't that right? You are just repeating what your boyfriend told you!"

Liam jumped from his seat. "Objection!"

"Overruled," Judge Carter said, giving Camille Reichland a look of disdain. "I'll allow the witness to answer your questions, Ms. Reichland."

"I think I heard her ... she ..."

Damn Dumay for putting Mena through this.

"No further questions, your honor," Camille Reichland said, turning to walk back to her table with a smug look on her face.

Chapter Ten

Liam Bishop stood and announced he wanted a redirect of Mena.

Mena looked up, staring straight at Julian. Humiliation and shame clouded her face.

She looked like she'd been dragged through hell and back.

He could almost read her thoughts.

She wanted this to be over.

Now.

Mena was one of the most private women he knew, not one to dwell on negative events. She was always pushing forward, focusing on the future and not letting anything hold her back. One of the things he loved most about her was also the one thing that caused him the most worry. He hated that she kept her feelings bottled up inside, without seeking an outlet to help her process what she was feeling. Putting pressure on her to talk when she wasn't ready was something he had never done. Julian was content to just be there, however she needed, to see her through. And that's what he'd do once she stepped off that witness stand.

He gave her a reassuring nod, strength to endure the last round of questioning.

The judge acknowledged the District Attorney's request, and Liam Bishop took Mena through a series of questions to clarify certain statements she'd made. The medical records were reviewed once more to highlight that the rape kit performed on Mena had come back negative. Then Liam revisited the reason Zak caught Mena in the first place. The conversation she'd overheard between Adam Russell and Priscilla where they discussed killing both Irving Bond and Ella to keep the criminal activities a secret.

Mena regained a bit of her confidence during the re-examination.

After twenty minutes of detailed questions, Liam Bishop finally uttered the words Julian had been waiting for.

"No further questions, your Honor."

Mena stumbled slightly as she stepped down from the witness stand. Her steps were slow and heavy as she walked across the courtroom, her eyes cast down.

She stopped at the bench, reaching a hand for him. He grabbed it and stood. Leading her out of the courtroom, he closed the door behind them and steered her toward the witness holding room where they could be alone.

Mena's haunted eyes stared back at him as she leaned into his embrace. "The jury doesn't believe me. They think I was too drugged up to remember what happened. What if Priscilla gets off because my testimony was useless? What if I'm the reason—"

Julian pressed his lips against the top of her head, whispering into her hair. "It's over now."

"It won't be over until Priscilla is behind bars for good," Mena said, pulling back from him.

Julian couldn't agree more. "How about I take you home, treat you to a decadent bubble bath and wash away everything that happened today?"

Mena inhaled deeply. "That sounds good. I'm going to run to the washroom before we leave. Can you let Kendrick know we'll have to meet up another time for drinks? I'm just not in the mood anymore—"

Julian couldn't take his eyes off of her. What torment of emotions was she hiding behind those stunning brown eyes? Would she open up and share her fears with him?

"Don't look so upset. I'm okay, really," Mena said, leaning in to kiss him quickly on the lips.

Julian reluctantly released her from his grasp and watched as she exited the witness room. He reached for his cell phone to send a quick text to

Kendrick. It buzzed in his hand. Staring at the screen, he didn't recognize the number. Aerie Islands area code. Could it be about Broman?

Pressing the green button, Julian answered the phone.

"Poor Mena. How is my sweet former conservator recovering from that disastrous testimony? The jury walked out of there thinking it was impossible for her to remember anything clearly from that time. And your testimony was no better. The D.A. is going to have a hard time proving beyond a reasonable doubt that I'm guilty of anything," Priscilla Dumay taunted.

"How are you calling me?" Julian growled into the phone.

"The more important question is why I'm calling you, don't you think?"

Julian was in no mood for Dumay's games, but he wouldn't deny his curiosity. "What the fuck do you want?"

"When I was locked up in Tiverton, I had a very interesting conversation with a woman who was serving time for smuggling guns with Enrique Rivera Ortiz. You know who that is, don't you?"

Julian gripped the phone tighter. "Why the fuck would I care about your conversation with one of El Mago's mules?"

"She told me an interesting story about a clash between his rebels and the SEALs about five years ago in Central Sulawesi."

Julian frowned. What kind of interesting story could some gun smuggler have told Dumay? The fight in Central Sulawesi wasn't a secret. The only secret was what he'd done. What he'd covered up. What no one could ever know. The mule couldn't have found out about that.

Julian said, "What the fuck are you talking about?"

"El Mago ambushed your SEAL team in the jungle because of what you did."

Julian remained quiet.

"I have unmistakable proof that you committed treason against the United States of America."

"There is no proof," Julian said, growing annoyed with her.

"Are you sure about that?" Dumay asked.

"What the fuck do you think you have?" Julian asked, his pulse quickening. He'd erased all traces of what he'd done in the jungle. Nothing was left behind that would implicate him. Testimony from El Mago's team wouldn't stand up in any naval court.

"An official U.S. Navy laptop assigned to Chief Petty Officer Julian Montgomery."

"So what?" Julian forced the words from his mouth as his blood ran cold. He was sure he'd corrupted the files on the laptop. There wasn't anything left on that computer to prove he'd handed over the location of a confidential informant to El Mago. There couldn't be. Could there?

Dumay continued, "Corrupting files is a painstaking process. Very hard to do thoroughly, especially when you have four mutilated SEALs dying on the floor around you. In the best of circumstances, you probably wouldn't have made the mistake you did, but saving that one SEAL that was still alive became your top priority, didn't it? And you left the laptop behind. Very sloppy."

"What do you want from me?" asked Julian, his mind racing. How the fuck did she know so much about what happened back then. Did the bitch really have his laptop? Or was she bluffing? He didn't know, but he had to find out.

"I want to make a deal," Dumay said.

"What kind of fucking deal?"

"Come to Anteroom F and find out," Priscilla demanded.

Chapter Eleven

Stepping outside the witness holding room, Julian glanced quickly to his left and right, before darting down the back hallway that led to the anterooms behind the courtroom. No one was allowed back there except for the defendants, their attorneys, and the correctional officers assigned to guard them. Reaching the end of the narrow corridor, he glanced around the corner. Voices floated from the two anterooms closest to where he stood. No sign of guards. Nothing to stop him from getting to Anteroom F, where Priscilla Dumay was waiting for him.

With silent, quick steps, he approached the door.

Julian hesitated.

He'd always assumed the laptop had been lost or destroyed. Had he left some evidence behind on the laptop? Did Dumay really have it? Could he afford not to find out?

Julian slumped against the wall, the wood paneling pressing against his back. Head hung low, he monitored the empty hallway. The air was heavy with silence.

Four years ago, Julian wouldn't have cared if the truth had come out. Hell, he probably would have been relieved to not carry the burden. Guilt had forced him into exile as he remembered every single mistake he'd made. Intercepting the communication between El Mago and the rebel group was exactly why they were in the region. The discovery should have been reported to his SEAL Team leader. But Julian had thought he knew better. He'd wanted to be the hero. To prove his old man wrong and show everyone that he could bring down one of the world's most wanted shadow facilitators for terrorist groups.

Sabotaging the Navy's efforts to protect the confidential informant, he'd used the informant's location as bait. With no way of knowing when his SEAL team members would return, he'd convinced himself that he could take down El Mago on his own. The prospect was foolish and reckless in hindsight. A mistake that landed Broman in a coma and sent four members of his SEAL team to premature, unnecessary graves.

If there was even the slightest evidence of what he'd done on that laptop, it could destroy the life he and Mena were building together.

He wasn't going to risk losing everything because of the mistakes of his past.

Whatever Dumay wanted, he would do it to get the laptop back.

Which made him no better than Dumay.

Disgusted, Julian reached for the knob and turned it slowly, pushing the door inward.

"I was beginning to think you weren't going to show up," Priscilla said, her lips in a tight line and her green eyes hard and cold, laced with hatred.

"Where the fuck are your guards?" Julian said. Stepping inside the room, he closed the door behind him.

Priscilla's legs were propped on top of the table, crossed at the ankles as she glared at him. The innocent, demure expression she'd projected to the jury was long gone. "The guards will come when I tell them to."

She lowered her legs to the floor and waved a hand toward him.

Julian approached the table, stopping short of the chair across from Dumay. Crossing his arms over his chest, he quickly checked the room. No sign of any video or audio surveillance.

"Where's the laptop? I'm not doing anything until I get proof you have it."

"You hacked into secure Naval databases to find the location of a confidential informant and used that information to lure El Mago out of hiding in Central Sulawesi. Is that enough proof that I have evidence that will obliterate your life as you know it? No more playing house with Mena. You'll be rotting in a prison cell for the next fifty years if I hand it over to the Navy," Dumay explained.

"What do you want from me?" Julian asked.

"You need to make amends for derailing my life's work. Critical work to better humanity is in jeopardy because of you. I often wondered why you were so determined to find Ella Sapphire. She was an unremarkable and useless bitch. The laptop helped me understand you better. Guilt can be a powerful motivator."

"Ella didn't deserve to be kidnapped, and she sure as hell didn't deserve to be murdered."

"Neither did your SEAL team."

Grasping the back of the chair, Julian leaned toward Dumay. "Stop fucking around and tell me what you want?"

"I had this amazing plan to kidnap sweet Mena from Africa. I knew you would come after her and I had laid a perfect trap for you. She would watch you die, then I'd ship her off to my new facility to be the first surrogate to restart the production of genetically enhanced infants. That was what I wanted. But you thwarted that plan, didn't you?"

Julian lifted the chair and hurled it toward the back wall. Priscilla Dumay didn't even flinch as the sound of the crash exploded within the room. The chair tumbled to the floor within feet of where Dumay sat.

"If you ever try to hurt Mena again, I will kill you. Do you hear me? I will end your miserable life!"

Priscilla raised her hands in mock surrender. "Relax. Now that I have the laptop, you are much more useful to me alive than dead. I must admit, I underestimated you, Julian. I thought you were just another fallible, brain-washed military operative who could be easily tricked and silenced. But you are so much more than that, aren't you? I wonder what goodies lie within your genetic code?"

"You want my DNA? Is that what this is about?" Julian asked.

"No, although it is an interesting prospect."

"I'm sick of this bullshit. Either tell me what you want or——"

"I want you to break me out of here. I have no plans to go back to Tiverton tonight. You secure my freedom and I give you the laptop. Simple transaction. And you have my word that I didn't even make a copy of the contents. Do we have a deal?" Priscilla asked.

Julian recoiled. He'd spent over a year working to ensure this bitch would go to prison for every crime she'd committed, and now he had to help her escape? Dumay had done her research on him and knew what he was capable of, what he'd done before. Extraction of captives with little time and even less to plan had been the hallmark of many of his SEAL missions. Even as he spoke, a plan to smuggle Dumay out of the courthouse undetected had taken root in his mind.

"How can I get you out of here with all the police and guards around? Not to mention the security cameras." Julian stalled.

"With this," Priscilla said. She reached into her pocket and pulled out an object. A small spray bottle filled with a white substance.

"What the hell is that?" Julian asked, stepping closer to get a better look.

Dumay raised the bottle and pressed the nozzle, sending a fine mist of powder toward him. Instinctively, Julian ducked. His movements weren't quick enough. The fine powder settled on his face. Dumay stood, continuing to spray him with more of the powder.

"What did you ... do to ... me?" Julian's words grew slurred as he lost the ability to control his mouth. Numbness raced through his body. His limbs tingled, then lost all feeling as he watched his arms collapse at his side. Julian felt nothing as the room shifted from upright to sideways. The floor rushed toward him as he landed with a loud thud. His body didn't register any pain from the impact. What the fuck had she done to him?

"Lazirprene is an amazing biotoxin. One of the best in existence. Capable of a targeted attack on the human body, it shuts down skeletal muscle of the extremities, leaving the victim fully conscious, breathing and aware of what's happening around them." Priscilla nudged him onto his back with the tip of her Chanel ballerina slippers, then stepped over his body to open the door.

"Don't worry. I carefully determined the exact dosage that would render you immobile for only a few minutes. You'll regain your ability to move soon." Priscilla dropped to her knees next to him, jerking his hand forward. Julian felt nothing as her pale, veined hand gripped his. Dumay lifted a syringe from the inside hem of her white dress and pressed it into his palm. Maneuvering his thumb onto the plunger and his fingers around the cylinder, she brought the syringe to her chest.

Julian tried to snatch his hand away, but his muscles weren't responding.

Dumay guided his hand and forced him to push the thin needle into her skin. Resting her thumb on top of his, she depressed the syringe, sending the clear liquid in the plastic cylinder into her body. Priscilla laid next to him and gave him a sinister smile. "Now let's see who ends up in Tiverton first."

An anguished scream erupted from her mouth. Seconds later, Dumay's body jerked and convulsed. Frothy white foam gurgled from her lips. Her face grew pale, flushed with sweat.

Julian's mind was a jumble of confusion and bewilderment. He couldn't make any sense of what had happened. A sharp pain seared through his body, jolting him. Racing from his feet toward his face, he regained sensation in his limbs. His arm was draped across Dumay's chest, still holding the syringe. If he could move his fingers, try to remove the syringe, he might be able to undo whatever Dumay had done to herself.

Intense shooting pain pricked his muscles as his nerves reawakened. Julian clenched his jaw as the sensation heightened. The pain was damn near unbearable, but he pushed through, struggling to move. His body responded with stiff, uncoordinated movements. The pain subsided, and Julian could feel again. He tightened his grasp of the syringe and yanked it from Dumay's chest. Flinging it into the corner, he reached for Dumay's head to prevent her from choking on her own vomit.

"Freeze!!! Hands in the air! Step away from the prisoner!"

"Call 9-1-1!" Julian turned his head slightly and saw Kendrick standing in the doorway. The police issued Glock was firmly in his friend's hand and pointed directly at him.

"Julian, step away and put your hands up!" Kendrick commanded.

"Kendrick, it's not what it looks like—"

Two guards rushed past Kendrick and dragged his body backward, slamming him against the floor as they pressed a knee into his back. His arms were pinned behind him. The cold metal handcuffs tightened against his wrists.

"You saw what he did. He stabbed her with that syringe. Read him his rights," one guard barked.

Kendrick's voice was low and hollow as he uttered the words. "Julian Montgomery, you have the right to remain silent."

Chapter Twelve

The tick of the second hand of the clock echoed in the interrogation room. Each movement triggered a pounding in Julian's ears that grew louder, drowning out the sounds of the police department on the other side of the door.

Popcorn textured beige walls surrounded the closet sized space. Julian slumped over the table, nestled in the corner of the room. A single desk chair floated in the center of the space, where Kendrick sat across from him. The dark globes in the corner of the rooms flashed a small red light intermittently. The room was being video recorded.

"This part is similar to the States," Kendrick said, sliding a single sheet of paper toward him. He explained his rights, emphasizing the right to an attorney and for the attorney to be present during any interrogation if Julian chose. "Do you understand those rights?"

"Yeah," Julian said, disgusted that he was in an interrogation room for the first time on the opposite side from Kendrick. "I didn't do—"

"You have the right to remain silent," Kendrick implored. Julian knew his friend didn't want him to say anything that could be used against him later. The charges of aggravated assault with a deadly weapon were serious.

Kendrick asked, "Do you have an attorney that you can call?"

"No. Never thought I'd need one," Julian admitted. After Kendrick and the correctional officers had burst into the anteroom, four other police officers rushed in within seconds. Julian was hauled into a police cruiser and ushered to the police station as journalists and paparazzi followed, clamoring for details on what had transpired at the end of Dumay's trial.

Julian had been in an angered daze as he was booked and processed before being led to a holding cell. The whole situation was a nightmare.

Dumay had toyed with him, using details from his past. One thing was clear. Dumay knew far too much about what had gone down in Central Sulawesi. But that didn't mean she had any proof of his crimes. The laptop was just a carrot dangled in front of him to get him to fall into her trap.

She wanted everyone to believe he'd tried to kill her. The diabolical bitch was focused on exacting revenge, staging the poisoning and risking her own life to put him behind bars.

His thoughts shifted to Mena. She had to be confused and bewildered. One minute they were planning a relaxing night at home after her testimony, and the next she'd watched as the police arrested him for attacking Dumay.

"Look," Kendrick said, leaning toward Julian. "It's no secret that I'll be yanked from this case because of our friendship. Des Francois will probably takeover. So, I'm not breaking any rules by helping you get a lawyer and I know exactly who to call—Octavia Constant."

"The better suspect lawyer?" Julian asked. "Fuck ... you really think it's that bad. I need someone of her caliber?"

"Whatever went down in that room is complicated and could be hard to prove. You need the best on your side to make sure you have a fighting chance," Kendrick explained.

"You think she'll take my case?" Julian asked.

"I'm good friends with her cousin, Icarus. I'll call him and get him to put in a good word for you. Her offices are in St. Mateo, but hopefully she can get over here in a few hours."

"Thanks," Julian muttered.

"It's the least I can do for arresting you." Kendrick patted Julian on the shoulder.

"Hey, what about Mena? Any chance I can see her?" Julian asked.

"Last I checked, she still hadn't made it to the police station. It's a madhouse out there. Let me see what I can do to get her in for a visit," Kendrick said, then exited the room.

After three hours, Octavia Constant, the "Better Suspect Lawyer," showed up.

"Did you do it?" Octavia asked, slipping her glasses from her face as she scrutinized him. "I'm not in the business of defending the guilty. My success is directly attributable to the fact that all of my clients have been wrongly charged with a crime. I don't plan to taint my track record, not even for a high-profile case like yours."

Undeterred, Julian stared back at the petite, curvaceous attorney as she stood in the corner near the door. Ms. Constant was a straight shooter who didn't mince words, or waste her time with criminals.

"No," Julian said.

Stepping inside the room, she stood on the opposite side of the table with her arms crossed over her chest.

"Tell me what happened," Octavia said.

Julian explained everything from the moment he got the phone call from Priscilla Dumay to the minute handcuffs were slapped on his wrists.

Octavia narrowed her eyes and watched him for a long moment. "I believe you. I will take your case, Mr. Montgomery. I'm sure you are aware of the seriousness of the charges against you. The doctors have confirmed that Priscilla Dumay was stabbed with a syringe that contains a yet unknown poison. She's in a coma and in critical, but stable condition. You need her to stay that way or--"

"I'll be charged with murder," Julian said.

"That's right. I will inform Detective Francois that you won't be answering questions. You have nothing to gain and a lot to lose by being questioned by the cops, even with me present. Proving that the victim framed you is a long shot, but there are other ways to prove reasonable doubt, which my team and I will begin working on immediately."

"What happens next?" Julian asked.

"You spend the weekend in jail and I negotiate to get you a bail hearing first thing Monday morning. This looks really bad, but I need you to maintain a positive outlook and trust that I can get you through this."

As the door closed behind Octavia, Julian rested his head against the cold, hard table. Staying positive would be easier said than done.

Chapter Thirteen

The door creaked and Julian glanced up.

"Here to take me back to the holding cell?" Julian asked as Kendrick poked his head in the door.

"No, you'll be going to lock up after you have one more visitor." Kendrick opened the door wider.

The love of his life peered around the heavy door.

"Get in here," Julian said, rising from the chair.

Mena pushed the door open and ran into his arms. "Are you ok?"

"I didn't do it," Julian whispered.

"Hey, I know you didn't," Mena pressed her hands on the sides of his face and looked up at him. Her beautiful dark eyes shone with love. Leaning forward, she kissed him softly on the lips. Julian pressed her close to him, deepening the kiss. He savored the taste of her, desperately trying to memorize what she felt like. He might not get a chance to be with her again for a while.

Breaking the kiss, Julian pulled Mena toward him and sat down. Balancing her on his lap, he went through the same details he'd shared with Octavia.

Julian said, "But there's one thing I left out of the story when I told it to Octavia."

Mena frowned. "Julian, you need to tell your lawyer everything. How can she defend you if you're holding back from her?"

"This I can't tell her. It's the reason I went to the room to see Dumay. She knows what I did in Central Sulawesi," Julian said, rubbing a hand roughly through his hair. "Apparently, she met a woman in prison who worked for El Mago and gave her proof that I committed treason."

"She's lying. There is no proof. You told me yourself that you destroyed all the evidence of what you'd done."

"Dumay claims to have my Naval laptop, which I left behind when I realized that Broman was still alive. From that point on, everything else flew out of my head. All I could think about was getting him to safety. Saving his life. I thought I completed the corruption of the files, but what if I didn't?" Julian said.

"That's what Prissy wants you to believe. If she really had that proof, why wouldn't she use that to get revenge on you instead. I don't believe it—"

"Maybe because she couldn't verify if the Navy already knew about it," Julian guessed, in no mood to figure out how that evil woman's mind worked. "Or maybe she's saving it for part two of whatever revenge she has planned for me. Who the fuck knows? All I know is that I need to find out if Dumay has the laptop."

"How can we do that now that you've been arrested?" Mena asked, sliding off his lap. He watched as she paced back and forth across the small room. "If Priscilla has the laptop, she will use it to manipulate you. We can't let her blackmail you into doing God knows what."

Julian stood and stepped in front of Mena. He grabbed her hands and lifted them to his lips. Kissing her knuckles slowly, he stared into her eyes. "You will not get involved in any of this. Not this time. I learned my lesson and I will never put you in danger again."

"Julian—"

"I'm serious, Mena. Do not do anything to find that laptop. I can handle it, as long as you're safe. Octavia is the best attorney I could have. Let me focus on beating these charges first. Then I'll figure out if Dumay is lying or telling the truth about the laptop," Julian said.

"I won't sit by while you do this on your own—"

Julian laughed, cupping her face with his hands. "I love your fierceness, but baby, this is one battle that you have no skills to help fight. Dumay has proven over and over again how dangerous and ruthless she is. She's kidnapped you more times than I want to count. Promise me you'll stay out of this. I'd rather not spend our last moments together talking about Dumay, anyway."

"Our last moments?" Mena asked.

An adorable frown creased her face. She was so fucking beautiful. How had he ever gotten so lucky to have this woman fall in love with him? She trusted him and believed in him completely, and he'd let her down by letting Dumay dupe him.

Julian reached into the pocket of his pants, his fingers gripping the tiny charm. "The earliest Octavia can get a bail hearing is Monday."

"I can't believe you have to spend the weekend in jail. That's not fair," Mena insisted.

Julian took her hand in his and placed the charm in her palm.

"You're not supposed to give me another charm until next January,"

"I know, but I need you to have that now."

Mena stared at the rose gold charm in the shape of a small key. "The key to your heart."

"That's right. And it will always be yours, no matter what."

Chapter Fourteen

Judge Diana Carter conferred with the bailiff and Stella Young, the court reporter.

The waiting was torture.

Mena sat rigid, legs numb from the uncomfortable worn wooden benches in the courtroom. She hadn't even allowed herself to consider that Julian wouldn't be coming home with her tonight. The hearing had been short and concise. Liam Bishop had argued, almost half-heartedly, against granting Julian bail. Octavia had shined in her delivery of why Julian wasn't a flight risk, laying out the terms of her bail proposal. Everything seemed to be going smoothly until now.

Julian sat still, less than an arm's length in front of her. If she stretched her arm, she could stroke his hair. Caress the soft skin of his neck. Comfort him as the minutes ticked by. But she didn't dare break formality of courtroom decorum, no matter how she ached to slip her arms around him and pretend like this nightmare wasn't happening.

Sitting in the courtroom alone had been her choice, but now she regretted insisting that she didn't need Regina or Omar by her side. They'd reluctantly agreed to stay away, and she was without her fierce support system when she needed them the most. She'd give anything for a hug from Regina or an encouraging word from Omar. Instead, she was surrounded by strangers, legal assistants and clerks on Octavia Constant's team assisting with Julian's case.

Behind her, curious locals packed the rest of the benches, watching like vultures as if Julian's problems were prime time entertainment. Last year, Julian had been the golden boy, the island hero. Now the newspapers depicted him as the fallen hero, attacking Priscilla Dumay to exact vigilante justice and revenge.

And then there was Quentin Tufa. Priscilla's adopted brother sat behind the prosecutor table, glaring at Julian with unrestrained hatred. He played the part of distraught brother, scared for his sister's life. Mena wasn't buying his act. Priscilla wouldn't kill herself to get revenge on Julian. More likely, Prissy would emerge from the coma in time to spout more lies about Julian attacking her.

Slipping her finger underneath the rose gold links of her charm bracelet, she twisted the jewelry around her wrist until the key rested against her palm. The key to Julian's heart. Mena would give anything to get Julian out of this situation, but this was a new battle unlike any they'd ever had to fight before. He could take out any rebel group threatening to hurt them, but how could they fight a methodical and manipulative attack by a psychopath.

Judge Diana Carter stacked the papers into a neat pile on the podium, then cleared her throat. "I have reviewed the arguments presented by both the defense and the commonwealth attorneys. While Julian Montgomery has obtained status as a permanent resident of the Palmchat Islands and has freely agreed to surrender his U.S. Passport as a sign of good faith of his intent to remain in St. Basil until his trial, there are other concerning facts about his situation."

Mena clasped her hands tightly in her lap. The room spun. She struggled to breathe.

"First, the financial records presented to the court indicate that he is a man of considerable wealth and means to fund an escape from the islands. Mr. Montgomery's training as a Navy SEAL indicates an extraordinary skill set to evade capture."

Mena leaned forward, sliding her hand along Julian's arm. He didn't turn around, but his strong hand cover hers. Intertwining their fingers, Julian rested the back of her hand against his heart. She felt the slow, steady beats in contrast to the pounding of hers.

"Finally, Mr. Montgomery has no roots in this community or reason to stay in St. Basil, other than a girlfriend, who is also not native to the Palm-chat Islands. For these reasons, I am denying bail and remanding Mr. Montgomery to Tiverton Prison to await his trial."

The bang of the gavel exploded within the room.

Chapter Fifteen

The photograph on the *Palmchat Gazette's* website only caught a partial view, but Michael knew it was her. His wife. Mena. Sitting behind Julian Montgomery in the courtroom as the judge denied him bail for attacking Priscilla Dumay.

Michael clicked on the photo, zooming into Mena's face. Reaching a hand toward the computer screen, he traced a finger around her jawline. She was hiding it well, as she always did, but Michael knew that testifying against Dumay and that bastard's arrest was taking its toll on her.

How could he add to everything that was going wrong in her life? He didn't want to lose her, but maybe agreeing to the divorce would prove to her he'd changed. With Julian in jail and likely to be convicted for the attempted murder of Priscilla Dumay, he could finally get the second chance he wanted.

Giving in wasn't the same as giving up, especially if he could make her life easier. He wanted her to see that he was still the man she fell in love with. He'd made some mistakes, but he knew deep down she hadn't really stopped loving him. She was angry and hurt, but that was something they could get past with time.

Michael stared at the phone.

Signing the divorce papers was an enormous risk. It could backfire and he could lose her for good, especially if that bastard fucking his wife weaseled his way out of the charges. He had to try. Nothing in her life was going right. He could change that and maybe change how she felt about him. He wanted to talk to her and not hear the loathing and annoyance in her voice. They'd been lovers, great friends and partners once upon a time. A connection like that didn't die.

Reaching for the phone, he lifted it and dialed Mena's number.

"Please ... don't hang up." Michael took a deep breath, then clicked away from the Palmchat Gazette website and back to the Genesis Gallery. Her bio picture on the gallery's website was stunning. She was still the most beautiful woman in the world to him. Why did she always make him feel this way? Punch drunk with love.

"What do you want, Michael?"

Michael exhaled slowly. Mena's voice was laced with irritation. He should have grown accustomed to her anger by now. But it still hurt. Shit. It stung like hell.

She didn't think she needed him, but he knew better.

"To tell you, I'm sorry," Michael said, his voice low and steady.

"You called to apologize to me?"

"When I saw you at the Genesis Grill, I didn't know about Priscilla's trial and your testimony. Now I see all this in the news about ..." Michael paused. He could barely force the words from his mouth. "Julian being arrested for trying to kill her after her lawyer dragged you through hell on the stand."

"He didn't do it—"

"I would've done the same thing if I was there. Priscilla deserves to die because of what she did to you," Michael insisted.

"Stop pretending like you care anything about me. If you really cared so much, you wouldn't—" Mena inhaled sharply.

Seconds filled with silence as he waited for her to continue. Waited for her to say the one thing he could do for her that no one else could. He could bring a smile back to her life. He was willing to make that sacrifice for her happiness. He'd find another way to win her back.

Mena said, "I can't do this right now. Goodbye Michael."

"Wait," Michael said, standing from his seat. He walked around the desk and leaned against the edge, wrapping the telephone cord tightly around his hand. Pain pierced his skin from the wire digging into his flesh. "I know what you're thinking. If I truly loved you, I would let you go. Give you the divorce and you're right."

Mena's shaky breaths calmed. She was still on the line. Listening. Waiting for him to say what she hoped he would. He would give her what she wanted, but he wanted something in return.

"The conference ends this week and I'll be going back to New York on Saturday," Michael said. "Can we meet? Talk about how to get the divorce finalized here before I leave."

"All of a sudden, you're willing to sign the divorce papers. I'm supposed to believe that?" Mena scoffed.

"I promised myself that I would never knowingly do anything to hurt you again. Not being honest with you about my marriages was a mistake that will haunt me forever. It cost me you and that is a devastating fact that I live with every day."

Mena said, "I've trusted you too many times in the past, just to be made a fool of, Michael. With everything I'm dealing with, I can't take one more setback, one more let down. Don't do this to me."

"When I read about your testimony, what Zak Webber did to you, it sickened me. I wanted to take away every bit of pain you'd gone through, but my love isn't what you want right now. What you want is a divorce. I realized that I love you enough to sacrifice what I want for what you need. If this is how it all ends, I want to see you one last time before I'm no longer your husband."

Mena sighed. "You stopped being my husband the moment I found out you had three other wives in three other states."

Michael yanked the phone base from the desk, then paused. His hand frozen in mid-air. Throwing it wouldn't solve anything. He had to stay calm.

"Listen, there's a little restaurant called Mama Lisa's Kitchen on the outskirts of Cashew Groves, not far from the resort where the conference is being held. It's discrete and pretty empty in the afternoons, so you don't have to worry about anyone hounding you or seeing us together. I'll be there at 3. Meet me, okay. Let's talk about everything so we can both get closure on our past and move on."

Michael held his breath, waiting for her to respond. She was still on the phone with him and that spoke louder than anything she said. If she truly hated him, she wouldn't talk to him at all. Lowering the phone back to the desk, Michael sat on the edge of the chair.

"Fine." Mena said.

The call ended.

A smile played at the corners of his mouth. Michael lowered the phone onto the cradle, then glanced at his watch. He'd need to catch the ferry from the Aerie Islands back to St. Basil now if he was going to make it in time.

Slipping out of his white coat, he hung it on the hangar in the corner and grabbed his briefcase. Everything was looking up. In a few hours, he'd be face to face with his wife. He would not blow it this time. He'd keep his cool and show her she was wrong about him.

Walking toward his office door, Michael stopped as it flew open.

Dr. Quentin Tufa barreled inside, almost colliding with him. The poised, professional demeanor was gone. Dr. Tufa looked haggard, salt-and-pepper gray stubble on his face. His clothes disheveled and wrinkled. What the hell was going on?

"I'm having my sister transferred here this afternoon. I need you to start your protocol on her and bring her out of the coma." The desperate words rushed out of Dr. Tufa's mouth.

Michael shook his head. He didn't care about the resources Dr. Tufa had promised him. He'd give it all back before he helped the woman who'd tried to destroy Mena's life. "You'll have to find another doctor. I don't have room for a psychopath in my clinical trials."

Dr. Tufa glared at him. "My sister is the only one keeping your clinical trial supplied with embryonic stem cells."

"I doubt you'd want a doctor under the distress of being blackmailed responsible for treating your sister. That wouldn't be a wise move on your part to put her life in my hands," Michael countered, unfazed by Tufa's threats. He wasn't going to be beholden to anyone for his groundbreaking research.

Tufa's anger was palpable. Michael had gotten his point across.

"It's wise if you think more clearly about what you have to gain by bringing Priscilla out of the coma," Tufa said, a hint of taunting in his tone.

Michael wanted to walk away but couldn't resist finding out what angle Tufa was working. What could he possibly gain by bringing back the woman who'd terrorized Mena?

Dr. Tufa continued, "Priscilla can give you exactly what you really want—your wife. Mena."

Michael lowered his briefcase to the floor. How the hell did Dr. Tufa know about his marriage? "How so?"

"You wife's new boyfriend tried to kill my sister. He's in jail right now and will stay there until the trial. There's only one person who can confirm the heinous crime he committed."

Michael whispered, "Priscilla Dumay."

"You wake her up. She testifies of Julian's attempt to murder her and he goes to jail for a very long time, leaving Mena Nix available for you to rekindle your defunct marriage. Sounds like a win-win all around. Now, let's try this again. My sister will be transferred here this afternoon. Will you treat her with your protocol?"

Chapter Sixteen

Staring at the window, a four-inch slit within the concrete wall in front of him, Julian flinched as the steel bars slammed shut. A tiny sliver of sun shone through the glass.

Another loud thud.

The outer door of his prison cell. Closed and locked.

Standing in the center of the room, he vaguely registered a man on the concrete bed to his left. Julian wasn't in the mood to play nice or make friends. He closed his eyes and took a deep breath.

Mena's gasp rang in his ears, over and over, drowning out every other sound. Her pained reaction to the Judge's ruling. The confusion in that simple sound had resonated from her to him. He'd let her down. He'd lifted her hand to his lips and kissed her palm, inhaling the intoxicating scent of sandalwood and orange from her skin. Walking out of the courtroom, he didn't dare look back at her. He couldn't let his last glimpse of her face be one etched with fear, worry and disappointment.

The prison guards had shackled him outside the courthouse behind the Governmental Promenade and forced him into the back of the van. In all the madness, he'd still felt her presence. Mena was standing across the street underneath the towering palm trees, alone. The hopeless and lost look in her eyes made him hate himself for what he was putting her through.

Opening his eyes slowly, Julian glanced to his right. A steel toilet rested against the stained concrete wall. Next to the toilet was a three-foot partition enclosing a shower stall. A mattress rested on top of a concrete slab inches from the toilet on the other side.

The gasp grew louder. Julian squeezed his eyes shut, tried to force it away.

"Fuck!" Julian yelled. Spinning around, he landed a fist against the wall. The sharp pain dulled the sound of Mena's voice. He swung another fist and another, pummeling the wall until he couldn't hear her anymore.

Blood smeared the rough surface.

His hands howled in pain, throbbing and aching from the force of the blows. Julian glanced down at his swollen, scratched and bloody fists, then leaned his forehead against the cold, rough concrete.

The mattress creaked from behind him. Slow footsteps grew nearer. A hand rested against his shoulder.

"It's good you got that shit out of the way. First couple of minutes were hell for me too, but it gets better. Kind of."

Julian glanced down at the hand resting on his shoulder. The forearm was emblazoned with a dark calligraphy tattoo of the word "Playboy." Julian looked at the guy he'd be sharing a cell with. He saw how he got the nickname. One of those GQ model types that the women swooned over.

"Almost time for lunch. You should rinse off that blood. No use getting on the guards' radar this soon, they'll think you've been up to no good," Playboy said.

Turning the faucet on, Julian winced as he allowed the ice-cold water to flow over his hands. Water tinted red with blood flowed over the stained basin and slipped down the rusted drain.

Playboy handed Julian a worn hand towel. Then reached under his mattress and pulled out a small pouch. Alcohol square. "Place is full of germs."

Tearing the pouch open, Julian pressed the small square over the raw and scraped skin. Blood soaked through the towelette. The blaze of stinging pain was no match for the sharp ache of his throbbing knuckles.

"Thanks," Julian mumbled. "Playboy."

"Don't start that shit. I get enough of it from the other fools in here. I'm Xander."

"So, Xander, if you don't like the nickname, why is it on your arm?" Julian asked.

"To make it clear to my female visitors that I'm not a one-woman kind of guy," Xander explained.

Julian laughed under his breath.

"I'm serious, man. I get about a hundred letters a week from females I've never even met wanting to set up conjugal visits with me. Shit, I can only fuck so much. I have to be picky about the ones I accept."

Julian slumped down onto the thin, hard mattress.

"Stop moping like your goddamn life is over. You won't be in here for long," Xander said.

"What makes you say that?"

"Cause you're my cellmate. We are what they call Errado Boys, wrongly accused of crimes and expected not to be here for long. Except my ass been up here for almost a year now."

"Who thinks I've been wrongly accused?"

"Well, some do and some don't. One side says you tried to whack her, and she deserved it. The other side, which I'm on, says you're an ex-Navy SEAL. If you wanted her dead, she would be. In the end, only one man's opinion counts. He thinks you're innocent, so you got put with me."

"And who the fuck is this one man?" Julian asked, frowning.

"Josue Chartres. The one man in this place that you don't want to piss off. A Vadaj. He executed people on the PC-5 death list, and he runs Tiverton," Xander explained.

The gang influence within Tiverton didn't surprise Julian. Many prisons had to deal with gang members who were just as powerful, or even more so, than they were on the outside. To keep the peace, prison wardens and guards kept a tight watch, limiting the interactions of rival gangs. No surprise that the PC-5 was a force to be reckoned with inside the maximum-security walls.

Julian said, "Guess rule number one is to always show respect to Chartres. What else do I need to know?"

"Josue expects prompt payment of a twenty percent protection fee on anything you buy or that gets sent to you while in here. Doesn't matter what it is. You get a pack of chewing gum with five pieces, one of those needs to be sent to Josue. You get a notebook with a hundred pages in it, you better rip out twenty and give them to Josue. Being Errado Boy and staying current on your protection fees will ensure you'll have no problems while you're here."

"Can't imagine that everybody follows those rules," Julian said.

Xander nodded. "Everybody don't follow them. The fee don't apply to motherfuckers on Death Row and it sure as hell don't apply to the Fury. Sick bastard went on a rampage killing people and eating them decades ago. He's in here somewhere, but his location is top-secret. I don't know anyone who's ever seen the hairy motherfucker, but it's still creepy as fuck to know we're locked up with someone like that."

Julian had heard the Fury suffered from a disease that covered most of his body with fur-like hair. He was a blight on the Palmchat Islands, which took a hit in tourism when he was on his killing spree.

A loud bell rang, followed by the sound of cell doors banging open.

"Lunch time?" Julian asked.

"We're up. We go by units. This is Epsilon Unit which houses all the Errado Boys plus some smaller gangs—Pandas out of Argentina, Ruffboys from Jamaica and Quattro. Got to watch out for Quattro. They're ruthless and stupid, bucking the PC-5 and trying to make a name for themselves. Josue keeps them in check. He and his leadership team stay out of the cells for the entire lunch hours to collect his protection fees from the other inmates," Xander said, then pushed open the inner door to their cell. "Come on, it's burrito day."

Julian walked side by side with Xander in the herd of inmates into the massive cafeteria in the basement of the prison. Guards toting assault rifles were stationed along the hallway and inside the dining area, keeping a close watch on the activities of the inmates. The plastic chairs and long rectangular tables were bolted to the concrete floor. Near the far left of the room, Julian saw a group of five men huddled over a table scattered with dominoes. Empty paper plates and cups lay littered toward the edge as they focused on their game.

"Which one is Josue Chartres?" Julian asked.

Xander turned and glanced at the table, then back toward the wall. "The one making those guards laugh over there near the doors."

Julian spied the imposing man, taking note as he crept through the line to pick up a paper plate that held a burrito and a small mound of refried beans. Near the end of the line, he saw plastic cups filled with jello and others with wilted lettuce for a salad.

"When's your next conjugal, Playboy?" one of the other inmates serving the food called out to Xander.

"Tomorrow," Xander said.

"She thick?"

Xander shrugged, "Not obese, but a healthy female, well fed. Big ass, big tits. I haven't been in the mood for skinny ones lately, nothing to grab onto if you know what I'm saying."

"Yeah, I like 'em thick too. My old lady's holding out, though, punishing me because I didn't respond to her emails quick enough when I got thrown in solitary for them three days. Hope she comes next week."

Julian's appetite waned. Conjugal visits. That couldn't become the future for him and Mena. He wouldn't put her through ferry rides to the prison for them to make love on a schedule dictated by the warden. Fuck. He didn't even want her to step foot in this hellhole. She was too good for a place like this.

"What the fuck you doing? The hero up here dreaming, holding up the line."

A hand slapped at the plate in Julian's hand, sending the burrito skittering across the floor.

Julian clenched his fists, trying to stay calm. Mena's voice flooded through his mind.

He forced his hand into my underwear and groped me ...

A swift pivot and Julian was face to face with Zak Webber, his hand clenched around the bastard's neck. A strained gurgle slipped from Zak's lips.

"I know what you did to Mena and you will regret it," Julian said, through gritted teeth.

Xander's hand clamped down on Julian's arm, wrestling it away from Zak's neck. "Not a good move, hero."

Zak's eyes bulged from the sockets as he gave him a sinister grin. "Never knew a good finger stroke could make a bitch moan that good."

"Montgomery! You starting trouble in your first hour here?" the prison guard asked, staring at Julian.

"No trouble, over here, sir," Xander said with a grin as he yanked Julian away.

Julian vaguely noticed the plate with a fresh burrito being shoved into his hands by Xander. Walking backward out of the food line, he kept his eyes on Zak Webber.

Chapter Seventeen

Mena brought the Maserati SUV to a stop near the back of the parking lot of Mama Lisa's Kitchen. She stared at the dilapidated building painted in the colors of the Palmchat Islands flag. A faded sign hung beside the door. The picture of a smiling elderly woman, likely Mama Lisa, next to a heaping plate of goat fritters, salad and a cup of goat stew greeted patrons.

Was this a good idea? Agreeing to meet Michael? Or was she just setting herself up for another one of his grand manipulations and more lies? Mena leaned her head back against the seat. A yawn escaped her lips. She was exhausted.

The last forty-eight hours had been the worst of her life. After the bail hearing, she'd kept her roaring emotions locked inside. Slipping past the crowds, Mena had made her way toward the back of the courthouse. She watched as the guards shackled Julian and forced him onto the prison bus. He hadn't seen her, and she was glad. In that moment, she'd hit rock bottom. Fear and hopelessness wracked through her to the point that she almost screamed out loud. Why did this keep happening to them? Why couldn't the world and fate and karma just allow them to be together in love and in peace? Around every corner was a different challenge, a new battle, another hurdle to overcome.

She was tired of fighting to be with the man she loved.

But in her heart, she knew she'd never give up.

Michael was another obstacle she and Julian had to face. Mena was in no mood to talk to the man who should be her ex-husband, but the alternative was even more daunting. She couldn't face going back to the penthouse knowing that Julian wouldn't be there. He wouldn't be coming home for weeks, if not months.

Focusing on getting the divorce from Michael was better than worrying about the days she had ahead of her without Julian. She owed it to their relationship to find out if Michael truly had a change of heart.

Finalizing a divorce in St. Basil was as simple as them signing the documents in front of a registered Palmchat Islands notary and one of them submitting the papers to the courthouse. Within six hours of submission, the divorce would be certified and that would be the end of the disastrous Michael Marsh chapter in her life.

Pushing the thoughts away, Mena watched as Michael appeared. He was walking from the base of the mountains down the narrow street, heading toward the small restaurant. As he approached the entrance, Mena exited the car and slammed the door shut behind her. Michael turned to look toward the sound, a glimmer in his eyes as he saw her.

Mena choked down the bile rising in her throat and warned herself not to botch this meeting. She knew what Michael expected, but perhaps she could convince him by showing him a side of her that he hadn't seen in years. Showing him the woman he'd fallen in love with. Anything to get him to agree to the divorce.

"Shall we go inside?" Michael asked as Mena approached him.

Mena nodded and followed him to the entrance of the restaurant. Stepping inside, Mena glanced around. Square tables and metal chairs with bright orange cushions were placed in each corner of the room. A single hibiscus flower in a tiny vase rested in the middle, surrounded by full place settings at each seat. Mena smiled.

"Reminds you of the original Kaleidoscope, doesn't it?" Michael said.

"Yeah, it does. Feels very familiar," Mena admitted, remembering the hole in the wall that was the first location of her Mother's iconic Jacksonville restaurant. Mena had ripped and run throughout the place, delighting the customers and driving her mom bonkers.

"Hello! Oh my, you said you'd be back by here, but that's what they all say.

Usually people end up eating at that fancy restaurant near the top of the hike and never make it back down to try any of Mama Lisa's food," a frail, skinny woman said, dabbing a towel across her forehead. "And you brought a lovely friend with you! Please sit anywhere and I'm going to whip up something that the two of you will love."

"Thanks Mama Lisa, we appreciate it," Michael said. He chose the table closest to the door and pulled out the chair, allowing Mena to sit down.

"Percy, get out here and get our customers some water and two Felipe beers," Mama Lisa called out.

Mena looked around, confused as to where Percy could be hiding. There didn't seem to be any other rooms in the restaurant. The front door swung open and a boy, probably only around twelve or thirteen, bounded inside, balancing two cups filled with ice and water in one hand and two bottles of beer in the other. After Percy had placed the drinks on the table, he gave them a big toothy grin, then ran into the kitchen as Mama Lisa barked more orders at him.

Mena took a sip of the refreshing water. "How was the conference?"

"Great, actually. I met a few potential investors who are interested in supporting my research," Michael said. He took a swig of the Felipe beer, his eyes scrutinizing her.

Mena figured he was thrown by her approach, but making Michael the enemy was pointless.

"You were always a very talented doctor," Mena said. "I'm glad that you're able to continue your work and help people after everything that happened."

"Rebuilding my reputation was hard, but it was my own fault. My lies destroyed both of us, our marriage. I get it now. It doesn't really matter if I was truly divorced from Courtney and Emma and Alexis in the eyes of the law. My biggest regret is not telling you about them. Not warning you so that Courtney couldn't have destroyed our marriage. If you'd known, things could be different now."

"You think our marriage would have survived?" Mena swirled her finger around the rim of the glass of water as the decadent smell of food permeated the air.

"Maybe it's just wishful thinking because I love you more today than the day we were married. I don't know how you turned your feelings off for me because I'm having a hell of a time trying to get over you, Mena," Michael said.

Mena resisted the urge to roll her eyes. "I guess we'll never know."

"At least this time, you have a chance to make a different decision," Michael said.

"What do you mean?"

Percy approached the table slowly. Michael waved at him to come forward. Mena's stomach grumbled from the delicious smell. Goat kabobs with rice and peas, goat fritters and a side salad.

"Thanks man," Michael said, then gave the kid a fist bump that caused his wide smile to get even wider, if that was even possible. Michael popped a piece of the succulent goat meat into his mouth, then turned his attention back to Mena.

"I know you don't want to hear this, but I love you. It's killing me to watch you tie yourself up in knots worrying about Julian," Michael said. "Did he even stop to think about how going after Priscilla Dumay could affect you or your relationship?"

"It's complicated. I can't expect you to understand. I'm not going to explain Julian to you," Mena snapped. Reaching for her fork, she plunged it into a goat fritter and stuffed it into her mouth. She understood exactly why Julian had taken the risk. Priscilla could have the one thing that could ruin Julian's life—evidence of the mistake he'd made in Central Sulawesi. Julian had no clue he was walking into Dumay's trap.

Michael raised his hands. "You're right. All I know is that I would give anything to have you back, but it doesn't feel right to try with everything going on with Julian. I want it to be a fair fight. Not me kicking a man when he's down and in prison."

"A fair fight has nothing to do with Julian. Fair is allowing me to make my own decisions about who I want to be with. Michael, I've already told you that it's not you," Mena said.

Michael sucked in a breath, and Mena was almost sorry for hurting him. Almost.

"How can you make a clear decision when you haven't even allowed yourself to think about the alternative I'm offering? If you spent just one weekend with me, without the chaos of Julian's legal troubles, you might find that we have way more in common than you and the ex-Navy SEAL," Michael said.

"And if I did and came to the same conclusion, then what?" Mena demanded. "Would you give me a divorce then?"

Michael hesitated, taking another long swig of his Felipe beer. "Yeah, I would."

"You're lying," Mena said.

"I want one last chance to show you why we belong together. Spend the weekend with me at the resort. After two days together, just the two of us, if you still wanted to be with Julian ... I wouldn't stand in your way," Michael said.

Mena stared at him, the face of the man she'd once loved, and couldn't quite reconcile the sincerity she heard in his words. Was he being honest with her? Or just setting her up? Was it worth finding out if it gave her a real chance to get out of this marriage?

"Would you consider it? If things go my way, then I'd protect you from all the scrutiny of Julian's situation and help you break the news to him. If they don't, I will go with you to the courthouse and have our divorce finalized," Michael offered, then laughed under his breath. "I'm the one taking all the risks here. It's really win-win for you. What do you say?"

Mena swallowed the lump of goat and glanced down at her trembling hands. Taking a deep breath, she rested her elbows on the table and stared at Michael as she gave him her answer.

Chapter Eighteen

Julian scratched at the scabs forming on his knuckles as he peered through the small window of the conference room door. The guards were doing their obligatory search and pat down of his attorney. He watched as Octavia Constant glared at the guard, daring him to make one move that could be considered even remotely inappropriate. He had no doubts she'd have him locked up in Tiverton in the cell next to his before the guard uttered the words, "I'm sorry."

The door swung open and Octavia walked in, slammed her attaché case in the chair and pointed a finger in his face.

"I told you to be a model prisoner," Octavia vented and sat down in the seat across from him. "What's this I hear about you attacking another prisoner, unprovoked, on your first day? You're lucky they didn't put you in solitary."

"Unprovoked is a stretch," Julian said, but didn't elaborate. The complex history he shared with Zak Webber wasn't worth bringing up to his attorney.

"Typically, new inmates have a seven-day waiting period before they can have phone calls and visitors. Guess what? Yours just got extended to fourteen days. That means two weeks before you can see Mena or your parents,"

"My parents?" Julian balked.

"I talked to your mom yesterday and gave her an update on your case—"

"Why the fuck would you do that?"

"She called and demanded information about your case. I divulged nothing that would breech our attorney-client privilege," Octavia said. "She said she would come to the island to see you as soon as you could have visitors ..."

Julian couldn't help but notice that she hadn't mentioned his old man. He was probably telling everyone that Julian would screw up eventually, and he'd been right about his son all along. Fucking asshole. He didn't want to see him, anyway. Dealing with his mom was going to be hard enough.

"How did Mena take the news?"

"She was disappointed but took it well. You don't have to worry about her. She's seems incredibly strong," Octavia said.

On the surface at least, Julian thought. Mena never showed much emotion, even as she battled internal turmoil.

"The main thing I need you focused on is staying out of trouble. I get it, skirmishes happen all the time in Tiverton, especially when some gang gets it in their head to torment a new arrival. The key is to only defend, never attack. Got it?" Octavia asked.

"Yeah, I got it," Julian mumbled. As much as he wanted to rip Zak Webber's jugular from his neck, Julian would have to play nice, or risk losing his freedom for good.

"Let me rundown some updates on your case. The police obtained a search warrant this morning for your yacht and the penthouse you share with Mena. Mena's going to stay with her friend, Regina, until the cops have completed the search."

"They won't find a damn thing."

"That's what I wanted to hear. Also, I asked my cousin Icarus—he's a P.I. —to see if he could find proof that Dumay framed you. He provided me with some interesting info last night."

"What did he find out?" Julian asked.

"We believe Priscilla bribed the two guards assigned to her at the trial."

"What makes you think that?"

"One of them is a young man named Whalum O'Keefe. Graduated from high school three years ago and completed the correctional officer training last year. He got hired by Tiverton Prison shortly after completing his training."

"Strange someone that inexperienced got assigned to a high-profile prisoner like Dumay."

"And it gets stranger. O'Keefe had been living with his parents until a week before the trial when he bought a house in Cashew Groves with cash. Icarus has a contact at the realty company who told him O'Keefe walked in with fifty thousand dollars in a backpack for the closing on the property."

"Cash?" Julian contemplated that angle. If Dumay was going to pay off the correctional officers, giving them cash reduced the likelihood of some investigator tracing a money trail back to her. "Bribing one officer doesn't help. What about the other guard? She needed both of them to pull off her little stunt."

"That brings me to the other officer, Farouk Essa." Octavia spread a series of photographs in front of Julian.

He lifted them from the table and stared at the picture of a little boy lying in a hospital bed with tubes going in and out of his tiny body. He had to be no older than five or six years old. His gaunt frame looked almost ghostly against the white sheets. "Who is this little boy?"

"Essa's son. The kid has a rare medical condition. He'd been in St. Basil General Hospital for months until he was transferred to the Rakestraw Blake Center over the weekend," Octavia said.

"This Essa guy could have been using the money to pay for the treatment that his kid needed," Julian said, staring into the face of the young boy.

"Or just to make a dent in the mountain of debt I'm sure he has from the months of his child being hospitalized. We believe Essa convinced O'Keefe to go along with Dumay's plan and accept the payout. He was clearly more desperate for the money than O'Keefe was."

Looking at the sick child, Julian understood why Farouk Essa would make a deal with the devil. "Nice story, counselor, but it proves nothing. There's a hundred different ways Whalum could have gotten the money to buy that house that don't have anything to do with Dumay. As for Essa, the RBC has plenty of compassionate treatment programs where patients are brought in and charged nothing for their medical care. We can weave stories for days on how both of them ended up in their situations. You haven't said anything that connects them to Dumay, so this theory won't fly with the cops."

"That's the same thing Des said when I talked to him," Octavia said, pressing her lips together in a thin line.

"Des? You on a nickname basis with one of the princes of Palmchat Islands law enforcement?"

"I grew up in St. X with the Francois brothers. We go way back. Lucky for you, I have a great relationship with all the Francois detectives. Des has agreed to look into the officers as a favor to me," Octavia explained.

"And if he comes up empty?"

"It doesn't change anything. That's our Plan B. Plan A is just to prove reasonable doubt."

"When will I get a trial date?" Julian asked.

Octavia hesitated. "Under normal circumstances, it would be two to three months."

"These ain't normal circumstances."

"I expect the D.A. to stall his case, hoping that either Priscilla dies and he can get you on premeditated first degree murder or she comes out of the coma and can identify you as her attacker. I'm doing everything to prepare to counter his tactics, but you should prepare to be here for three to six months. Maybe more."

"Fuck!" Julian slammed his fist against the table.

"Not what you wanted to hear. Listen to me. Stay out of trouble. Be the model prisoner for as long as it takes, and you'll be fine." Octavia grabbed her attaché case and exited the room, leaving him alone.

Julian dragged his hand down his face and took a deep breath. Three to six months away from Mena. How the hell was he going to break this news to her? Julian imagined her reaction and it made him sick, just thinking about it.

"Let's go Montgomery."

The door swung open and two guards entered, followed by another prisoner. "Webber has this room after you."

Julian looked up into the cold, dark eyes of Zak Webber. A deep bruise had formed on his neck from where Julian had grabbed him two days ago. Julian stood and walked toward one of the guards.

"Don't think I won't get you back for this, bitch!" Zak growled under his breath as his hand lingered near his neck.

"That's what you always say, isn't it? I kick your ass and you come back with words. Some badass you are," Julian said.

"Fuck you!" Zak screamed, then spat at Julian.

The warm, thick saliva hit Julian in the eye, then dripped down the side of his face.

"You're a dead man," Julian said, as the guard jerked him away and out of the room.

Chapter Nineteen

"Who did you sleep with to get us reservations during this prime hour?" Omar asked, slipping his sunglasses on.

Regina slapped at Omar's arm and rolled her eyes. "No salacious acts were required to get this reservation. When I told Beaujean we wanted to do something special to take Mena's mind off everything, he suggested Solar."

"Helps that the cops forced you out of the penthouse with that damn search warrant or we wouldn't have convinced you to come, would we?" Omar asked.

Mena remained quiet. A week ago, Julian had surprised her with a romantic dinner the night before they were due to testify against Priscilla. Mena never would have believed that Julian would be the one in Tiverton seven days later, and Priscilla would be in a coma at the Rakestraw Blake Center.

Her world had been knocked off its axis. Mena had taken the week off, unable to concentrate on work. She'd placed her phone on vibrate, checking in every few hours to text her family and friends back. They meant well, but she'd been in no mood to talk or be around anyone. Then without any notice, her morning moping had been interrupted by police pounding on her door. Shoving the search warrant in her face, they forced her out of her home. Mena had fumed in the lobby as she called Omar to tell him what had happened. As she expected, her best friends had left work immediately to support her.

"Mena, we're not expecting you to pretend like you're okay. Getting out of the penthouse and staying with me for a while will do you some good," said Regina.

Mena nodded. "I just don't know what they think they are going to find. Julian didn't try to kill Priscilla."

"Just a damn witch hunt." Omar said.

The maitre'd found their reservation and signaled for them to follow a waiter dressed in dark orange Bermuda shorts and a bright yellow tank top. Sandwiched between Omar and Regina, her arms looped between theirs, Mena took shaky steps forward. The waiter escorted them past a throng of locals and tourists waiting in a line that stretched across the rooftop of Harmony Towers to the side elevator. On the bottom level, hopeful restaurant patrons were wrapped around the block. Snaking through the opulent cabanas of Solar Restaurant, the newest and hippest restaurant and dayclub in the Palmchat Islands, Mena recognized several Caribbean celebrities lounging on the cabanas. Even CoCo had been spotted at the restaurant earlier in the week, sending the already massive reputation into the stratosphere.

Thankful that they were seated in a more discrete private area, Mena sat down on the cabana cushion and waved a hand for the waiter to lift the shade to shield her from the bright sun. She couldn't remember the last time she'd eaten. Her stomach was tied in knots, a dull ache that made the prospect less than desirable.

"You need a liquid lunch, my dear. You look like you haven't slept in days," Omar said as he ordered a round of Palmitos, his voice elevated to be heard over the loud music of the D.J.

"No, she needs food. You felt how shaky she was walking over here," Regina admonished. "Mena, we have got to get your energy up. Julian is going to kill us if we don't keep you fed and healthy while he's away."

Mena gave a small smile. "Why not both?"

"Let's do it!" Omar said, pounding a hand against the table.

Fighting over the menu, Omar and Regina debated what to try, then ordered enough food for a party of eight.

"The two of you are crazy. How are we supposed to eat all of that food?" Mena asked.

"Who said we have to eat all of it? The goal is to try the best of what Solar has to offer and to keep your mind off of Julian and damn Prissy for a little while," Omar said.

"Have you heard anything about her condition? Maybe from Charlie?" Mena asked, even though she wasn't sure she wanted more details. Octavia had explained the complexity of Julian's case. If Priscilla remained in a coma, there was a slightly better chance to control the narrative in Julian's favor. If she woke, Prissy would likely confirm Julian as her attacker. Octavia could then shift the legal strategy toward discrediting her based on the other crimes Priscilla was charged with. Neither option sounded like a slam dunk for Julian.

"Charlie's been swamped with making big money from that medical conference that's in town. He's closed on about a dozen deals for his medical supplies, worth about ten million in sales. If there's one thing my boo knows how to do, it's make that money, baby. But anyway, I did get an update when Katherine Pourciau stopped by the gallery yesterday," Omar said.

"Katey and Prissy were best friends," Regina remarked.

"*Are* best friends. Katey insists that Prissy is innocent and that the charges are all a big mistake. Her husband is the chief administrator at the Rakestraw Blake Center. Apparently, Prissy's adopted Ethiopian brother had her moved there. She's being treated by some hotshot doctor from the States as part of an experimental clinical trial. There's a good chance she'll come out of the coma in a couple of weeks."

Mena sat up straighter. Julian's best friend Broman Garrison was also at the RBC being treated in an experimental clinical trial. "Have they figured out what was in the syringe?"

"No," Omar shook his head. "Katey said they have the best researchers working on trying to identify what it is. They've never seen anything like it before. Katey says the unknown poison won't stop Prissy from coming out of the coma. They just aren't sure what other lasting effects could remain."

"I thought we were trying to get Mena's mind off the case for a while," Regina interrupted.

"Hell, she asked the question. What am I supposed to do? Ignore her?" Omar retorted.

"No, you're supposed to subtly direct the conversation toward another topic like this. So, Mena, did you ever talk to Uma? Any chance she'll be coming back to work at the gallery?" Regina asked.

"I left her a message, but she didn't call me back. Still can't believe Beaujean insisted that I try to get her back on the team with everything she did to help Irving Bond steal from the gallery," Mena admitted.

Regina said, "Beaujean believes in second chances. Uma made mistakes, but I really liked her—"

"Oh, Lord! Is that my husband walking in here with some fine ass man?" Omar said, rising from the cabana.

Mena looked up. Charlie Johnson was walking behind a petite waitress as he engaged in a lively conversation with ...

Forcing herself to breathe, Mena could barely hear over the pounding of her heart as Omar waved them over toward the table.

Charlie broke into a wide smile at the sight of Omar, tugging on the arm of his companion to approach the table.

"Hey hon," Charlie said, leaning over to give Omar a quick kiss. "Surprised to see you here."

"Who's your friend?" Omar asked, eyeing the man suspiciously.

"This is Dr. Michael Marsh, a neurologist in town for the medical conference I told you about," Charlie said, as he rubbed Omar's arm.

Omar visibly relaxed and greeted Michael.

"Glad to see you out and about, Mena," Charlie said. "If there's anything you need, please don't hesitate to tell us. We are here for you."

Mena nodded her head, then avoided eye contact with Michael.

"Good to see you again, Mena. I hope we get a chance to catch up before I leave town this weekend. My offer still stands," Michael said.

Mena raised her head and glared into Michael's piercing hazel eyes. "I won't be taking you up on that offer, but do hope you have a safe trip back to New York."

Awkward silence filled the air. The waitress broke the tension and beckoned for Charlie and Michael. The two men said their goodbyes and left the table.

Regina shrieked. "What was that all about?"

"How do you know that fine ass neurologist?" Omar asked.

"Long story," Mena said, exhausted by all the lies and the pretense. How dare Michael put her on the spot in front of her friends.

"Mena?" Regina said. "Honey, are you okay?"

"Okay, spill it. What's going on with you and Dr. Sexy?"

"He's ..." Mena swallowed past the lump in her throat. "My ... husband."

Chapter Twenty

Regina gasped, her hand flying to her mouth. Omar's mouth dropped open.

Mena looked back and forth between the two as silence stretched across the table. Neither of her best friends had moved a muscle, faces frozen in shock. The waiter approached the table with the pitcher of Palmitos and the first round of appetizers.

"Thanks, we're definitely going to need the drinks," Mena said.

Over the next hour, she told her best friends the unbelievable story of how she was still the legal wife of Michael Marsh. Meeting Michael was like a whirlwind romantic comedy, something too good to be true. And it was too good to be true. A year after being married to the charismatic neurologist, her world had been turned upside down when his wife, Courtney, showed up at their home. Mena had learned that not only was Michael still married to Courtney, but he had two other wives, Alexis and Emily.

As Michael's last wife, Mena had been told her marriage to him was voided by the previous three, so she didn't think she needed to get a divorce or an annulment. A mistake she regretted as she struggled to keep the truth from Julian.

"You must think I'm a horrible person for keeping all of this from you," Mena said, looking down at the food she hadn't touched.

"Start eating and let us talk now," Omar demanded, lifting Mena's fork and forcing it into her hand.

"You are not horrible for being lied to by your husband. Any creep that would knowingly marry more than one woman at the same time doesn't deserve a second chance or forgiveness," Regina said. Her face flushed red with anger.

"That slimy bastard is forcing you to stay married to him. None of that is your fault, Mena. I don't care if you didn't jump through all the legal hoops needed to officially annul the marriage four years ago. You are not that man's wife!" Omar said.

"I talked to three different lawyers, Omar. Legally, I am. The worst part is that Julian doesn't even know," Mena said.

"Mena! That's why you had to say no to his proposal. You want to marry him, but you can't until your divorce is finalized," Regina said.

Mena said, "I should have told Julian the truth then—"

"Wait a minute, now," Omar held up a hand.

Mena frowned, then glanced at Regina.

"I'm with Omar on this one. You did the right thing by not telling Julian. Best-case scenario, he's hurt because you lied and the two of you have to wait six agonizing months before you're free to get married again," Regina said.

"Worst-case scenario, he hauls off and murders the bastard for manipulating you and refusing to sign the divorce papers and spends the rest of his life on death row in Tiverton," Omar said.

"Either way, you put Julian through unnecessary pain when you don't really need to," Regina said.

"I can't believe what I'm hearing," Mena said, absently chewing on a tamarind glazed goat tender.

"I hate to say this, but Julian being locked up in Tiverton gives you a chance to get out of this mess without him finding out," Regina added.

"What was the offer your slimy husband was alluding to?" Omar asked.

"An indecent proposal," Mena murmured.

"He wants you to have sex with him to get him to sign the divorce papers?" Regina whispered angrily.

"Not that indecent. He wants me to spend this weekend with him at the Blue Moon Resort so he can convince me to give him a second chance," Mena said.

"And if you do that and still aren't convinced, then what?" Omar asked.

"He signs the divorce papers in front of the hotel's notary, and I get to file them first thing Monday morning," Mena said. "I just know he's going to find a way to weasel out of it. He can't be trusted."

Omar and Regina exchanged a conspiratorial glance.

"What are the two of you up to?" asked Mena.

"Sweetheart," Omar started. "Why don't you text Michael and tell him you reconsidered? You will take him up on his offer and check in at the resort tomorrow night. In your own room, of course."

Regina nodded her head. "I'll get the room booked for you now. There are ways to make sure Michael doesn't renege on his end of the bargain. With our help, you'll be a divorced woman after the weekend is over."

Omar reached over and gave Regina a high-five. "We guarantee it!"

Chapter Twenty-One

The twenty-foot barbed wire fence topped with spikes surrounded the expansive rectangle known as the yard. Gray clouds billowed across the sky, casting an ominous shadow on the inmates as they dispersed across the space that stretched the length of two football fields.

Julian trudged across the dirt worn path leading to the outer gravel running track. The meeting with Octavia had gone worse than he expected.

The look on Octavia's face when she entered the holding room of the prison had said it all.

"I got the report from Des about what the police found when they searched your penthouse and yacht," Octavia had begun, unable to hide the frustration and bewilderment in her tone.

"What are you talking about? There was nothing for them to find. Nothing that connects me to the attack on Dumay," Julian said, leaning forward. The search had started shortly after sunrise yesterday and had concluded earlier this afternoon. Almost thirty-six hours scouring through his home and yacht, the cops had forced Mena to stay with friends until they were done.

"If by nothing you mean the same poison that was injected into Priscilla Dumay, then yeah, you're right. The cops found nothing."

"What the hell?" Julian said, forcing himself to stay calm. "I didn't poison that bitch and I don't make a fucking habit of keeping poison lying around my home."

"On your yacht, the cops found a bloody shirt in the dirty clothes hamper. Inside one of the pockets was a vial that contained the exact same poison that put Dumay in a coma. Your fingerprints are all over that vial. The police are testing the blood to find out who it belongs to. Care to explain?"

Julian slumped into the chair as the memories hit him like a freight train. "It's Mena's blood."

"Mena? Your girlfriend?"

"I had that shirt on when Adam Russell kidnapped us in Kenya. After the pilot shot Mena in the arm, I had to get the bleeding under control. There was a first aid kit with the vials, gauze, wraps and the like," Julian said, remembering the odd configuration of six vials filled with clear liquid lined neatly inside the kit. "I put one of the vials in my pocket just in case her pain got too bad, but then I forgot all about it when the plane was going down. I didn't even remember I had that vial after we survived the crash."

"So, you thought the vial was a painkiller, and that's the only reason you had it?" Octavia asked. Her eyes bored into him, likely searching for any sign that he was lying to her.

"Yeah, but it wasn't labeled, which was why I didn't give it to Mena immediately," Julian explained, grateful he hadn't accidentally poisoned Mena.

"I may be able to use your version of events to help poke holes in the police investigation. I'm guessing Des feels like he found the smoking gun with that vial on your yacht. When you add that to the video footage from the courthouse showing how you bypassed the normal security entrance protocols with Kendrick to get inside, it looks a lot like premeditated attempted murder."

Julian took a deep breath. The soft drizzle of rain tapped against his skin as he jogged along the trail. Despite the gloomy weather, none of the inmates at Tiverton had opted to stay inside. Recreational time was the highlight of being in this hellhole. Pumping his arms faster, Julian increased his speed as thoughts hounded his mind.

Why the fuck had he kept that damn vial?

Octavia's ability to prove reasonable doubt was in jeopardy. Everything he'd been fighting for, the life he had with Mena, was slipping through his fingers. How the hell was he supposed to stop Priscilla Dumay from ruining his life?

What was even worse was how Mena would handle finding out about the vial. He couldn't even talk to her to explain. Would she still believe in him? Or would she think like so many others? That he'd taken justice into his own hands and kill Dumay for all the bullshit she'd done.

Honestly, the thought had never been too far from Julian's mind.

Only one thing stopped him.

Mena. Having her by his side meant he would never risk doing something that could separate them. He loved her too much to put their relationship in jeopardy, not even to punish Dumay.

Julian had to find a way to clear his name. Dumay's sick and twisted plans for Mena flooded his mind. Who would protect Mena from that bitch if he was trapped in a fucking prison cell in Tiverton for the rest of his life?

Mena was brilliant, smart and courageous. But Dumay had her kidnapped not once, but twice. If Julian was out of the picture, Mena would be a target once again. Dumay had admitted her original plans for them after the kidnapping in Kenya. Taking away Mena's livelihood and forcing her to be a surrogate was the worst thing that could happen to both of them. How the fuck could he stop that from happening now?

Julian would have to do the one thing he was never any good at—wait while others helped him out of this mess.

The sound of footsteps, mirroring his own, broke into his thoughts.

Someone was running behind him. Gaining ground. Julian increased his pace to gauge the reaction of whoever was behind him. The steps increased, keeping up with him as he made his way toward the eastern edge of the yard. Two armed guards looked past him at whoever was behind him. Their hands moved to grip the assault rifles draped across their chests.

"We don't want any trouble out here," one guard yelled as Julian passed by him.

A voice responded, "Won't be no trouble, sir."

Zak Webber.

Julian wasn't making any promises about avoiding trouble with the asshole. After everything Zak had done to Mena, Julian wanted to rip his heart from his chest. But he had to stay cool.

Julian slowed to a stop, then turned to face Zak.

The misting rain covered Zak's face as he shielded his eyes with one hand. He drew closer to Julian.

"Your days are numbered, hero," Zak glared at Julian with unrestrained hatred.

Julian responded with a fist to Zak's kidney and followed it with a knee to his stomach. Zak toppled over onto the ground, and Julian raised his hands in mock innocence toward the guards.

Zak coughed and writhed on the ground, stunned by the unexpected attack.

Lowering his face near Zak's ears, Julian pretended to help him up, which appeased the guards who remained at their stations. "I let you survive the last time I stabbed a knife in your chest. Keep fucking with me and the next time, you won't be so lucky."

Julian patted Zak on the face, then turned and jogged away.

Chapter Twenty-Two

Michael raised his hands in mock innocence toward Mena. "I promise, I won't try to seduce you. It's been a long time since we had a night without bitterness, blame and regret. I want to extend it a little longer."

Mena folded her arms over her chest and counted to ten in her head. Everything was going according to the plan that she, Omar, and Regina had outlined. Mena had maybe gone a little too far getting close to Michael over dinner, but she needed Michael to let his defenses down.

She'd endured his not-so-subtle attempts at affection and the repugnant trips down memory lane of their past, biting her tongue, telling herself not to mention all the times he'd lied and manipulated her.

"I suppose this is all a part of your plan to show me that I should give you another chance," Mena said, leaning against the door of the luxury casita nestled near the jungle at the Blue Moon Resort. The high-end accommodations were in the most remote area of the resort grounds, giving the perfect cover for what she planned to do next.

"I think it may be working, just a little bit." Michael flashed her that seductive, sly look that used to make her swoon. His hazel eyes intense with barely contained desire.

She didn't think he would cross a line and try to force himself on her, at least not before she subdued him.

"Fine," Mena said. "One drink only."

She opened the door and Michael walked inside.

He whistled under his breath. "Nice room. Better than mine."

Mena shrugged as Michael seemed to appreciate the massive stone fire-place nestled in the corner surrounded by impeccable furnishings, exotic Caribbean themed art and eco-friendly architecture reminiscent of Frank Lloyd Wright.

Mena walked over to the bar next to the kitchen nook and scanned the options. "No Bishops, but they have Appleton Estates."

"That would be perfect. Are you going to join me?" Michael asked, sinking down on one of the plush couches near the fireplace.

Mena reached for the remote control and the wood inside ignited, giving the room a calming, amber glow. "I'll have wine."

Slipping her hand into her pocket, she extracted the clear vial with the powder inside and tapped it into the tumbler. Hand trembling slightly, she poured the rum in the glass and watched the powder slowly dissolve.

She reached for another glass and filled it with pinot noir, then raised both glasses as she walked to Michael and sat next to him.

"To good memories of times past," Michael said, taking a large gulp of rum.

Mena took a sip of pinot, then placed it on the side table. "Tonight wasn't so bad, but I don't want to mislead you. A weekend at this amazing resort, just the two of us, isn't going to be enough to change my mind."

"How can you be so sure about that? You don't know what I have planned for tomorrow," Michael said. Finishing his rum, he placed the empty glass on the table. "I booked a helicopter tour of the Palmchat Islands followed by your favorite—"

"Skydiving?" Mena asked, stunned. Michael really was trying to win her back.

Michael playfully touched her nose. "You got it. I remember how excited you were after we went that first time. You kept bugging me over and over to go back."

"And you never quite mastered being able to tell me no," Mena said, with a laugh under her breath.

"Four trips in four months and I thought to myself, I've created a monster," Michael said. His eyes grew heavy as he blinked slowly.

"Come on, you enjoyed it as much as I did," Mena said, wondering how much time she had before the drug took effect.

"Only because I was with you." Michael trailed a finger along her arm, caressing her skin gently.

Mena took a deep breath. It was now or never. "This is what worries me, Michael. I don't believe you're going to hold up your end of the bargain if the weekend doesn't turn out like you want it to."

"I promised you I would—"

"You've promised me things before and broken every one," Mena reminded him, but there was no anger or sadness in her voice. She was resigned to their past, almost indifferent to the memories. The only lingering connection between her and Michael was the legal one that kept them as husband and wife.

"What would make you feel more secure staying the weekend with me? Tell me and I'll do it."

"Sign the divorce papers."

"Come on, Mena," Michael leaned back.

"Hear me out. I brought them here with me. If you sign them now in front of me and then take them to be held in the hotel safe until we check out, I will spend the weekend with you."

Michael scoffed. "Signing them without a notary won't make them valid."

His words were becoming slurred. She didn't have much time. Reaching for the stack of papers and pen resting on top of the coffee table, she handed them to Michael. "It's not about making them valid for filing. It's about proving to me that I can trust you."

Michael reached for the pen, but his hand fumbled it. She watched it fall to the floor as Michael stared down at the divorce papers.

"What did you do to me?" Michael's voice was cold. He shoved the papers to the floor. "Did you put something in my drink?"

"Stop being paranoid," Mena said, and picked up the divorce papers from the floor.

Michael slapped them from her hand, then gripped her wrist. His hand was unsteady as his body swayed toward her. His eyes grew hard. "I'm a damn neurologist! You think I wouldn't know when my faculties are impaired. What the hell did you put in my drink?"

Mena snatched her hands from his grasp and stood. Michael rose from the couch, then stumbled down to one knee. His breathing labored, he stood but struggled to maintain balance.

"Just sign the divorce papers, Michael. Do that and I'll stay here with you the entire weekend, I promise," Mena insisted.

Michael snatched the papers and ripped them apart. "I didn't know you had it in you to be so manipulative. You never had any intention of giving me a fair shot, did you? You just wanted to trick me into signing these fucking papers!"

Taking another step backward, Mena watched as Michael struggled to come after her. A few tentative steps and he collapsed down to the floor. Resting on his hands and knees, he resorted to crawling across the carpet until he slumped down in a heap.

"I trusted you," Michael said.

Mena squeezed her eyes shut and took a shaky breath. What the hell was she supposed to do now? She needed to call Omar. No, she needed to get out of the casita—

A hand clasped around her ankle, yanking her forward.

Mena screamed. "Get away from me."

"You owe me another chance," Michael said. His eyes were dark and haunted. "I love you, Mena. Why would you do this to me?"

Mena kicked at Michael's face, missing by inches, but freed her leg from his clutches. "You are delusional if you think I owe you anything. The only reason I agreed to meet you here was to get a divorce from you. I can't stand the sight of you! I don't want your love and I don't want you!"

Michael flipped over onto his back and stared at the ceiling.

Unable to contain her rage and disappointment, Mena fought the urge to scream. The plan had been so simple. Trick Michael into signing the papers, then take them to Omar's cousin in the PC-5 to have the divorce decree notarized. With the notarized documents, she could take them to be filed at the courthouse without Michael being present.

"Why won't you just give me the divorce?" Mena demanded.

Michael glared at her. "Because you're mine."

Chapter Twenty-Three

The concrete walls closed in on Julian as he was led to a chair near the wall by the prison guard. Octavia Constant, his attorney, was already seated at the table. A single manila folder rested on the table in front of her. With clasped hands, she glanced up at him.

Julian slumped in the chair. He wasn't expecting to get a visit from Octavia so soon after the depressing news she'd brought him on Friday. The weekend had dragged at a snail's pace. He'd kept his mind occupied, learning how to stay below the radar with the prison guards. Avoiding Zak Webber had been next on the list, with Xander helping to keep him out of trouble so he wouldn't murder the motherfucker. He had to keep his anger in check, or risk being thrown in solitary or adding to the charges already pending against him.

"Tell me you have good news this time."

"Potentially," Octavia said. "Des got back to me on his investigation of Whalum O'Keefe and Farouk Essa."

"Those were the prison guards assigned to watch over Dumay, right? Your cousin found out one bought a house with cash and the other paid off his kid's medical bills at the Rakestraw Blake Center," Julian said, remembering their discussion from last week.

"Yes, and my cousin was on the right track. Des brought Whalum and

Farouk in for additional questioning, and Whalum caved pretty quickly. He admitted to accepting a bribe," Octavia said.

"You serious? He told the cops Dumay bribed him to leave her alone?"

"I didn't say that." Octavia lifted a hand and sighed. "He claimed he was given fifty thousand dollars cash by Farouk to leave Priscilla Dumay alone for thirty minutes at the end of the first day of the trial. He wanted the money, and he didn't ask any further questions."

"Let me guess, Farouk stonewalled and didn't admit to anything," Julian shook his head. One step forward and two steps back. He needed a real break.

"Quite the contrary. Farouk explained someone using a voice distortion device called him to make the deal. The caller assured him that Dumay would still be there when he returned to get her thirty minutes later," Octavia said.

"He didn't know who he was talking to, but he agreed to do it anyway?"

"Farouk said that immediately after the call, a woman rang his doorbell. She had the fifty thousand in cash and asked if he would accept the terms of the deal. He couldn't walk away from that money with his son being so sick, but he knew he couldn't pull it off by himself."

"He needed to convince Whalum to go along with leaving Dumay alone," Julian surmised.

"And when Farouk told the woman this, she left and came back to his home with another fifty thousand to give to Whalum. The rest is history," Octavia said.

"But we don't know who Farouk talked to or who the woman was that dropped the money off."

"No leads on the caller, but Des will probably get copies of Farouk's cell phone records to figure that out. Farouk claimed the woman never gave him her name, but he provided video footage from his home security system that shows the woman at his door." Octavia slid the manila folder toward Julian.

Julian opened the folder. He stared at a black and white shot of a woman standing on the porch in front of the modest home. She was wearing dark sunglasses and holding a Gucci bag tucked under her arm.

Even with her face partially obscured, he knew exactly who she was.

"The cops are trying to figure out who the woman is. I'm going to get these to Icarus and see if he can identify her, even though it will be harder because of those huge sunglasses covering her face—"

"I can tell you exactly who she is." Julian closed the folder and stared into Octavia's stunned face.

"What do you mean, you know her?" Octavia's voice grew tense.

Julian nodded. "She used to work at the Genesis Gallery. Her name is Uma Fischer."

Octavia grabbed a legal pad and scribbled furiously as Julian gave her the background on the demure and devious former assistant conservator. He spared no details as he told Octavia how Uma Fischer had gotten caught up in Irving Bond's stolen art scam over a year ago. She disappeared, avoiding any prosecution for her role in forging the authenticity of the pieces.

"She's no stranger to working with criminals. The question is, how did she get caught up in working for Dumay?" Julian asked. Dumay had been oblivious to the scam Bond and Uma had orchestrated right under her nose. Julian was surprised that Dumay would trust Uma to handle bribing the correctional officers. But he didn't know what Uma had been up to after she moved from St. Basil. Anything was possible when Dumay was involved.

"How often did you interact with Uma at the gallery when you were a security guard there?" Octavia asked.

"Pretty regularly. Mena was her boss. Back then, all the conservators worked late hours after the gallery was closed. As the night security guard, I'd walk them to the employee parking lot when they were done for the night," Julian said.

"She worked for Mena?" Octavia said, biting her lower lip. "Were you friends with her?"

"Friendly. Not friends. I didn't hang out with her after work, and I don't think Mena did either. Why are you asking this? Shouldn't we be figuring out how she's connected to Priscilla?"

"From what you're telling me, both you and Mena had a professional relationship with Uma and interacted with her frequently at the gallery. Uma has a history of assisting with crimes. One could argue that it's not out of the realm of possibility that you and Mena supplied the funds to Uma to bribe the officers."

"Why the fuck would we do that?" Julian asked.

"The whole world knows you believe Priscilla Dumay terrorized the two of you. It's no secret that the D.A.'s case against the woman was weakening by the day. What was a strong case a year ago had become more of a gamble on whether Dumay would be convicted on any of the charges. The cops could just as easily pursue an angle that you wanted Dumay to be alone so you could punish her for everything she'd done to you and Mena."

"That's bullshit and you know it. If I wanted Dumay dead, she would be," Julian said.

"I hope you don't share that sentiment with anyone else," Octavia gave him a suspicious look.

Julian had crossed the line, but the idea that he'd constructed a sloppy plan to murder Priscilla Dumay after the first day of her trial was beyond ludicrous. Despite the case weakening, he still believed that the D.A. was likely to secure a conviction. Why would he risk it all by taking matters into his own hands? He had too much to lose now. Punishing Dumay was not worth risking his relationship with Mena.

"Once Des finds out about this connection that you and Mena have to Uma, he will get a warrant for your financial records. They'll be looking for any withdrawals that match the amount of the bribes. If you've moved that much cash in the past months, you better have proof for what you purchased or it's going to look very bad," Octavia explained.

"I did not bribe Uma. They can look at whatever they want. They won't find anything," Julian said.

"That's what you said last time and look what happened," Octavia said, sliding the folder and her legal pad into her attaché case.

"Fine. What's your next move?"

"I'm going to set up a meeting with the cops and tell them who the mystery woman is. The more we can show that you are cooperating, the better it will look for your case."

"Anything I can do?" Julian asked, although he doubted he could help stuck behind bars. What he really wanted to do was find Uma and force her to tell him that Dumay had instructed her to bribe the correctional officers. Uma could be the key to proving that Dumay had framed him.

"Yes. Stay out of trouble. No more run-ins or near fights with other inmates. Don't do anything that could jeopardize your case or add to your charges. Understood?"

"Yeah, I got it." Julian mumbled. Uma bribing the correctional officers had him on edge. Farouk Essa had received a phone call from someone giving him instructions on what to do. That call couldn't have come from Dumay since all calls made from the prison were monitored, except those made to lawyers. Had Uma made the calls? Or was there someone else involved in this scheme?

Some other piece on the chessboard Dumay had set up to bring him down.

Chapter Twenty-Four

The trail of ants marched across the dingy gray wall, methodical in their ascent to devour the dead spider trapped in its own web in the corner of the prison cell. Julian flipped over onto his stomach on the thin, hard mattress.

Finding out that Uma had bribed the correctional officers to leave Dumay unattended had his mind racing. He'd underestimated Dumay and the lengths she'd go to for revenge against him and Mena. He needed to go on the offensive, but he couldn't. He was trapped, just like she wanted. Stuck in Tiverton prison with no way to take her down.

Julian propped his head on his hands.

From what he remembered about Uma, she was just a pawn in Bond's game. The bastard had convinced Uma he was in love with her. That was the only reason she'd agreed to forge the authentication of the fake art. Once she found out Bond was screwing other women, Uma had walked away from Bond and his scam.

Was Uma clever enough to bribe the correctional officers on her own? Julian's gut told him hell no. Uma was a follower. Whoever had called Farouk using the voice distortion device was the real mastermind behind the plan. Uma was just the mule, delivering the cash. He was sure of it, but how the hell could he prove it? And who was the caller?

Two people came to mind—Adam Russell or Quentin Tufa.

Russell was in PIIB custody, so he was likely out.

But Dr. Tufa could be pulling the strings.

"You won't believe what I found out." Xander entered the cell, arms overflowing with envelopes of various sizes.

"What?" Julian asked.

"Zak Webber is going to try to kill you while you're in here."

Julian bolted up from the mattress. "Who told you that?"

"Little Rico. Josue Chartres' messenger. Seems the PC-5 got wind of it and Josue wanted you to have a heads up to watch your back. Word is, there's two million dollars in a bank account with Zak's real name on it—Teo Juarez, collecting interest," Xander said, sorting his mail into piles on the mattress. Postcards near the edge. Letter sized envelopes in the middle. Large envelopes by the flat square that served as his pillow. "Zak's in for twenty years. Compound that interest, bitch. That'll be a nice nest egg at the age of fifty when he walks out of here. And all he has to do to make sure that money stays put in his account is send you out of here in a body bag."

"No fucking way that bastard can kill me. He'd be stupid to even try," Julian said, shaking his head. There was only one person who'd pay Zak Webber to off him behind bars, and that was Dumay. Was that her fucking plan all along? Did she really think that punk Webber could get the best of him, even in here? Julian couldn't even pretend to be concerned, although he did appreciate the intel from Josue.

"Well, look-a-here. This one's for you," Xander said, extending a single brown, flat envelope toward him.

"Is it like that for you every time mail gets delivered?" Julian asked, reaching for the envelope. He glanced at the label and recognized Mena's handwriting. Inhaling slowly, he fought the smile threatening to spread across his face.

"This is a light day, but usually." Xander collapsed down onto his bed and opened one envelope. Lifting a picture out, he turned it toward Julian. A woman in a string bikini stared seductively into the camera for the shot. "Normally, these kinds of photos would never make it to me. They are real strict in here about mail, opening everything and throwing shit away they don't want us to have. But I pay a little extra to Josue and he makes sure I get all my mail. This beauty is Jamie, she wants to come in two weeks."

"You going to put her on the schedule?" Julian asked.

Xander shook his head. "Nah, not in the right head space with all this shit going on with my case. All my focus has to be on getting another lawyer to take me on pro bono."

"That's going to be tough," Julian said. Octavia Constant was a damn good attorney, but she didn't come cheap. Turning his attention back to the envelope from Mena, he hesitated. Was this what their relationship would come to? Exchanging handwritten letters like lovers hundreds of years ago? Did he even want that kind of life for her?

He knew the answer, and he didn't like it.

Flipping the letter over in his hand, he felt sick. Could he really end things with Mena? Put her needs before his own if he couldn't get out of this mess with Dumay. What other choice did he have? He wouldn't let her waste precious years of her life, clinging to a relationship, if he ended up stuck behind bars. But it would rip his fucking heart out. Without Mena, wasn't much left for him to live for.

Unclasping the metal prong, he opened the envelope and slipped a hand inside. Julian's fingers slid across a stack of glossy paper. He lifted them out and stared at the first photograph.

A sensual look graced Mena's face in the photo as she looked into the face of the man standing next to her. The guy's arms were wrapped around her waist in an intimate embrace as he stared back at Mena, enamored and full of lust. In the background, Julian could barely make out the illuminated name of the Blue Moon Resort on the side of the building. The only five-star hotel on the island was tucked away in the St. Basil Mountains.

"What you got?" Xander's question floated across to him, but Julian couldn't answer. He didn't know what the hell he was looking at. Why would Mena send him a photo of her and another man?

Julian flipped through the other pictures. The man with Mena looked familiar, but Julian couldn't quite place where he'd seen the guy before. Dark brown skin and intense hazel eyes. The position of their bodies suggested an intimacy that sent a swell of jealousy pumping through Julian.

Standing, Julian arranged the pictures across the mattress and stared at them.

The guy kissing Mena's neck as she laughed.

Mena resting her head against the guy's shoulder as they walked away from the resort restaurant.

Mena and the man outside a casita in an embrace, his hands resting against her ass like he owned it.

The two of them walking into the casita.

Julian grit his teeth, running a hand over his head. He wanted to rip each of the photos into a million pieces. What the fuck was this?

"You got a P.I. following somebody? Wait, is that your girl? With another dude?" Xander asked.

"Private investigator?" Julian echoed, thoughts forming in his head. The one thing he knew for certain was that Mena's heart belonged to him. She wasn't fucking around on him with another man. Never. But what the fuck was he looking at in these photos? Was someone following Mena? Watching her, taking photos of her when she didn't realize it.

Was Dumay be behind this?

Julian nodded. "That's Mena, but I don't know who the fuck this guy is or why she's with him."

"Who sent you this shit?"

"Envelope says they came from Mena."

"Bullshit," Xander picked up one of the photos.

"What are you looking at?"

"Trying to see if I can tell if these pictures have been manipulated. I get tons of photos. The ladies go through a lot of trouble to make themselves look better than they do in real life. Trust me, I can tell if a photo has been enhanced. I bet you somebody put Mena's face onto another woman's body just to fuck with your mind."

Oh, they were fucking with his mind, but Julian didn't believe for one minute that the photos were fake. What he thought was more dangerous than someone tricking him into thinking Mena had moved on with another man. He'd welcome that over what was haunting him.

"Mena is in danger," Julian said, turning to pace across the cell.

"You serious?"

"Wouldn't be the first time that Dumay sent somebody after her." Or the second time, Julian thought glumly. He'd always been there to rescue Mena from Dumay. How the fuck was he going to do that now that he was trapped behind bars? If that guy in the photos did anything to hurt her, there'd be no limit to the terror he'd rain down on Priscilla Dumay and anybody who'd ever worked for her.

"That's fucked up. What are you going to do?"

Julian glanced at the small digital clock resting against the sink. Almost rec time. "Go to the one person in this place who can give me some fucking answers."

Chapter Twenty-Five

The silence was deafening.

Mena grabbed the cashmere blanket and wrapped it around her body as she eased down onto the sofa. Taking a sip of Riesling, she closed her eyes and tried to imagine what she and Julian would do on an afternoon like this when Mena left work early.

Normally, the surround sound speaker system would blast the rapid-fire bullets and intense drama of some military action show they ignored as they talked about anything and everything. She and Julian never seemed to run out of things to discuss. Mena loved to hear Julian's perspectives on current events and debate with him when they didn't see eye to eye. He even managed to be riveted when she talked about the most mundane aspects of restoring a difficult piece of art. Everything she'd ever wanted in a man, he embodied. Even the things she didn't like about him were more endearing than annoying.

She sighed, resting a hand against her forehead. Another night without Julian. Each one harder to endure as the pain of missing him grew stronger. What she should have been doing tonight was celebrating the end of her marriage with Michael, but that had blown up in her face.

After Mena's attempts to trick Michael into signing the divorce papers had failed miserably, she'd watched him sink into unconsciousness on the white sheepskin rug in the casita. Leaning over his body, Mena pressed her fingertips against his neck. The strong pulse had sent relief coursing through her. Staring at the ripped shreds of the divorce papers still clutched in his hands, she'd gathered the pieces and threw them into the fireplace.

Getting out of the situation would prove to be trickier than Mena would've imagined. Even though Regina had booked the casita under an assumed name, Mena feared what could happen if someone from the hotel found Michael passed out in the room. She hadn't exactly been discreet as they visited the hotel bar and then the restaurant for dinner. The cops would be called and several witnesses at the hotel would be able to describe her as the woman seen with Michael that night. What would she do then?

With trembling hands, she called Omar and gave him the details of how the night had fallen apart. He hadn't hesitated to tell her that his cousin in the PC-5 would be at the casita within the hour to help her clean up the mess with Michael.

Almost an hour to the minute, there was a knock on the casita door.

"Can I help you?" Mena asked.

"Hey, I'm Athena," she said.

Mena stood there for a moment dumbfounded by the woman with the smooth dark caramel skin and gray doe-like eyes. She had the body of a dancer and a sweet, girl-next-door look and charm that left Mena confused.

"Is this the guy forcing you to stay married to him?" Athena asked, pressing the tip of her Nike tennis shoes against Michael's face.

Mena nodded, then shut the door.

"You have a few options here. He's a doctor. I could make it look like he overdosed on prescription meds."

"I don't want him dead," Mena shrieked.

"You sure? That's the best way to get rid of this problem. Not my normal M.O., but it fits for this situation."

"Your normal M.O.?" Mena asked.

"I'm Vadaj."

"What does that mean?"

Athena chuckled. "Omar didn't tell you what his cousin in the PC-5 does?"

Mena gave a blank stare, unsure that she wanted confirmation of what she expected Athena to say.

"I'm an assassin for the gang. I kill people, quite effectively, too," said Athena.

"This is a mistake. I didn't know that's what—"

"Relax. Vadaj doesn't just kill. We are cleaners too. I'll make sure none of this is connected to you. But I'm doing this for family and can't call my normal crew to help, so you're going to have to get your hands a little dirty."

"What do I have to do?"

"Erase yourself from this room," Athena reached into her pocket and tossed a small spray bottle toward her. "Spray everything down with that solution in any area that you were in. You don't have to wipe it away, just let it dry naturally and it will eat away any oil or dirt that would make your fingerprints cling to surfaces."

Mena caught the small bottle, then walked over toward the bar where she'd made the drinks for her and Michael.

"A shame, you didn't get him to sign before he passed out."

"He figured out what I was doing and came after me. If the drug hadn't kicked in, I'm not sure what would have happened next," Mena admitted.

"Good thing it did. Trust me, hurting another person leaves a mark on you, even if you feel justified in doing it. I wouldn't want you to live with something like that."

Mena didn't want Michael's blood on her hands either. All she wanted was to be legally divorced, but Michael had made it clear he would not let that happen.

Because you're mine.

"Where are your clothes? You have a suitcase somewhere?" Athena asked.

"Michael thought I would stay the weekend with him before he flew back to New York, but I had no plans of doing that."

Athena slipped a phone from her pocket and typed quickly.

"What are you going to do to him?" Mena's finger grew numb from pumping the spray bottle. The fine mist glistened across the surfaces of the furniture in the casita.

Athena glanced up and gave her the most innocent look. "Fly him back to New York."

Pushing the memories from her mind, Mena stood from the couch and stumbled into the kitchen. Reaching for the bottle of wine, she filled her glass, then jumped as her doorbell rang. Taking a quick sip, she left the glass on the kitchen island and peeked through the peephole.

Athena.

Why was she here?

Mena opened the door. "What's wrong?"

Athena raised an eyebrow. "Can I come in?"

"Of course," Mena stepped back and allowed the petite woman into the penthouse. Athena was dressed in yoga pants and a hoodie. Her dark brown locks cascaded around her face, making her look younger and more innocent than she had the first time Mena met her.

Gray eyes intense, Athena said, "There's no easy way to say this, so I'm just going to get to it. I'm here to warn you that your husband arrived on the island this morning from New York--"

"He's going to come after me," Mena whispered.

"Don't panic. He's not going to remember anything that happened within a couple of hours before you gave him the drug."

"Are you sure?"

"He won't. He's here to do the same thing he was trying to do last week, convince you to give him another chance. This is the story you need to tell him. After dinner, he started to look ill. He walked you to your casita, and that was the last you saw of him. He didn't show up the next morning for whatever activity he had planned for the two of you, so you stopped by his room and he told you to go home because he was sick. So you did. End of story. Got it?"

"You really think it's going to be that simple?" Mena asked.

"If you let it be," Athena said, then walked toward the door.

Mena dragged her hands down as her cell phone rang.

"You going to get that?" Athena asked.

Slipping the phone from her back pocket, Mena stared at the caller ID.

"Oh God. It's the St. Basil Police Department," Mena said, staring back at Athena.

"Whatever you do, keep my name out of your mouth. You understand me?" Athena warned.

Mena nodded, then answered the phone.

"Ms. Nix, this is Detective Desmond Francois. I was hoping you wouldn't mind coming down to the station this afternoon. We have reason to believe that you may have information about a crime that was committed and wanted to discuss this with you."

"What crime?" A chill ran down Mena's spine.

"I'd prefer to give you all the details when you get to the station. Can you be here in the next hour?"

Mena took a deep breath. "Yes, detective. I'll be there."

Chapter Twenty-Six

Michael traced his finger along her face, longing to feel her in his arms again.

"Mena, do you take Michael to be your husband? Do you promise to love, honor, cherish, and protect him, forsaking all others, and holding only unto him forever more?" the minister asked.

Her expression grew serious and confident. He remembered how she'd squeezed both of his hands as she answered, "I do."

Michael paused the video. He and Mena stood facing each other in profile. The love emanating between them was strong, stronger than anything he'd ever felt in his entire life. She'd made a promise before their friends, family and God. She'd loved him more than anyone ever in her life. That kind of love didn't just fade away, no matter how many mistakes were made.

He could forgive her for getting swept away by Julian. Hell, the man had saved her life. It wasn't a stretch for the damsel in distress to believe she was in love with the hero. Michael knew whatever Mena thought she had with Julian was fleeting. She was trying to forget about him, but she couldn't. He wouldn't let her.

Leaning back in his chair, Michael closed his eyes and tried to remember what the hell had happened over the weekend at the Blue Moon Resort. He remembered walking Mena back to her casita after an intensely romantic dinner at the resort's upscale restaurant. She hadn't fought his attempts to take her back down memory lane. She'd smiled and laughed and teased him, just like she used to do when they were together in Florida. All the years of them being apart had faded away. He'd wanted nothing more than to spend the night with her, making love to her like he did in his dreams almost every night.

Mena had agreed to have a drink with him in her casita.

And that was the last thing he remembered.

Three days later, he'd woken up in his bed in his apartment on the upper west side of New York City. He didn't know how he'd gotten there or how he'd lost three days of his life. Although he suspected the truth.

Mena had lied to him. She'd pretended she was willing to spend the weekend with him, when the truth was she'd had no plans to give him a fair shot of winning her back. He still couldn't believe she'd pulled off something so cruel. Had she drugged him? If it was that simple, why hadn't he woken up at the resort. How the hell had he gotten all the way back to New York City when he'd had no plans of returning? His relocation to the Aerie Islands was almost finalized. The apartment in New York was listed for sale, and the realtors expected for it to go quickly. Did Mena know that?

Michael opened his eyes and closed the browser on the laptop. Shutting the lid, he slipped it into the bottom drawer of his desk. What was he thinking? Mena would never do anything to hurt him. She was probably worried about him, wondering why he didn't show up for their skydiving trip the next morning.

Reaching into his pocket, he checked his cell phone again. Still no message or text from Mena. That was odd. Why wasn't she worried about him? Why hadn't she been trying to figure out what happened to him? Why he disappeared?

Because the bitch did this to you, that's why.

She'd live to regret rejecting him again. After everything he'd done to prove his love to her, she still resisted coming back to him where she belonged. He had no plans of walking away from her ... ever. He'd be damned if he let her move on with another man when she belonged with him.

Michael stood and flung his white coat onto the floor. It was time to pay Mena a visit. She'd promised to spend the entire weekend with him, and he was going to make sure she followed through on her word.

Grabbing his keys from the top of the desk, Michael strode toward the door and flung it open.

"Where have you been?" Dr. Tufa stalked into his office, slamming the door behind him.

"I don't have time for this," Michael said, reaching for the door.

Tufa gripped his forearm, yanking him back. Michael stared at the man as rage flooded his body.

"You better make time." Tufa released his grip, then turned and sat in the chair across from Michael's desk.

Ignoring Priscilla Dumay's adopted brother, he opened the door, then stopped. Two enormous bodyguards blocked the opening, each revealing pistols with a silencer on the end tucked discretely beneath their sport coats.

Michael exhaled, then shut the door. He turned and walked back to his desk and sat down.

"What do you want?" Michael asked.

"You've been missing for the past five days while my sister is still languishing in a coma. What is going on with her treatment?" Tufa asked, rubbing his temple. His eyes were bloodshot and weary. The stubble on his face more unkempt than before.

"Priscilla is responding well to the protocol—"

"What the hell does that mean?"

"It means your sister will be out of the coma in the next few days," Michael said.

Tufa raised an eyebrow. "That soon?"

"Yes." Michael bristled at Tufa's doubt of his assessment. He'd told Priscilla's brother that his protocol would be even more successful on patients with no physical trauma, and he'd been right. His colleagues at the RBC had minimized the effects of the poison in Dumay's body, which made the treatment protocol work even faster.

"And if a delay in bringing her out of the coma was needed, could you make that happen?"

"Why would you want to do that?" Michael asked.

"Just answer the question."

"Reducing the dosage of the daily treatments would prolong the date that she emerged from the coma, but I wouldn't recommend it."

"Any fatal side effects?"

Michael reflected on his protocol, which was damn near perfect. There wouldn't be any risk to Priscilla's life if he were to decrease the dosage, or increase for that matter, within reason. But did he want Tufa to know that? What was Tufa trying to do? "You're a medical professional. You know that any change to an established treatment plan introduces risks to the patient. Would they be life threatening to your sister? Probably not, but I couldn't give you a guarantee."

"Based on her current treatment plan, do you have an exact date of when she should be out of the coma or are there other factors that come into play?"

"I'm working from an extremely small sample size, as you're aware. But, based on the results of the last patient and Priscilla's progress, we can estimate the time of when she will come out of the coma to a thirty-six-hour period."

"I'm impressed, Dr. Marsh," Tufa said, then reached into his pocket.

Michael flinched, almost expecting for Tufa's hand to emerge holding a gun instead of the small business card. Tufa handed it to him. Michael grabbed the stiff paper and turned it over, glancing at the note scribbled on the surface. "What is this?"

"That is the exact day I want you to bring my sister out of the coma. Not a day earlier and not a day later. Understood?"

Michael thought about the goons lurking outside his office and instantly regretted the day he'd agreed to meet with Dr. Tufa. Would the ends justify the means? They would, especially when Priscilla woke up and told the cops that Julian Montgomery had attacked her. Mena's new boyfriend would spend years in prison, and she'd be his again. The embryonic stem cells Tufa provided for the protocol had given Michael professional security beyond his wildest dreams. But more than that, Michael wanted Tufa and his diabolical sister, Priscilla Dumay, to help him get his wife back.

Michael opened the desk drawer and slipped the card inside. "Consider it done."

Chapter Twenty-Seven

Breaking away from the other inmates, Julian approached the exercise station. He walked by Josue Chartres, as the man regaled the gang members with a comedic tale of one of his killings that almost didn't happen. Laughter permeated the air as the leader acted out the actions of his victim. Julian shifted a hand inside his shirt, maneuvering the envelope with the photos to a more comfortable position.

Staring at the pictures of Mena and the unidentified man for hours, Julian had become convinced that she was in danger. Mena's facial expressions looked forced. Her smile never quite reached her eyes. She was pretending. But why? Was the asshole trying to hurt her?

Julian had seen the man before but couldn't place from where. He wasn't going to waste time trying to figure that out. Zak Webber could give him the answers he needed. The only person who would pay Zak two million dollars to kill him was Dumay. That meant Zak knew a lot more about that bitch's plans than Julian realized. Zak had to know something about the man in the photos with Mena and what Dumay was up to next.

The prison yard was crowded on the perfect Caribbean afternoon. Fluffy white clouds provided respite from the sun as cool breezes wafted from the ocean. Near the center of the yard, Julian saw a group of inmates discarding their shirts and rolling up their pants as they prepared to sunbathe on towels.

Other inmates gave them disgusted stares as they crossed the plush grass toward the basketball courts. Near the corner, Julian spotted Zak and the other members of Quattro lounging at a picnic table under the shade of a grapeseed tree. The group of three huddled close together as a guard stood about fifty feet away watching the area. Julian made a beeline in their direction, stopping at the edge of the table.

The three men halted their conversation, staring up at Julian with loathing in their eyes. Julian wrestled with the deep-rooted hatred he had for Zak Webber. Julian wanted to choke the life out of him. But he couldn't kill the bastard. He had to find out if Zak knew anything about Dumay's plans for Mena or the identity of the mystery man in the pictures with her.

His back to the guard, Julian slipped the envelope from under his shirt and pushed it across the table.

Zak reached for the brown envelope. "What the fuck is this?"

"Open it," Julian said through gritted teeth.

Annoyed anger flashed in Zak's eyes, but Julian knew he'd be too curious not to comply. Slipping the photos from the envelope, a sly grin spread across Zak's face. Zak tossed the photos back toward Julian.

"Looks to me like she's done with you, white boy." Zak chuckled, eliciting laughter from the other Quattro gang members. "Don't know why you're showing me that shit."

"Who's the guy in the photo?" Julian asked.

Julian watched as Zak glanced down at the photos once again. A flicker of recognition flashed in his black eyes. "What makes you think I'd tell you?"

"Does he work for Dumay? Did she send him after Mena? Tell me!" Julian said, his voice rising. He didn't have time to play games with this asshole when Mena could be the target of some attack. Julian forced himself to calm down. He had to find a better way to get what he needed from Zak. "Look, Dumay is the reason you're in this hell hole—"

"And she's the reason you're in here too. So, the fuck what? She and I have an understanding. You and I ain't never been friends. I could give a rat's ass what happens to Mena Nix. If Dumay has Mena in her sights, then there's nothing your ass can do about that while you're locked up in here."

Zak's dark eyes were cold with malice as he smiled at Julian. The bastard knew exactly who the guy was. He was taunting Julian by not telling him.

Rage coursed through Julian's body as he glared down at the man who'd kidnapped and tried to violate the woman he loved.

Julian slammed his fist in the middle of Zak's face. Blood splattered on his skin as throbbing pain detonated through his hand, snaking its way up his entire arm. Zak stumbled backward, falling off the bench.

"Truth hurts, doesn't it bitch?" Zak said. Blood poured from his bruised nose, dripping over his lips as he revealed a bloodstained, toothy grin.

Julian charged forward, landing a second punch to Zak's temple and following it with a combination punch to his kidneys. Zak cowered in the fetal position, coughing and sputtering. He spit blood onto the pale green grass, then glared up at Julian.

The other members of Quattro stood. Zak raised a hand, stopping them. "Don't bother with that punk bitch. He ain't worth it."

In his periphery, Julian saw two prison guards, with assault rifles raised racing toward them. He should have known better than to attack Zak, but the truth in the man's words had stung, shining a light on all of Julian's fears. There was nothing he could do to protect Mena from inside the prison. With the so-called evidence the police had, the likelihood of beating the charges and outwitting Dumay wasn't likely. He was out of options and the thought was about to drive him insane.

Julian stuffed the photos back in the envelope. He shouldn't have wasted time with Zak Webber. He needed to call Octavia and tell her about his suspicions. She could send someone to check on Mena and make sure she was alright—

A sharp pain sliced through his abdomen. Julian took a step back, his eyes focused on the shiv in Zak's hand. The blade had ripped through his shirt and disappeared into his flesh. Hot, sticky moistness poured from the wound. His shirt stained dark red. His body spasmed as he doubled over. Sharp, stinging pain radiated from the wound. Sweat beaded on his face. He dropped the envelope, clutching at the torn flesh of his abs. Frantic shouts of the prison guards grew louder, clouding his thoughts. Dazed, Julian crumpled to the ground.

Breathing heavily through his mouth, Zak stood over him with the canvas of bright blue sky and stark white clouds behind him. "Cha-ching!"

Chapter Twenty-Eight

Mena struggled to keep up with Octavia. The powerful attorney stomped down the hallway toward one of the interrogation rooms within the bowels of the police station. After getting off the phone with Detective Francois, Octavia had been Mena's next call. Luckily, Octavia had still been in St. Basil and agreed to represent Mena during the interrogation.

Octavia stopped in front of the door and spun around to face her. "If the detective asks you anything that could be detrimental, I'll instruct you not to answer. Otherwise, be concise, honest, and direct. It's a common tactic of cops to lure you into saying more. Don't fall for it."

Mena sucked in a sharp breath as Octavia opened the door. She wasn't sure how the interrogation would play out, but she had a feeling Michael was in the station somewhere. Her only priority was to make sure she didn't say anything to incriminate herself or Athena before she had a chance to tell Octavia what happened and why.

Even with the prospect of criminal charges facing her, Mena thought of Julian. If she was arrested, he would find out about her marriage to Michael in the news. She hoped that somehow, someway, Julian could forgive her for not telling him the truth.

Crossing the threshold, Mena stepped toward the metal table in the center of the room and sat in the chair near the end. The room was large and virtually bare. Three chairs. One table. Nothing on the surface and no decorations. Not even one of those see through police mirrors Mena had seen on police T.V. shows countless times. Searing fluorescent bright lights illuminated the stark white walls, giving it an intense, claustrophobic feel.

"I see you phoned a friend," the detective said, with a slight chuckle.

Mena glanced up and stared into the ruggedly handsome face of Desmond Francois, one of the famed Francois detectives. Almost all of the Palmchat Islands had one of the Francois Brothers, as they were affectionately called by islanders, working in the local police departments. Their father and grandfather were police officers integral in capturing the heinous serial killer, The Fury, catapulting the family of law enforcement into Palmchat Islands royalty.

Francois gave her a wry smile as he rocked on the back legs of the metal chair. His friendly demeanor made her wary. He was playing the good cop, trying to weaken her defenses and trick her into admitting that she'd drugged her *husband* to force him to sign divorce papers.

Octavia said, "Detective Francois, you wanted us to come to the police station. We're here. Why don't you skip the comedic preamble and get to your questions? I don't want the rest of Ms. Nix's night to be ruined by this inconvenient summons."

"Wow, so formal, Tavie? I thought we were closer than that. Or do you save all of your warmth for my brother, Richland?" Detective Francois asked. His smile grew sexier as Octavia grew visibly irritated.

Octavia clasped her hands as she leaned across the table. "Please explain why we are here. Why does the St. Basil Police believe my client has knowledge related to a crime?"

Mild amusement played across his face as he turned his attention to Mena. "Ms. Nix may know more about her boyfriend's plan to kill Priscilla Dumay than she previously indicated."

"What?" Mena asked, stunned. She wasn't here about drugging Michael. This was about Julian and the charges against him for allegedly attacking Priscilla. "I don't know anything about Julian's plan to kill Priscilla because there was no plan. Julian didn't try to kill her—"

Mena saw Octavia's raised hand in her periphery, urging her not to say another word. The lawyer looked more amused than concerned by Detective Francois' announcement.

"You remember Uma Fischer, don't you, Mena?" the detective asked.

"My former assistant?" Mena asked, confused. "What does Uma have to do with any of this?"

Octavia turned toward Mena and explained, "Yesterday, with Julian's help, I informed the detective that the woman suspected of bribing the correctional officers assigned to Priscilla Dumay was Uma Fischer."

Mena was shocked. How had Uma gotten involved in bribing officers for Prissy? Priscilla was livid when she learned of Uma's role in helping Irving steal art from the gallery. Why would they work together now?

Detective Francois recounted how the two officers had accepted a bribe in exchange for leaving Dumay unattended at the courthouse for thirty minutes. The woman who paid the bribe was believed to be Uma.

"We've found additional footage from CCTV cameras around Farouk Essa's neighborhood that allowed us to positively ID Uma Fischer as the woman who showed up on his doorstep with the bribe," the detective added. "Now I just need to figure out who put her up to it. I took a glance through her phone records. One number showed up several times over the past two months. That number belonged to you, Mena. So, what have you and Uma Fischer been talking about?"

"I only called Uma once. My boss wanted me to rehire her. I left her a message, but she never called back," Mena explained.

"The phone records show you called her six times in two months—"

"No, I didn't!" Mena insisted. "My boss asked me to call the day before Dumay's trial, and I did. Since then, I've had a lot more to deal with then trying to give Uma her old job back."

"The only reason you called Uma to offer her the job was at the request of your boss. Is that correct?" the detective asked.

"Yes, it is. She wasn't a very strong conservator. Her work was average at best, and she lacked the focus that I expect for those working within my group. If Beaujean hadn't pushed me to make the offer, I never would have considered working with Uma again."

The detective sat up straight in his chair. A pensive look spread across his face. "Did you say Beaujean? Beaujean Ali?"

Octavia stared at Mena in shock.

Mena's eyes darted between the detective and her attorney, confused by their reaction. "Yes. He purchased the gallery in a private sale about a month before I returned from Kenya."

"When did he get out of the coma?" Octavia asked, the question directed at the detective.

"I don't know. But I can tell you no one told us he was awake—"

"Coma? Beaujean was in a coma?" Mena stumbled over her words as the question blurted from her mouth. "I don't understand."

The detective grew serious. "You understand a lot more than you want people to realize, don't you, Mena? Come clean and tell the truth."

"Everything I've told you is the truth," Mena said.

"I subpoenaed your phone records. You made two calls to Uma Fischer within a couple days after you and Julian survived the plane crash. You blame Priscilla Dumay for kidnapping you. I believe that's true, even if we haven't been able to prove it. And because of that, you and Julian made sure Priscilla was punished for everything she did to you. Isn't that right?"

"I never called Uma after the plane crash. I wasn't even working at the gallery then—"

"Mena, don't answer that question," Octavia interjected.

Detective Francois smirked. "Julian Montgomery got a multi-million-dollar payday from saving an African heiress's life, but he couldn't use his normal contacts to exact revenge. That would be too obvious. So, you reached out to your unemployed former assistant and offered her a chance to make some quick money, didn't you?"

"No, that's not true," Mena shook her head.

"Despite the fact that some of the most horrific moments of your life happened at the Genesis Gallery, you quickly agreed to work there again. I'm supposed to believe that had nothing to do with the new owner. Beaujean Ali is a money launderer and financial crimes expert trained by the PC-5. What better person to work for than a man that could help lay the groundwork for Julian's plan to exact his vigilante revenge on Priscilla Dumay, isn't that right?"

Octavia interrupted. "Do not answer that! Detective Francois, you're tossing a lot of accusations at my client. Is it your plan to arrest Mena Nix for any crimes this evening?"

"Tavie, I have phone records that show Mena called Uma Fischer within a few hours before she went to the bank to withdraw money for the bribes.

The next call from Mena to Uma came a couple of days later, which happened to coincide with the day Uma showed up on Farouk Essa's porch to pay him," Detective Francois said.

"That doesn't answer the question, Des," Octavia said.

"Your client is free to go ... for now. I shouldn't need to say this, but I will. Don't leave the island."

"I'm not going anywhere. I didn't do any of those crazy things you're accusing me of and neither did Julian," Mena said standing. "I want you to find Uma because when you do, she'll tell you exactly what I've told you. I'm not sure what's going on with her and Priscilla and these bribes, but I had nothing to do with it."

"Your evidence is weak, Des. Conjecture, assumptions and hearsay. It proves nothing," Octavia said, gathering her purse and briefcase from the floor. "You're wasting time investigating the wrong people. Put your efforts where they belong and figure out who was really behind these bribes and the attack on Priscilla Dumay."

The door to the interrogation room opened with a loud thud.

"Des, there's been an attack outside Tiverton," Kendrick said, rushing inside. "Three masked unidentified perps hijacked a water ambulance docked at the prison. The Chief wants you out there with the PIIB since the inmate abducted in the attack was--"

Kendrick paused. Mena stared into the detective's eyes. Heart racing, she could barely breathe as he frowned at her.

"Mena? What are you doing here?" Kendrick asked, then glanced over at Octavia.

Mena tried to remain calm, forcing the panic away. "You said an inmate was abducted. Which inmate?"

Kendrick shook his head. "I'm so sorry, Mena. I didn't want you to find out like this."

"Who was it?" Mena screamed.

Kendrick pinched the bridge of his nose and said the one name Mena prayed he wouldn't.

"Julian."

Chapter Twenty-Nine

Julian grunted in pain, his hand clenching the thin mattress of the cot as two prison guards rushed him past the crowd of gawking inmates. Both of his wrists were handcuffed to the rails of the stretcher, preventing him from checking the stab wound himself.

"What the hell happened out there?" The head of prison security ran a hand over the bald spot of his head, eyes darting across the yard as he approached them.

The gurney slowed to a stop in front of the head of security. He lifted Julian's shirt and cursed under his breath. "Nasty gash."

Straining to lift his head, Julian glanced at his wound through blurred vision. Blood coursed down his side, dripping onto the grass.

"Webber got Montgomery with a shiv, but Montgomery attacked him first," the guard said, breathing heavily as he gave the cot a shove to get it moving again. A second guard jogged along the side of Julian with one hand gripping the side railing and the other resting against his assault rifle.

"Damn it! Again? How the hell is he getting this past you guys?" the head of security asked.

The jogging guard shrugged, then trudged ahead.

The doors to the prison opened. The gurney shot over the lip of the entrance, bumping over the uneven terrain. A sharp pang shot through his abdomen. Julian let out a low growl. The guards didn't bother to check on him as they maneuvered the cot down the hallway.

"Where's Webber now?" the head of security asked.

"Headed to solitary," the guard behind Julian responded as he steered the gurney down another long hallway that led to the infirmary. Moments later, the cot rolled to a stop inside the cramped room that served as the clinic for the inmates.

A man leaning over the back counter spun around and looked up, startled. His pale-yellow afro and pink-tinged skin indicated he likely was a person with albinism. Julian leaned his head to the side, peering at the letters stitched on the white lab coat. Physician's Assistant.

The PA dropped the tablet he'd been typing on to the counter and turned toward Julian. "What happened here?"

"Webber at it again," the head of security said. "Make sure this one survives. Don't want the *Palmchat Gazette* writing about a pattern of inmate deaths at Tiverton. Got it?"

Concern creased the PA's face as he took a pair of scissors and cut Julian's shirt open. "What did he use? Do you have it?"

"Metal shiv, pretty ordinary. It's probably still out in the yard—"

"Find it now!" The PA screamed, then turned toward a phone on the wall. Pressing the buttons, he tapped his fingers impatiently then barked into the phone, "I need a water ambulance to transport a stabbed patient to Felipe Memorial with possible poisoning."

"Poisoning?" Julian said, raising slightly from the cot. He glanced at the guards, who looked just as confused.

"Wait a minute," the head of security said, holding up a hand. "Montgomery's just stabbed—"

"Webber poisoned that last inmate you so crudely referenced earlier. I found aconite on the glass shard he used to stab the guy, which is why he died. I'm not letting that happen again. This inmate will be treated at a suitable facility in case poison was on that shiv."

"You sure that's really necessary? He doesn't look like he's been poisoned," the head of security said.

The PA glanced at Julian. "I'm not taking a chance. The stab wound could mask the symptoms of poisoning. I'm telling you, that is exactly what happened last time. I will not let another man die on my watch because I didn't recognize what was happening until it was too late. He needs to be transferred now!"

"Fine," the head of security said, shaking his head. "But the warden won't like this."

The guards huddled with the head of security for several minutes as he gave final instructions that Julian couldn't quite hear. He clenched his jaw against the white-hot pain blazing through the wound in his side. He'd definitely need stitches, but he didn't think the shiv had been laced with any kind of poison and definitely not aconite. He'd be in worse shape right now from that fast-acting poison if it had been on the shiv. But Julian wasn't going to argue with the PA's precautions. In fact, he quite liked the idea of being transferred to a hospital in St. Felipe. The move could work to his advantage.

Julian shifted slightly, forcing his body to shake and spasm to support the PA's fears that he'd been poisoned. The PA rushed over to the gurney and wiped at the sweat rolling down Julian's face. He never thought of himself as an actor, but he needed to play the part to make sure he was transferred to the hospital in St. Felipe. Once on the water ambulance, he'd gauge whether it would be easier to take out the guards on the boat or wait until he was at the hospital to escape. Either way, he had no plans of returning to Tiverton until after he'd proven his innocence.

"Ambulance is here!" one of the guards yelled.

Pounding steps grew closer. Julian glanced behind him as two EMTs emerged and entered the infirmary.

The PA rushed toward them. "I didn't stitch up the wound. Made that mistake last time. Need him to be checked for poisons first and then, if clear, they can stitch him up at Felipe Memorial. A doctor needs to be involved in this case, so get him there as fast as you can."

"What kind of poison are we checking for?" the EMT asked.

"Last time it was aconite, but hell if I know this time," The PA said, then lowered his voice. "These inmates can get their hands on all kinds of weapons, and the guards couldn't care less if they kill each other. I just can't have another inmate die on my watch. My nerves can't handle that."

"We'll take it from here," the EMT responded. The two EMTs placed a white sheet over his exposed abdomen, then wheeled the stretcher out of the room.

Escorted by the guards, Julian moaned and writhed as they exited the side door of the prison that led to the boat dock. The pain was intense, but nothing compared to some of his injuries when he was a SEAL. But the guards and the EMTs didn't need to know that. Julian wanted them to believe that he was weak and knocking on death's door. A cool sea breeze swirled in the air. Birds squawked and circled overhead, as a large white cloud moved across to block the sun.

A whizz zipped through the air.

The guard walking on his left stopped suddenly. His hand flew to his neck as he looked around dazed before falling to the ground. Two more whizzes and the other guard tumbled forward, his assault rifle releasing a spray of bullets.

The EMT at the front of the gurney screamed. He spun around slowly. Bullets from the guard's gun had ripped through his torso, leaving the EMT's scrubs stained dark red.

Rocking against the cot, Julian jerked at the handcuffs that kept him immobile and toppled it onto the side. He fell hard, banging his shoulder. Pain exploded through his arm as his head snapped back against the cot. One of the fallen guards was a few feet from him. He didn't see any blood or wound, but the guy was definitely unconscious from whatever had shot him.

The prison was under some kind of attack.

But by who and why?

The second EMT scrambled forward toward the water ambulance. Three armed, masked forms emerged from the boat. One of them raised a weapon and shot the man in the chest. The EMT stumbled from the blow, then fell to the ground. The three figures stalked forward, stepping over the man's body toward Julian.

Jerking his wrists against the handcuffs, Julian tried in vain to free himself from the stretcher. Three masked forms converged around him. Julian grew still. His hands were bound, but he could make a surprise attack with his legs if they came closer. It could be the only chance he'd get to stop them from putting a bullet in him, too.

One of the masked attackers squatted in front of him. The subtle curves of the body and the breasts bulging within the skintight top were definitively female. He gazed up into her piercing green eyes through the rectangle opening of the mask. The only part of her face that was uncovered.

A spray bottle emerged in her delicate hand. The white powdered substance sparkled within the clear container. She wiggled it back and forth in front of his face.

Fuck! Not again. That bitch—

A poof of white cloudy powder coated his skin.

A soft chuckle escaped her mouth.

"Good night, Mr. Montgomery."

Chapter Thirty

Julian jerked at the I.V. piercing the vein of his left arm, removing it slowly. A drop of blood oozed from the prick, which he swiped at quickly, pressing his thumb against the bend of his elbow. "Let me get this straight. Sunny found out I got arrested and the entire TIDES team came to the Palmchat Islands to break me out of prison?"

When the masked woman had thrown powder in his face, he'd been convinced it was Priscilla Dumay coming after him again. He'd never expected TIDES had planned his escape.

Azalea "Zale" Newton nodded. "We split up and headed to different islands to stay off the cops' radar."

"We put our bloody lives on hold, waiting for the opportunity to bust you out of prison," Simon Newton added with a surly expression.

Hakeem Underwood crossed his arms over his chest. "The three of us have been in St. Felipe since we arrived. When we heard you'd been stabbed in Tiverton and were going to be transferred to a hospital here, we were ready."

"So that's why the three of you broke me out of prison," Julian said, staring at the last three people he'd ever expected to help him. Julian hadn't exactly endeared himself to the trio when they'd worked together in Africa. Simon, Zale's husband, had decided Julian was a foe and not a friend when Julian embarrassed the team during his first workout with them in Nairobi.

Hakeem was an entirely different story. He and Sunny's brother still weren't on good terms after Hakeem had used Mena as a pawn in his revenge against Tubeec Hirad. They tolerated each other for Sunny's sake, which made it even more surprising that he was one of the TIDES members who had freed him from prison.

Zale was the exception. She was the only one who didn't have a beef with him.

Zale said, "We'd been training for a possible prison break since we got here. Hijacking the water ambulance after we intercepted the call from the prison to St. Felipe Memorial Hospital had been the easy part."

"Deciding whether to let you in on our plans almost stalled everything," Hakeem said. "Ultimately, Sunny decided we should sedate you and make it look like an abduction. That way you have plausible deniability if you get caught."

"Not a bad plan, if Zale hadn't been so heavy-handed with the powder and knocked me out for almost two damn days," Julian said.

"You're welcome, asshole," Simon said, taking a step toward Julian. "Zale risked her life and her freedom to help you, and you want to be pissed off because you got a few extra hours of sleep? Extra hours that helped that nasty gash heal after I stitched you up, by the way."

Julian raised his hands, regretting his outburst. Simon was right. He was being ungrateful. The entire TIDES team had put their assignments on hold to come to the Palmchat Islands and lie in wait for a chance to help him. The least he could do was show appreciation for the risks they were taking. Risks that could land all of them in a maximum-security prison for years.

Julian said, "I'm sorry. I appreciate everything that all of you have done to help me. But it's time that I step up and do more to help myself."

"We agree," Hakeem said. "The heat is on now that every Caribbean law enforcement agency is looking for you. We need to get back to Kenya. It's only a matter of time before they connect you to us and cops show up at our doorstep with questions."

"Which means, we need to be at our doorstep, if you get our drift," Simon added.

Julian nodded. Going back to Nairobi was the right move. Time wasn't on their side. They needed to head back to Africa tonight. He couldn't be the reason any of them ended up in prison for helping him or worse—headed back to Kenya in body bags.

Julian glanced around the room. Four beds were stationed along two of the walls. In the middle of the room was a round table covered with monitors, computers and surveillance equipment. Across from the bed where he lay was a studio sized kitchen next to a full-sized bathroom. A step up from his accommodations in Tiverton.

"So, where am I? What is this place?" Julian asked. There were no windows, and he suspected he was in a hidden bunker.

Zale smiled, then said, "In a place you discovered about a year ago. No one would look for you here."

"I discovered this place?"

"It's where Dumay hid the surrogates, mate. The basement of the Genesis Gallery in St. Basil," Simon explained.

"How the hell did you pull this off?"

Hakeem shrugged, "Not without a lot of help. You know how persuasive Sunny can be. She struck a deal with the owner and arranged for this room to be set up in case we were able to break you out of Tiverton."

"Does he know I'm here?" Julian asked. He'd never met Mena's boss, Beaujean Ali. Even though Mena had spoken highly of the man, Julian wondered what kind of owner would harbor a fugitive? Why would Beaujean take the risk?

"He doesn't want to know, that's part of the deal," Hakeem explained. "As you can see, everything that you need to investigate and figure out what Dumay is up to is down here. Sunny made sure we got the best computers and hooked you up to a high-powered network to perform your search."

Simon said, "Getting in and out of this place will be tricky. Security won't be looking to bust you, though. Just don't get caught by any of the museum visitors. The last thing you need is one of them to report a sighting of the fallen hero on the grounds."

"Trust me, I won't be seen," Julian said.

Zale walked over to a small file cabinet and opened the bottom drawer. "You got a couple of Beretta M9s, enough bullets to last for months, a few burner phones and some clothes in here."

"Looks like I have everything I need." Julian swung his legs out of the bed and stood slowly.

"There's something you need to know," Hakeem said as he walked to the computer and opened a file from the desktop. "Glaze hacked into the St. Basil Police Department servers and found out that the cops brought Mena in for questioning a couple nights ago."

"Mena?" Julian said, heart thundering in his chest. "What did they want to talk to her about?"

"They think she hired her former assistant, a gal named Uma Fischer, to help the two of you bribe the guards assigned to watch Dumay. Last we heard, they will issue an arrest warrant for Mena as soon as they locate Uma," Simon said.

"Fuck!" Julian slammed his fist against the table, sending office supplies to the floor. "She wasn't involved in any of this."

"Phone records show calls between Uma and Mena around the time that Uma was getting cash to bribe the officers and meeting with one of them to deliver the money," Hakeem said.

"The cops aren't close to finding Uma and without her to corroborate their theory, they won't arrest Mena," Zale said.

Hakeem added, "Problem is, we haven't been able to find Uma either."

Simon said, "I know you need to get your own ass out of trouble, but you might want to spend some time helping your lady out of this jam."

"This changes everything," Julian said, resisting the urge to slam his fist through the wall. "Dumay tricked me and got me arrested in the courthouse. Now she's going after Mena and she's using Uma to do it. If the cops find Uma, she'll probably lie and tell them that Mena was involved in the bribes."

Zale nodded. "You've got to find Uma before the cops do."

"That's exactly what I'm going to do," Julian said.

Chapter Thirty-One

The circular driveway of Harmony Towers was more crowded than normal. Drivers honked and valet attendants raced through the gridlock, frantically trying to retrieve cars for waiting residents and park the cars of those arriving.

Leaving the penthouse hadn't been Mena's idea. Beaujean had summoned her to his home to discuss important gallery business. After learning from the cops about Beaujean's connection to organized crime, refusing to meet him wouldn't be in her best interest. She wanted nothing more than to remain camped out by her phones and computer, hoping and praying that Julian would try to reach out to her. But she knew in her heart the call wasn't coming. There was nothing she could do to help Julian.

Mena motioned for the attendant, then asked for her car to be retrieved. The young man nodded, then sprinted along the sidewalk toward the entrance to the underground parking lot. Rubbing her arms, Mena stepped out of the way of a stream of tourists heading toward the front doors of the tower. The group was rowdy and likely headed to join the hundreds of others waiting to get into Solar After Dark.

"Mena?"

Turning toward the soft voice behind her, Mena groaned inwardly as Stella Young walked toward her. Life had been much simpler the first time she'd met Stella the morning of Priscilla Dumay's trial. Mena had plans to help the woman make a love connection with Kendrick, but that had all faded away when Julian was arrested.

"Hi Stella," Mena said, then glanced backward, hoping the attendant would pull her car into the driveway soon.

"Hi, I thought that was you. I've been watching the news, I can't tell you how sorry I am for what you must be going through," Stella said, her eyes creased with concern and sympathy.

"Thanks," Mena mumbled.

"Do the cops have any more news about what happened to Julian? Where he could be?"

"There are no leads. The police don't know who took Julian or why. But I know who was behind this. Priscilla," Mena said, venom laced in her words.

"But Priscilla is still in a coma," Stella responded

"You think that really matters? Priscilla still wants to kill us. She doesn't need to be conscious when others are so willing to sell their souls for money and do her dirty work. I just hope and pray that Julian is okay. That Priscilla didn't give the orders for him to be—"

"Oh God, don't say that. Don't even think like that. I'm so sorry," Stella said, tears welling in the woman's eyes. "I didn't know. I'm really sorry—"

The sleek silver Maserati SUV curved to a stop in front of Mena. She didn't have time or energy to deal with Stella's sympathy. Mena exchanged a quick goodbye with the court reporter, then handed the valet attendant a tip before she closed the door.

Thirty minutes later, Mena was on the opposite side of the island. Applying pressure to the gas pedal, she gripped the steering wheel tighter as she navigated the sharp S-curves leading up the northeastern section of The Meadows. The neighborhood, born from the hallowed remnants of the volcanic crater, was now covered with beautiful vegetation, winding streets and mini mansions. The desert ironwood trees were full with pink blossoms as she drove along the winding road.

Glancing down at the GPS, Mena paused at the stop sign, then turned on Meadow Desert Lane. The houses grew fewer and farther in between, replaced with a series of wrought iron fences interrupted by gates brandishing the occasional family crest or initials. Beaujean lived along the edge of the crater, which granted him sweeping views of the Caribbean Sea—one of the most coveted areas of St. Basil.

Mena steered her car toward the guard booth outside the gate emblazoned with the Ali name. She lowered the driver's side window.

"Ms. Nix, once you go through the gate, take the fork to the left and park near the Range Rovers. You can't miss them. Beaujean is at the lookout," the guard said, then gave her a small smile.

Seconds later, the gate slid open, allowing her entry onto the property. Mena drove for several minutes until she saw three Range Rovers parked in a lot on the side of the single lane road. Easing her Maserati next to them, she exited the car and walked along the narrow dirt path crowded by wild growing hibiscus and frangipani bushes. After about a quarter mile, the bushes cleared to an open grassy meadow with a dazzling view of the Caribbean Sea as the sun dipped behind the horizon. To the right was a stunning glass-enclosed structure about the size of a bedroom. Mena watched Beaujean sitting inside, propped on pillows lining the floor as he whittled away at a piece of wood.

As if sensing her presence, Beaujean looked up and stared at her. His gaze was neither foreboding nor welcoming. Mena felt like an intruder to some sacred place. Beaujean exited the glass room and walked toward her, brushing wood shavings from his linen pants.

Turning to look at the glass structure, she asked, "What is that place?"

"An artist studio. I had it built for someone a few years ago. She was an artist, and this place inspired her," Beaujean said.

"I take it you two aren't together anymore," Mena said.

"No. It was a volatile relationship. We were always breaking up and getting back together. I thought she was the one. But then I did the one thing she couldn't forgive, and she left me for good. I tried to get her back, but she was stubborn and unforgiving and that was that," Beaujean said.

"Sounds like you still love her."

"A part of me always will." Beaujean's eyes softened, reflecting a pain and sincerity she'd never seen in him before.

"Sorry, I'm sure you didn't ask me to come here to discuss your past love life. What's going on at the gallery?" Mena asked. The fact that Beaujean wanted to speak to her outside of the gallery was concerning. She hoped nothing illegal was happening on her watch again. With Julian missing, she was barely hanging on. Losing herself in her work had been a saving grace as she waited for any word on Julian's whereabouts.

"Things have been difficult for you since Julian was abducted from Tiverton. Everyone at the gallery is worried about you. Omar. Regina. Your team," Beaujean said.

"Being with Julian over the past year has taught me that I'm much stronger than I realized. This situation is horrible, but I won't let it get me down. Julian needs me to stay strong, and that's exactly what I'm doing," Mena said.

"Do you need a few days or weeks off?"

"No. I need to stay busy. Coming to the gallery gives me a chance to take a break from worrying. The work is good for me and I assure you, there won't be any decline in the quality of my work."

"I know how professional you are," Beaujean said.

"So, what's the problem? Why did you ask me to come out here?"

"To set your mind at ease."

"What does that mean?"

Beaujean said, "Julian wasn't abducted. He escaped from Tiverton and is alive and safe."

Chapter Thirty-Two

"Hey hon, you feel like a visitor?"

Mena looked up from her computer. Omar stood in her doorway. "Only if it's you."

Omar crossed the large office and walked around her desk, reaching toward her. Mena placed her hands in his and allowed him to pull her up into a bear hug. Placing his hands on the sides of her face, he turned her head from side to side then raised an eyebrow.

"You look like you're doing a lot better today. Any news?" Omar asked.

Mena shrugged and looked away. She couldn't confide in her best friend the amazing news she'd gotten from Beaujean. Julian had escaped from prison. He was safe. She didn't know the details and frankly, she didn't need to know. She just hoped Julian could find proof that Dumay had framed him so he could come back home to her.

Mena said, "Still no word from Michael. Not a call or a text. I talked to Athena this morning, and she got some intel. Apparently, he charted a private yacht and left St. Basil a couple of days ago, but she couldn't find out where he was headed."

"Well, thank God for small favors. The last thing you need is to be worried about your H-U-S-B-A-N-D showing up while you're worried out of your mind for Julian. I checked the *Palmchat Gazette* this morning and the police are still baffled by his disappearance and who attacked the prison," Omar said. He walked back around her desk and plopped down onto the cushioned chair.

"I doubt it's the first time Julian has found himself captured by an enemy. Omar, the things he did in Kenya went beyond heroic. He's skilled and smart and relentless. He can get himself out of whatever situation he's in. He just needs time," Mena said.

"And so do you. Sweetie, why don't you take next week off. You've been working nonstop through this madness."

"To do what? Sit alone worrying?" Mena asked.

"Fine. I know that tone. You won't listen to reason. I guess I should just be satisfied that Regina and I can keep an eye out on you while you're here. Now let's talk shop," Omar said.

"Let's not. A totem pole carved by indigenous people in British Columbia is arriving this weekend. It was painted black decades ago, covering the original colors. The province wants to see if my laser conservation techniques can remove the outer layer of paint. My entire team will be here working with me through the weekend to see if it can be done," Mena said.

"If anyone can do it, you can. But before it gets here, can you put a rush on authenticating the Mayan relief Beaujean wants to purchase? The owner will only let us keep it for a few more days to run the tests."

"I'll get the report to you later this afternoon."

"Thanks, hon. Don't forget, if you need anything, I don't care how big or small, please let me know. Or Regina. We're here for you."

Mena pressed her fingers to her lips and blew him a kiss. As Omar walked out of her office, Mena turned her attention back to the computer. The website of the company Athena said Michael had chartered a private boat from was on the screen. What was her *husband* up to? Now that she knew Julian was safe, she turned her attention back to trying to get Michael to sign the divorce papers.

Leaning back in her chair, Mena stared out the large window onto the manicured lawn below. She suspected that Michael had returned to the island to figure out what happened to him over the weekend. Athena had made it clear Michael wouldn't remember what she'd done to him. Mena didn't know how Athena had gotten Michael back to New York City. She imagined he was baffled by the abrupt change in location once the drugs wore off.

For a neurologist, the gap in his recall was probably driving him crazy. Why hadn't he called her to figure out what happened over the weekend? Did he suspect she'd drugged him?

Mena jumped, goosebumps peppering her skin, as her cell phone vibrated on the desk. She reached for the phone and glanced down at the screen.

Private number.

Must be Athena with more news.

Mena answered, "Hello."

"Go close your office door." The voice was unmistakable.

Pushing up from her chair, Mena raced to the door and slammed it shut, then pressed her back against the cool wood.

Heart pounding in her throat, Mena whispered, "Please tell me it's really you."

Chapter Thirty-Three

"Julian? Are you there?" Mena asked, then glanced at the screen. No bars. She'd lost her cell phone signal at the worst possible time. "Damn it!"

Mena threw the phone across the room. The small device slammed into the back wall of bookshelves, then clattered across the rug. Sinking to the floor, Mena covered her face with her hands and willed herself not to cry. She'd been so close to talking to Julian. So close to being able to tell him how much she missed him and loved him. He'd taken a risk by calling her.

Go close your office door.

That's what Julian had said to her. But how could he have known—

Mena's eyes flung open. She stared across the room.

Julian stood in the open entrance to the secret stairwell that led to the basement of the Genesis Gallery.

His seductive brown eyes were cast down toward her, alluring and mesmerizing. A sexy smile played at the corners of his mouth.

Julian looked damn good and not like a man who'd just escaped from a maximum-security prison. His body was relaxed, slouching against the edge of the wall. Dressed in a dark t-shirt and basketball shorts, Mena's eyes lingered for a moment on the bulge in his pants. She scrambled to her feet and walked toward him.

He put a finger to his lips. Mena slipped her hand in his. The warmth of his touch sent a jolt of excitement racing through her body. Easing the bookshelf closed behind them, he led her into the stairwell, down the steps and through the steel door. Memories of the first time they'd discovered the basement flooded her mind. The search for Irving Bond and the missing baby. Seeing Quentin Tufa for the first time and overhearing Quentin and Zak Webber talking about Operation X. Back then, they'd had no clue Priscilla Dumay was hiding three kidnapped women in the basement and forcing them to be surrogates.

The hallway was as she remembered, dark and narrow. Julian moved quickly, steering her around one corner, then another before stopping in front of a dead end. Pressing a hand against the wall, it gave way and opened to a large room. Her eyes took a moment to adjust to the brightness.

Mena glanced around at the furniture arranged like a war room. Computers littered a table in the middle. To her left were four beds arranged in an L-Shape along two of the walls. To her right was a bathroom and a small kitchenette. Off to the side of the kitchen was a round wooden table adorned with a bouquet of red roses, a bottle of champagne protruding from an ice filled silver bucket and a tray of cheese, fruit, cold cuts and crackers.

Julian grabbed a rose, snapping the stem between his fingers. They hadn't said a word since he'd appeared in her office. The silence between them was comforting as she basked in being in his presence again. The sheer proximity of him set her nerves on fire, an insatiable burning desire roaring within her to touch him.

Julian tucked the rose behind her ear, then leaned forward. The gentle pressure of his lips against her forehead made her knees weak. Mena leaned into him, savoring the feel of his body against hers. She slipped her arms around him. The taut muscles seemed even harder, stronger than what she remembered. Resting her head against his chest, she felt his heart beating faster than expected as his arms enveloped her, holding her tight.

"Oh God, I've missed you. How long has it been?" Mena asked. Her mind floating back to the morning before their testimony in Priscilla's trial. The last time they'd touched, kissed, made love.

"Thirteen days," Julian said, as his soft kisses trailed excruciatingly slow along the side of her face, sending a flurry of pleasure in their wake.

"How many hours?"

"Twenty-one," Julian's tongue slid along the edges of her lips.

"Minutes?"

"Four," Julian paused. His lips barely brushed hers. "And fifty seconds."

"Well, that's too damn long," Mena said, a soft chuckle escaping her mouth.

"Tell me about it."

Mena shrieked as Julian lifted her in the air, crushing her mouth with an intense kiss. She melted into the passionate caress of his tongue as her hands roamed and gripped his body. She clung to him in sheer passionate desperation, squeezing her thighs around him as he stalked across the room and laid her down on the bed.

Against her protests, Julian broke the delicious kiss, resting his hands on the side of her face.

"What is it? What's wrong?" Mena asked, panting.

"You're fearless and strong and so fucking beautiful. What did I do to deserve you?" Julian asked, tracing his finger along her eyebrow then to the bridge of her nose.

"I ask myself the same question about you."

Julian gave her that sexy smirk that drove her wild. Her body responded as it always did, flooding her with desire.

"How are you here right now? How did you pull this off?" Mena asked.

Julian propped himself on his elbows, robbing her of the delicious weight of his body pressing against hers. "Do you really want to waste this precious time we have together talking?"

Mena raised an eyebrow and shook her head vigorously. Grabbing the edges of his t-shirt, she pulled it over his head. Her hands groped his broad chest, roaming and stroking his body as she shifted underneath him. Lacing her fingers through his dark hair, Mena pulled him down toward her. Their lips crashed into each other. Mena hungrily devoured the intoxicating taste and feel of his tongue in her mouth, sucking and swirling in concert with him as her mind went numb, overwhelmed from the intensity of the emotions rocking within her.

Julian's hands inched along her thigh, pushing her shirt dress up toward her waist. His fingers lazily circling around her belly button, before easing further south. Yanking her dress over her head, Mena lifted her hips. Understanding her subtle cue, Julian hooked a finger along the edge of her lace panties and tugged them down her thighs. He eased out of his shorts, tossing both garments across the room.

His touch was delicate as he unclasped her bra. His hands circled around her breasts, squeezing them between his fingers. Mena involuntarily moaned in ecstasy. Julian dipped low, flicking his tongue against her nipple, then taking it fully in his mouth as he sucked hard.

She moaned his name as he shifted focus to her other breast, delighting it in the same manner. His fingers danced across her stomach. Mena giggled from the tickling sensation as her hands caressed Julian's hair. Julian slipped his arms under her legs, pressing them up in the air. He gave her a deliciously naughty look before he delved between her legs, licking along her swollen clit. Mena rode the wave of pleasure slamming through her body as she bucked and pressed against him.

Spasms of heat rolled through her. Grabbing a pillow, she pressed it against her face to muffle her moans, which grew louder and louder with each tantalizing move of Julian's mouth on her. Slipping his fingers in her, Julian ratcheted up the sensory overload, sending her over the edge of desire. Mena felt out of control as her body shook and trembled from the intense orgasm. Gasping for air, she tried to get her bearings, but could barely see straight as Julian pressed his cock against her opening.

Her body responded faster than she'd expected, craving his manhood inside her. Lowering her legs, she wrapped them tightly around Julian's hips as he began the slow push and pull of entering and exiting her. The friction building was driving her crazy.

"Faster, harder, faster," Mena cried out, digging her nails into Julian's back.

"You think you're in control here? I got news for you," Julian said, continuing the tortuously slow stroking into her. "You're not. I'm going to do this my way and you're going to like it."

"Just like it? You better make me love it," Mena quipped, synchronizing her movements to Julian's. Her muscles contracting around his cock, intensifying her pleasure. She ached for him. She wanted all of him now and forever.

"Have I ever let you down?" Julian teased, biting her softly along the edge of her neck.

Mena gasped for breath as her pleasure threatened to drown her. "No ... never ..."

She was deliriously and completely at his mercy, surrendering all control and benefiting from his targeted seduction. He lengthened and grew harder inside her, pushing deeper within, giving her no relief, no reprieve from the pleasure.

Mena lifted one leg, allowing Julian deeper access as he increased the speed of his movements. She loved looking into his eyes as he made love to her. The desire and passion pouring out of him heightened every nerve ending in her body. His intensity swelled and sent her crashing toward another blissful orgasm. Before she cratered over the edge, Julian tightened a grip around her back.

"Hold on," he whispered. In one fluid motion, he rolled their bodies until Mena was straddling him. Her knees pressed against the mattress while still holding his cock tight within her.

"Ride me, hard, make me come, Mena," Julian demanded.

That was all she needed to hear. She leaned back slightly for the perfect angle to drive him wild, then bounced and gyrated on his cock at a feverish pace. His face registered every ounce of his desire.

As she brought him to the brink, he grabbed her ass, squeezing tight as a low growl eased from his lips. She felt him come within her as his body arched and shuddered underneath her. Mena held him tight, squeezing until Julian's head arched back.

"Fuck! I love you so fucking much. You're killing me."

Mena eased off of him, then collapsed beside him, wrapping her arms around his neck. The sounds of their panting filled the room. Their breathing synchronized, then slowed into a low hum, as Mena settled within Julian's strong arms. Sadness pooled within her. This moment was temporary. Fleeting. He was a fugitive, trying to clear his name. Despite the setup in the basement of the gallery, Julian wouldn't be sticking around here for very long. It was too dangerous, too risky. Mena couldn't fathom how she'd ever survive being without him again.

Chapter Thirty-Four

The clock on the computer monitor read fifteen minutes after ten. Julian leaned against the back of the chair, shifting closer to the table as his fingers lightly tapped on the keyboard. He'd overindulged, keeping Mena in the basement of the gallery with him for this long. He hadn't wanted to tell her the truth of what lay ahead for them. He didn't want to see the disappointment on her face when he told her he couldn't guarantee that they would see each other again over the next several days, weeks or maybe even months. He couldn't emerge in public without proof that Dumay had set him up and that she'd likely arranged for Uma to do the same to Mena.

Mena's naked body was twisted between the sheets. Snoring softly, her hand dangled over the edge of the mattress. The rose gold Tiffany bracelet rested against her wrist. He loved that she never took off the only symbol of their commitment that she'd allowed him to give her. A wedding band would have been his preference, but Mena wasn't ready for that. Maybe she would never be ready. Julian had come to terms with that fact. It didn't change anything.

Mena yawned and stretched, blinking as her eyes focused on him.

"Your stitches. How did you get hurt?" Mena mumbled, rising slightly from the bed. She tucked the sheets under her arms, robbing him of the chance to see her voluptuous breasts.

Julian thought about the fight he had with Zak Webber. The reason he'd confronted him. Photographs of Mena with another man. He didn't think for one minute that Mena had sent them. Dumay or some other mindless fuck on her payroll was trying to get into his head.

It worked.

Why else had he believed that Zak Webber would tell him anything about what Dumay was doing? He knew better than to trust any lies the bastard might have told him. Seeing the mystery man with his hands all over Mena in the photographs had driven him crazy with jealousy. The jealousy had quickly been replaced with worry that Dumay was targeting Mena again.

But Mena was safe. He'd seen her scared for her life before. She wasn't. She was more concerned about him than herself, which made the photos even more confusing. Who the fuck was that guy in the photos with her? And why did the man look familiar to him? He had a chance to ask her now, but for some reason he was hesitating.

"Julian? Did you hear me?" Mena asked, scooting toward the edge of the bed.

"Yeah, I got into a fight with Zak Webber and he stabbed me," Julian said, turning away from Mena. He knew what was coming next, and he wasn't sure how he'd respond.

"Why did you fight?"

Julian paused, his heartbeat quickening. "You know why."

Wrapping the sheet around her body several times, Mena shuffled toward his chair and stopped behind him. Her arms circled around his shoulders as she leaned down and pressed her lips against his neck. The sensual scent of her sandalwood and orange perfume hypnotized him, forcing the questions from his mind.

"I'm sorry I never told you what really happened back then. There's so much I wish I'd told you earlier—"

"Hey, it's okay," Julian said. Swiveling around on the chair, he pulled her down into his lap. "That's in the past. Zak can't hurt us. No one can."

"Dumay definitely tries, doesn't she?" Mena asked, leaning her head onto his shoulder.

"I think she's using Uma to frame you."

"The cell phone calls," Mena said, running her hands through her thick tresses. "Beaujean wanted me to hire her back at the gallery. That's the only reason I called her."

"Why?"

"He didn't say, and he made it clear I wasn't to question him. I found out he has connections to the PC-5. When the cops brought me in for questioning, they said he was a money launderer and financial crimes expert with the island gang," Mena explained.

Julian said, "I want you to be careful around Beaujean. If he told you about me, he might want something in return, and I don't like that—"

"I don't think he would try to use me."

"But you don't know for sure."

"Maybe he knows Uma authenticated the fake art for Bond and wanted to get someone on my team to run a new art scam," Mena said.

"Another reason for you to keep your guard up until I can clear my name."

"He's not the one we need to worry about. Uma is. The cops have my cell phone records, but the calls they say I made to her I didn't make. They think I called her shortly after our plane crashed, but that isn't true."

"I saw those records."

"How?" Mena leaned back, then a look of realization crossed her face. "I forgot. You're not just a badass ex-Navy SEAL. You're an intelligence expert able to hack into any computer in the world."

"I'm not that good," Julian said, tapping Mena on the nose. "The dates and times of those calls were manipulated. A few of them were when you were still in the hospital recovering from the gunshot wound to your arm."

"I find it hard to believe that Prissy is working with Uma to frame me. After she found out about Uma's role in Bond's art scam, she was livid. She hated Uma. Why would she work with her now?"

"Uma wasn't arrested for her part in Bond's scam. Maybe Dumay has evidence on her and blackmailed her."

"You could be on to something. Omar and I saw proof of Uma's involvement when we inventoried the pieces, but Priscilla didn't want to inform the cops. She didn't want any more bad press for the gallery."

"Maybe she wanted a way to control Uma in the future," Julian said.

"To make it look like you and I paid the guards to leave her alone after the trial," Mena said, shaking her head.

"And if Uma's involved in trying to frame you, she could also know more about how Dumay set me up. I need to find her and see exactly what she knows about Dumay's plans."

"Julian, we have to be careful. We need a rock-solid plan to find Uma and get her to help us prove that Dumay set you up."

"We don't need a plan," Julian said, forcing Mena to look at him. He needed her to understand the situation was serious. "I need a plan. You are going to go back to the penthouse and keep living life normally. I don't want you doing anything to help me."

"If the cops catch you, then you'll never get out of prison. You'll be charged with the escape on top of attacking Priscilla. The best thing is for you to stay here in the basement and let me be your eyes and ears on the outside. I promise it could work," Mena said.

"No, it won't. The cops are watching your every move. They don't know where I am, and I know how to keep it that way. The best way you can help me is to pretend to be the worried girlfriend. You can't give the cops any reason to believe that you know where I am."

"I don't like this."

"I know you don't, but it's the way it has to be."

"You don't know how long it's going to take to find Uma. Julian, we could be apart for months while you try to prove your innocence. I can't be without you for that long—"

"You're so much stronger than what you realize. You survived being kidnapped in Kenya. You survived me being in prison. You'll survive this. When I'm out there searching for the truth, the one thing that will drive me is knowing that I'm doing all of this so I can come home to you. The beautiful love of my life," Julian said. He leaned over and kissed Mena softly on the lips. The tension dissipated from her body as he deepened the kiss. God, he was going to miss those lips.

Mena pulled away and stared into his eyes. "We'll do it your way. What's your next move? Do you really think you'll be able to find Uma before the cops?"

Julian gave her a wink. "I already have."

Chapter Thirty-Five

Julian looked up at the thick copse of trees obscuring light from piercing through the gloomy darkness of the jungle. His combat boots sank into the muddy road leading to the faded yellow house, stained and cracked from what he guessed was years of lack of care. The horses in the stable across the wide road huffed and wailed at the intruder in the Tango Lowlands on the island of St. Felipe. A small community cut off from the rest of the island nestled in a gorge between the mountains and a stunning black sand beach that merged with the Caribbean Sea. There was no electricity, internet or phone lines or even addresses. It was a haven for people who didn't want any connection to the outside world. The perfect place for Uma Fischer to hide.

After making love to Mena one more time, Julian had given her one of the burner phones and a gun for protection. Mena insisted she would be fine and that he should leave before she changed her mind. She'd almost changed his. How easy would it have been to sneak away with Mena and disappear? Too damn easy. The trouble with Dumay would be behind them. They could start fresh in a different part of the world. His parents would never be surprised if he disappeared, but Mena was a different story. She had family and friends she talked to daily. People she'd miss and would regret leaving behind. He could never ask her to walk away from her life for him. He wanted only the best for her. Convincing her to live a life in the shadows, never being able to see her mom or Omar or Regina wasn't any kind of life she'd want to live. Not even for him.

With one last kiss, Julian had trekked through the underground tunnel connecting the basement of the Genesis Gallery to the opposite side of Dumay Park. He'd emerged near a beaten path wide enough for trucks to enter, yet remain hidden from any cars driving on the major roads. The entrance was how Dumay had smuggled the surrogates and the medical equipment onto the grounds of the gallery.

Hiking his way toward The Bluffs, Julian arrived at the exclusive neighborhood of the island's richest families several hours later. Stealing a small catamaran from the dock of one of the private mansions had been easy. He sailed around St. Basil to St. Felipe. Dropping anchor a couple hundred yards away, he'd swum to the black sand beach that marked the seaside entrance to the Tango Lowlands.

Glancing toward the yellow house, Julian trudged across the road into the small yard. Chickens squawked and fluttered as he entered, scrambling away to safety. The quiet pre-dawn morning was unsettling. Stepping onto the concrete slab of the porch, Julian bent over to examine the lock on the door. Standard deadbolt. Easy enough to pick, even in the darkness. A minute later, he was twisting the knob slowly as the door creaked open.

Julian entered the dark room. Sliding his foot along the floor, he eased the door closed behind him. Moonlight shining through the open side windows illuminated the tight space. A quilt, discarded needles, and swatches of fabric littered the coffee table in front of a worn, patchwork sofa. The house was the shotgun variety with a single hallway. He could see only one door to the left before the hallway opened up into a medium-sized kitchen in the back.

A small tray rested on a stand next to the couch. An empty plate with remnants of food lay in the center with a paper towel crumbled up on the side. Julian scanned the room for any sign that there could be more than one inhabitant of the home. From what he could discern, it seemed she lived alone.

Stalking toward the single door that likely led to her bedroom, Julian paused. The door was slightly open. Pressing a palm on the door, he pushed it open and stepped inside.

He eased closer to the bedside table. A box of matches rested next to an old-fashioned lantern. Sliding the box open, Julian grabbed a match and struck it against the side. A yellow flame burst from the end. Lighting the lantern, he peered at the woman sleeping in the bed. It was definitely Uma Fischer.

Julian sat near the end of the bed and grabbed Uma's ankle through the sheets. Squeezing slowly, he waited. Uma squirmed, then screamed as she awoke and found herself not alone in the bedroom. Eyes wide with terror, she stared at Julian. Frozen in place, she blinked several times before a look of recognition passed through her eyes.

"Julian? Is that you? What are you doing here?" Uma asked. Her fingers moved slowly toward her throat, gliding across a key hanging from a chain around her neck. She squeezed the small key, then slipped it underneath her nightgown, out of sight.

"I need information."

"What kind of information? What are you talking about?"

"You paid Farouk Essa fifty thousand dollars to leave Priscilla Dumay unattended at the end of the trial," said Julian.

"No, I didn't. Who told you I did that?" Uma stammered. She recoiled toward the headboard, pulling the sheets to cover her body.

"Farouk Essa told the cops you did," Julian said, pausing to let his words sink in.

Uma was quiet. Her hands fidgeted with the frayed ends of the blanket covering her body.

"Whoever he is, he must have me mistaken for someone else," Uma whispered.

"And I guess the home security footage he handed over to the police showing you on his doorstep is wrong," Julian asked. "And the police facial recognition software that matched your driver's license photo is wrong too."

"How are you even here right now? Aren't you supposed to be in Tiverton? I could call the cops and tell them where you are," Uma said, shifting in the bed. The demure innocence replaced with vengeful desperation.

Her face grew pale as her eyes darted around the room. Was she looking for a weapon? The thought that she could overpower him was laughable.

"Do it. The cops would love to get a phone call from the woman they're trying to find. By the time they show up, I'd be long gone, and you'd be arrested," Julian said.

Uma glared at him.

"Go ahead Uma, make the call."

Uma sighed, sniffing away her tears. "What do you want from me?"

"Already told you. I want to know why you bribed the guards to leave Dumay unattended," Julian said.

"I didn't know what the money was for. I was told to deliver the package to an address at a certain time and that's what I did," Uma said.

"Who told you to do that?"

Uma avoided his gaze. "I can't tell you."

"That's too bad. Maybe the cops can get you to tell them after I call in this anonymous tip on your location." Julian took his cell phone from his pocket.

"You can't do that. You don't understand what's at stake here," Uma pleaded.

"Let me tell you what's at fucking stake here. The cops are circling Mena right now because they think she hired you to bribe those officers. They are building a case against her as my co-conspirator, and I'll be damned if I let that happen."

"Mena? Why do they think that?" Uma asked.

"Because of those phone calls between the two of you. You're trying to frame her, make her look guilty—"

"I would never do anything to hurt Mena. She left me a message, but I never talked to her. She offered to rehire me at the gallery. If I wasn't in this mess, I would've gladly accepted her offer," Uma said.

The confusion in Uma's eyes was real. If she was being used to set up Mena, then she was clueless about that part of the plan.

Uma continued, "Look, it would be best for Mena if I stay here and not talk to the cops. I'm sure this will blow over and they won't be able to arrest her. Just don't tell anyone you found me. If you do, it could be the end for me."

"What are you saying?"

"My life is on the line here. I can't give you any information or even be seen with a cop or I'm a dead woman."

"Who would kill you? The person who forced you to pay the bribes to the officers?"

"No, not him. Who do you think?" Uma screamed back at him. "You know firsthand how crazy that bitch is! How she doesn't stop until she gets revenge for however you've wronged her. As soon as she found out I'd helped steal art from her gallery, that sealed my fate. Priscilla wanted me dead. She still wants me dead."

"A guy told you to pay the bribes. Who is he?" Julian said, catching her slip.

"Please don't do this. You don't understand—"

"Tell me or I call the cops. Your choice."

Heaving breaths through her sobs, Uma closed her eyes as tears flowed down her cheeks. Swiping at her face, she looked at Julian, defeated. "Priscilla told Zak Webber to kill me for helping Irving steal art from her gallery. He was hunting me. Watching my every move. I knew he'd killed Ella, and that I was next. So, I went off the grid. I thought no one could find me once I rented this house in Tango Lowlands. The people who live here don't want to be found. They don't want a connection with the outside world. They don't snitch. And they don't get into anyone else's business. I was finally safe from Priscilla. But you're never safe from Priscilla."

"Zak was arrested and has been in Tiverton for almost a year. You should have been safe, unless she sent someone else after you?"

Uma said, "I made the mistake of going into town one weekend to get groceries. Here we grow our own fruits and veggies, kill our own animals for food. Everything you need to survive is contained within the Lowlands. It had been months since Priscilla had been arrested. I thought I might get my life back once she was convicted. I figured everyone she would have sent to look for me was behind bars, but I was wrong."

"Go on." Julian wondered who Dumay had enlisted.

"When I was in the grocery store, I could tell a man was following me. He was subtle, not too obvious, but I wasn't safe. I left without buying anything and when I stepped outside, he was waiting for me. It was Adam."

"Adam Russell." Julian spat the name.

Damn it. He should have put those pieces together. Russell had escaped from PIIB custody shortly after Dumay was arrested. The man had made a habit of doing Dumay's bidding for years. He'd orchestrated Mena's kidnapping by Tubeec Hirad in Kenya, all while the PIIB was clueless as to his whereabouts. Russell had months to terrorize Uma and force her to help him with the next phase of Dumay's revenge.

"He pressed a gun in my side and forced me to get in his car. I was scared to death. He was going to murder me and dump my body in the ocean just like they did Ella."

"What happened? Why didn't he kill you?" Julian asked.

"I don't know what made him hesitate back then. He wanted me to show him where I'd been hiding out this whole time. He drove us back here to my house. I watched as he went through all the rooms, looking at my things. He asked me questions about my life, before I went on the run. My dreams, my hopes. Hours passed, and I relaxed with him. I saw a real man with feelings and not just a trained killer next to me," Uma explained.

"And this went on for how long?"

"Days, weeks, then months. He told me I was a beautiful soul and that he didn't believe I deserved to die for being used by Irving. And somewhere along the way, he fell in love with me and I fell in love with him."

"You and Russell are in love?"

"It seems crazy, but he's the most amazing gift I could've ever gotten out of this whole sordid mess. Of course, when he told me he was in trouble, I had to help. He saved my life, there's no way I wouldn't do anything and everything within my power to help save his."

"Let me get this straight. Russell forced you to bribe the guard because his life is in danger?"

"Adam didn't force me to do anything. Priscilla was going to kill him if he didn't follow her directions exactly. It was too risky for him to deliver the money to that guard himself. So, I told him I would do it. He never asked me to. I insisted that he let me help him," Uma said.

Julian resisted the urge to roll his eyes at Uma's staunch defense of Adam Russell. She hadn't changed since the last time he'd seen her. She had a knack for falling for men who used her. He didn't believe for one minute that Russell was being threatened by Dumay. He was her most loyal employee, collecting large payoffs for wreaking havoc at her commands.

"Did he tell you what Dumay asked him to do? What directions did she give him?" Julian asked.

"He wouldn't tell me. It was hard enough to get him to let me help deliver the money to that guard. I don't know what else he was doing for her. What I do know is that even with Priscilla in a coma, she has the power to kill Adam. She's set things in motion that can't easily be undone. Adam is trying to figure out how to stop her plans, but until he does, we have to keep following her instructions. Doing things that both of us hate."

"Do you have more instructions from Dumay? Something else Adam has told you to do?" Julian asked.

Uma was quiet.

Julian grabbed his cell phone and dialed Kendrick's number. Uma hadn't told him anything that helped clear his name. If he gave her up to the cops, Julian was certain she'd clear any suspicion surrounding Mena. The person he really needed to find was Adam Russell.

"What are you doing?" Uma asked, panic creeping in her voice.

"If that's all you have to tell me, then I'm calling the cops to let them know where you are—"

"No. Don't call them. There's a second payoff I'm supposed to make. I'm not sure what they're supposed to do to get it. Adam communicates with them, not me. Once they've done what he's asked them, he's going to text me with a location to meet them with the cash."

"No chance that's happening now that they've confessed to the cops."

"That's not what Adam told me. He texted this morning to confirm that he'd still need my help to deliver the second payment," Uma insisted.

"How are you communicating with Adam?"

"I have a small generator that I use to keep my phone charged," Uma said.

"And what happens if you don't make the second money drop?"

"Priscilla will kill Adam. If he dies, then I'm next. I can't lose him. So, nothing will stop me from delivering the cash once I hear from Adam."

"Where is he now? I need to talk to him," Julian said.

Uma scoffed. "I won't let you hurt Adam just to get Priscilla off your back. If it comes down to his life or yours, I have to make sure I protect my man."

Julian reached behind him, lifting the Beretta from his waistband, and pointed it in Uma's face. "You think I won't shoot a woman?"

"I know you won't," Uma said, flinging the blanket at Julian.

He scrambled off the edge of the bed, batting the cloth away. Uma extended her arm toward him. Julian ducked as a stream of mist landed across his face.

Fuck! Pepper spray. The mist blazed through his nose, sending him into a spasm of coughs as he struggled to breathe. Julian stumbled down to one knee as Uma leapt over him and raced out the back entrance of the house.

Chapter Thirty-Six

Julian was off his game.

Rattled. Unfocused. Mistake prone.

Uma never should have got the jump on him.

Quick reflexes saved his eyes from the onslaught of the pepper spray. His lungs still burned from the mist. Deep coughs racked his body as he stumbled out the back door of the house.

Up ahead, Uma ran through the jungle. The dark night sky transitioned to a hazy purple as Julian burst forward. Single dirt roads and clusters of jungle separated the ragged homes of the Tango Lowlands.

Uma moved fast. But not fast enough. Making it to another house was risky for Uma. There was no guarantee the recluses that lived among the closed off community would open their doors to help her. The one shot she had to get away from him was the black sand beach. A rowboat was moored along a dock when Julian had approached on the catamaran. If she got to it before he caught her, she might row faster than he could swim. Maybe.

The humid jungle air soothed his passageways as he sprinted across the yard, taking a circular arc through the trees. The pale-yellow nightgown Uma wore almost glowed against the dark backdrop of the jungle foliage, making her easy to see. Not only would she not be able to see him, Uma wasn't even trying to look back to gauge his position. She was taking the most direct route from her house to the beach. The same one he'd taken to get to her.

Julian zigzagged between the towering, lush fruit trees and palm fronds, closing the gap between him and Uma. Her breathing was heavy and ragged. Her speed slowing as her energy waned. Stumbling, Uma tripped and plunged head first into a mud puddle on the trail. A soft muffled cry escaped her mouth. Pushing up from the ground, Uma swiped at the dirt covering her face as she struggled to crawl to a stand.

Slowing his speed, Julian approached her from the left. Uma was barely jogging, head cast down as she walked gingerly over the tangled brush of the jungle floor. He stalked behind her, following the sounds of her whimpers as he grew nearer to her. Where would Uma go once she reached the beach? Could she lead him to Adam Russell? Or would she circle around aimlessly, hoping to lose him before returning to her home in the heart of the Tango Lowlands? Julian pondered his options. Even with Uma believing that she and Adam were in love, Julian doubted that Russell told her the details of what Dumay had planned for him and Mena. But he couldn't shake the feeling that Uma had some information he needed. Something that could help him dismantle Dumay's attack on him.

Darting across the jungle brush, Julian clamped a hand on Uma's arm, yanking her backward. Arm gripped around her waist, he lifted her from the ground as she squealed and kicked against him.

"Let me go!" Uma said, jerking in his grasp.

"Tell me where Adam is, and I'll leave you alone."

"Never!" Uma said, increasing the intensity of her fists beating against his arm. Her legs swung wildly as Julian turned and carried her back toward the house. He almost chuckled at her futile attempt to get him to release her.

A swing of her heel connected with his groin. Pain shot through him as he released his grip on Uma, his hand catching on the necklace she wore as she fell to the ground.

"Fuck!" Julian muttered, instinctively grabbing his nuts. In his hand was Uma's necklace with the rusted bronze key he'd seen earlier around her neck. Bent over from the throbbing pain, he glanced to the right and watched Uma running back toward the beach. Frustrated, Julian stood slowly, waiting for the pain to subside. Even with a bruised dick, he'd be able to catch her before she got away.

Staring at the small key in his hand, Julian raised it to eye-level. It looked old and worn. Definitely not a house key. Perhaps it opened a mailbox or safe deposit box? He slipped the burner phone from his pocket and snapped a couple of photos of the front and back side. He could email the jpeg files to the computer in the basement of the Genesis Gallery and start the search remotely. By the time he got back there, he would know what the key opened and if that information could be useful to him.

Julian turned to check Uma's location and stopped. She was running back toward him. What the fuck?

"Give me the key," Uma panted as she reached for his hand.

Julian jerked it away from her grasp, lifting his arm high in the air.

Desperation clouded her eyes as she jumped and scratched at his arm.

"There's only one way you're getting this key back," Julian said. "Tell me where Adam is."

"I don't know where he is! Give me that key!" Uma screamed, her face red and splotchy as tears flowed down her cheeks.

"That's too bad," Julian said, then pushed past her, headed for the trail to the black sand beach.

"No! You can't take that. It's too important," Uma insisted, rushing up behind him. She grabbed at his shirt, trying to slow his speed.

Julian kept walking, increasing his pace as Uma struggled to keep up. She slipped to his right and stepped in front of him, placing her palms against his chest. Her eyes pleaded with him.

"Wait. Please. I'll tell you what you want to know, just give me the key," Uma said.

Julian looked down at her. The key was more important than he'd figured if Uma would give up Adam's location to get it. What secrets did it unlock?

"Why is this key so important?"

Uma paused, glancing up at the canopy of tree branches overhead. She took a deep breath, then said, "It's a key to a locker where the money is hidden. The money that I have to pay those two men. If I don't have that key, I can't get it and Adam dies. You know what it's like to protect someone you love from dying. That's what I'm trying to do. Protect the man I love from the same bitch that's terrorizing you and Mena."

Uma was lying. The key led to something more important than money.

Something that made Uma desperate to get it back. But Julian needed to find Russell more than he needed to figure out what the key opened.

Snatching one of her hands from his chest, Julian squeezed her wrist as he turned it over. Dangling the key a few inches above her palm, he said, "Tell me where Adam is hiding?"

Chapter Thirty-Seven

Mena's sight grew blurry as she stared at the computer screen. Glancing down at her notepad, she checked her calculations. Punching numbers into the calculator, she confirmed the optimal setting for the laser. Turning toward the laser, she entered the parameters that she hoped would be successful in removing the outer layer of black paint from the totem arriving at the gallery later that morning. The meticulous work had been a distraction from worrying about Julian.

Finding out that he'd been in the basement of the Genesis Gallery since the attack at the prison had been bittersweet. She was happy she'd gotten a chance to be with him again. To make love to him. But she regretted not knowing sooner.

Closing her eyes, she allowed the memories of Julian's hands on her body to soothe her. They'd made love over and over throughout the night, each desperate to sear the memory of the other on their minds and bodies. Neither had said it out loud, but she knew they were thinking the same thing. Last night was likely the last time they would see each other for a long time. The thought made her heart ache with yearning to be with him again.

At least she had the burner phone.

Julian could call her when it was safe.

Until then, she would wait and convince the world that she was still upset and concerned over his abduction from prison. She couldn't mess up. One wrong move and the cops might figure out she knew Julian was alive and safe. She wasn't going to do anything to put his life on the line.

Her cell phone lit up near the edge of the table, the ring filling the silence inside the Conservators Workshop. She glanced at the caller ID.

Uma Fischer.

Rushing forward, Mena grabbed the phone and answered. "Hello, Uma?"

"Try again, gorgeous."

"Hey, you found Uma? What happened?" Mena asked, lowering her voice and checking over her shoulder to make sure she was still alone in the workshop. She hadn't bothered to go home after Julian left to find Uma. Mena had taken a shower, then slipped back upstairs and changed into the set of workout clothes that she kept in a gym bag in her office.

"Let's just say she wasn't the wealth of information that I was hoping for, but I learned that Russell told her to bribe the correctional officers."

"I should have guessed that Adam was involved. Is she okay? What does he have on her to force her to do that?" Mena asked.

Julian chuckled. "She did it willingly. They fell in love after he refused to carry out Dumay's orders to kill her."

"You've got to be kidding me," Mena said, pacing around the workshop. "Uma really knows how to pick them, doesn't she?"

"Yeah, and interestingly enough, she's waiting on one more call from Russell for another payoff to the guards. Russell gets instructions to them, but Uma wasn't sure how. Once they've done their part, Russell calls Uma and tells her where to deliver the money. They were paid half the fee up front and will get the other half after they finish all the tasks. But Uma said Russell hasn't told her to make the second drop yet."

"The guards admitted to the bribes. The cops know that they were paid off to leave Dumay alone in the courthouse. Adam's not going to give them the rest of the money now," Mena surmised.

"That's what I thought too, but Uma heard from Russell this morning. He made it clear the deal was still on and that she'd have to deliver the second payment. I'm sure Russell knows about the guards' confession," Julian said.

"What do you think is going on?"

"My guess? The confession was part of what Russell told them to do. It's no secret Dumay wants revenge on both of us. I get thrown in Tiverton to await trial for attacking her, then the cops find out about the bribes to the guards. Conveniently, Uma—your former assistant—was the one who gave them the money."

"And it looks like we orchestrated all of it to try to kill her," Mena said, pacing across the workshop toward the window. A shimmering orange glow spread across the sky as the sun began to rise. "Now those two guards are probably waiting for the rest of their payoff."

"Money they haven't gotten yet. I'm sure the more time that passes, the more anxious they'll be," Julian said, then paused. "I hate to do this, but I need a favor."

"There's nothing I wouldn't do for you," Mena blurted.

"Really?" Julian's question lingered in the air.

Guilt slammed into Mena as she realized what he must be thinking. She had turned down his marriage proposal when she knew it was the one thing he wanted most for them. She hadn't told him the truth. She couldn't marry him when she was still legally married to someone else. A situation she still hadn't figured out how to resolve. Knowing that Michael was somewhere in the Caribbean could work for her. What would happen if she called him? Pretended to worry about how he disappeared over the weekend. Could she still trick him into signing the divorce papers?

"Yes," Mena whispered. "I would do anything for you. Just name it."

Her heart pounded in her chest as she waited for his response. Julian was quiet for longer than she expected. He cleared his throat and said, "Kendrick needs to know about this second payment and use that as a reason to put some pressure on the guards. If one of them cracks, they could tell the cops the truth. Adam Russell is the one who orchestrated the bribe with Uma and not me and you. That's why I called you from Uma's phone. You'll have to tell a little white lie and say she admitted all of this to you. Think you can do that?"

Mena exhaled slowly. "Piece of cake."

An hour later, Mena rehearsed the details of her modified plan as she drove her SUV onto the ferry to the Aerie Islands. She was taking a risk, going rogue from what Julian expected her to do. Julian never would have agreed to let her help him like this. But Mena knew in her heart this was a better approach than trusting the cops to do the right thing. She had to give

Kendrick something more concrete and definitive to prove Julian's innocence.

Placing the car in park, Mena stared out the window at the deep turquoise waters of the Caribbean Sea. St. Basil grew smaller in the distance as the ferry chugged across the open waters toward the Aerie Islands. She didn't have much time. Grabbing the printouts, Mena studied Julian's notes. He had meticulous intel on both Farouk Essa and Whalum O'Keefe. Research he'd left behind in the basement of the Genesis Gallery—addresses, phone numbers, family members, friends, frequent hang out spots. Mena didn't believe for one minute that either officer would flip on Dumay under police interrogation.

They would need a better reason to tell the cops what they knew. She planned to make sure they had one.

Her plan had come together when she'd read a critical detail in Julian's notes. Farouk Essa's son had a rare medical condition. He was transferred to the Rakestraw Blake Center the weekend after Dumay's attack. Julian believed that Farouk was using the money to help his sick son. If the second payment hadn't been made yet, Farouk was likely the more desperate of the two officers. She could appeal to his better nature, helping him to understand how his actions to save his son were going to put an innocent man in prison for years. Maybe if he listened to her, she could convince him to come clean to the police about Adam Russell.

As the ferry docked, Mena started the SUV and drove across the island to the Rakestraw Blake Center. Julian's notes had indicated Farouk was on medical leave since the trial. She couldn't imagine he'd be any other place but at the hospital with his son.

The pediatric ICU was on the fifth floor. Mena stepped into the elevator and pressed five. She took a deep breath and said a silent prayer.

The door to the fifth floor opened. A man stepped inside, then paused.

"I'm sorry. Ladies first," the man said. His voice low and pained.

Mena recognized him. The man she'd come to see—Farouk Essa.

"Mr. Essa," Mena said.

"Yes, do I know you?" Farouk asked.

"No, but I have information to share with you from Adam," Mena had chosen her words wisely, in case the man was concerned about further implicating himself.

Farouk nodded slowly, then stepped inside the elevator. "Let's talk outside."

Mena rode down the elevator in silence with Farouk. Fingering the charms on her bracelet, she rehearsed her next move as the elevators opened. Farouk led her outside to a deserted outdoor sitting area that surrounded a wishing well.

"Where's my money?" Farouk asked.

"There won't be any more money. You didn't hold up your end of the bargain—"

"The hell I didn't! I confessed to the cops like Adam told me to and kept his name out of my official statement. I told them it was a voice distorter, and I didn't know who I was talking to. I could still get fired for what I did, and now that bastard is trying to renege on paying me. What the hell? Do you understand that my son is dying in there? The treatments that are saving his life cost five grand a day! The Rakestraw Blake Center doesn't do charity. Once the initial 10-day payment is up, they will ship him right back to St. Basil General where the disease will start back ravaging his body. I need that money," Farouk said.

"I'm sorry about your son," Mena said, regretting her decision to try to get Farouk to help her and Julian. They weren't the only ones fighting for their lives. Farouk's son needed the money that Farouk was expecting from Adam.

"You tell Adam he's the one who's going to be sorry. Payment for the next round of my son's treatments is on Monday. If I don't have the money in my hand, I'm going to the cops with evidence that could put him in prison for a very long time," Farouk said.

"What kind of evidence do you have?" Mena asked.

"I'm not stupid. I know Adam was just following Priscilla's orders. He's been her head of security for years. Everything that happened in that anteroom was exactly what she wanted,"

"What do you think you know?" Mena asked, heart pounding in her throat.

"I heard Priscilla make a phone call to that ex-SEAL who was arrested for attacking her. She lured him back there and I'm guessing everything played out exactly like she planned. Now, I don't know what went down in that room while I was gone, but I don't believe for one second that he tried to kill her. When we rushed into the room and saw her convulsing on the floor, I knew I was dealing with some dangerous people. I figured it might come to this, so I made sure I had some insurance. I saw the cell phone in her pocket as I helped the EMTs get her on the gurney. I grabbed it and hid it in my pocket."

"You have the cell phone," Mena whispered, stunned.

"Damn right, I do. You know what else is on that phone? Texts between her and Adam talking about setting the guy up. So, you tell Adam that my fee has doubled to a hundred grand. That will pay for all the treatments my son needs and I'll hand over the phone," Farouk said, then stood.

"Wait a minute," Mena grabbed his arm. "Where is the phone now?"

"A place where I can easily get it," Farouk said.

"I'll have a cashier's check within the hour," Mena said, grateful that Julian had put her as a secondary owner on a few of his local bank accounts. "You better have that phone when I get back."

Chapter Thirty-Eight

Mena pounded her fist against the door. Again. Her hands aching, she glanced at the SUV in the narrow driveway of the modest home in Cashew Groves. Hands on her hips, she stepped toward the window to the left of the door and tried to peek inside. Curtains blocked her view. Mena raised her fist to knock again as the door opened slightly.

"Mena, what are you doing here?" Kendrick asked, frowning.

Pushing the door open wider, Mena forced her way past him into the living room.

"I have evidence that proves Julian is innocent," Mena said, spinning around to face him. "I need you to get it authenticated so the charges can be dropped."

"Wait a minute. What kind of evidence?" Kendrick asked, crossing his arms over his chest. He was closed off, guarded, his eyes wary as he stared at her.

Mena reached into her purse and pulled out the quart sized Ziploc bag with the burner phone inside. "This is the phone that Priscilla used to call Julian. There are also text messages on here between her and Adam discussing their plan to set Julian up."

Stunned, Kendrick took the bag from Mena. "How did you get this?"

"Does that matter? Why can't you just trust me and take it to the station?" Mena asked.

"Because evidence needs to follow a chain of custody to be certain it hasn't been tampered with, Mena. Where did you get this burner phone?" Kendrick asked.

Mena stifled her rage. The look on Kendrick's face frustrated her. He didn't believe she was telling the truth. Taking a deep breath, Mena said, "I got the phone from Farouk Essa. He took it from the courthouse after Julian was arrested to use it as blackmail to get more money from Adam Russell."

"Adam Russell?" Kendrick asked.

"Let me start from the beginning," Mena said, sitting down on the leather recliner. Over the next thirty minutes she told Kendrick everything Julian had found out from Uma, except she told Kendrick that Uma had called and given her the information. Then she explained how she met up with Farouk at the Rakestraw Blake Center and got the burner phone.

"So, Adam Russell is behind the bribes. He got his new girlfriend Uma to deliver the cash to Essa. A second payment is owed to both men, but Uma hasn't received directions from Adam on when to deliver it. You went to Essa and confronted him about this and he hands over the burner phone he was holding to blackmail Adam? Something's not adding up here," Kendrick said.

"I paid him to give me the burner phone. He needed the money to pay for the last round of treatments for his son," Mena explained.

"Damn it, Mena. Why didn't you come to me the minute Uma called you?" Kendrick threw his hands in the air and stalked back toward the kitchen.

"Because Farouk Essa wouldn't have admitted any of that to you and you know it. He was desperate to save his son's life. Coming clean to the cops out of the goodness of his heart wouldn't pay the medical bills at the Rakestraw Blake Center," Mena insisted. "So, what does this mean? You can't use the evidence?"

"I only have your word that Dumay used this phone. How do I know you didn't place all these texts on here to make it look like Dumay set Julian up? That's what Detective Francois is going to think."

"Oh my God, Kendrick! You act like you don't even know me. Do you really think I would do something like that?" Mena turned and walked toward the small kitchen. Two wine glasses sat on the edge of the glass table, one stained with red lipstick. Remnants of plates cluttered the kitchen sink. The bedroom door was slightly ajar.

Kendrick's silence spoke volumes.

He walked toward her and steered her back toward the living room.

Finally, he spoke. "I know you're worried sick about Julian since he went missing from Tiverton. The PIIB and every police station in the Palmchat Islands are searching for him with orders to bring him back alive. I want to prove that Julian is innocent just as much as you do."

Mena glanced back at the bedroom door. "What are you going to do with the phone?"

"I'll take it to the station and have it checked out. Let me ask you this. If I bring Farouk Essa in for questioning, what is he going to say?"

"Exactly what I just told you. He's so grateful to have the money to pay for his son's treatments that he doesn't care about keeping secrets anymore," Mena said.

"You asked me to trust you. Now I'm going to do the same. What you did, going to see Essa by yourself, was reckless. It could harm Julian's case. You need to trust that I'm doing everything I can to clear his name."

"Kind of hard to trust you when you're too busy hooking up with someone while one of your closest friends is still missing," Mena said, anger boiling within her. She jerked her arm from Kendrick's grasp and stomped over to the kitchen table. Lifting the wine glass smeared with dark red lipstick, she shook her head. "Hope getting laid while Julian is fighting for his freedom was worth it."

"Mena, come on, it's not what it looks like," Kendrick said.

"Mena?" A woman's voice called from behind her.

Mena turned and stared at Stella.

A bitter laugh erupted from Mena's lips as she looked at the woman, dressed in one of Kendrick's t-shirts and leggings. "Stella. I guess you got your man. Normally, I would be happy for you, but your timing stinks."

"It's not like that," Stella shook her head as tears filled her eyes. "Kendrick and I aren't together. He's trying to help me."

Mena stared at Stella as she twisted the ends of the t-shirt between her fingers. Her makeup was smeared around puffy eyes. She'd been crying. "What happened?"

"Don't say anything, Stella," Kendrick warned.

"I have to. This pain that Mena is going through is my fault," Stella said. "She deserves to know the truth."

Mena stalked toward Stella, staring the woman in the eyes. "What is your fault? Tell me what you did."

Stella's body wracked with sobs as she leaned against the kitchen counter. Sniffing, she rubbed her hands across her face, gulping air as her tears subsided. Mena's heart pounded in her chest, adrenaline flooding her veins in anticipation of what Stella was about to say. It had to be related to Julian. But what could Stella have done? And why was Kendrick helping her and not hauling her down to the police station?

"One of you better tell me what's going on!" Mena said, glancing back at Kendrick.

Kendrick's shoulders slumped as he joined them in the kitchen. He reached a hand toward Stella protectively as he helped her to a chair at the table.

"You probably should sit down for this." Kendrick motioned toward the chair.

"Stop stalling," Mena said.

Stella said, "I had an accident months ago. It was my fault, and I didn't have enough insurance to cover the damages to the family that I hit. The family sued me. They wanted fifty thousand to settle out of court. Fifty thousand dollars that I don't have. A man came by my house. I thought he was a lawyer or insurance agent, so I let him in. But he wasn't. He knew about the lawsuit and handed me an envelope with fifty thousand dollars in cash to make all my problems go away," Stella said, looking out into the distance.

"And what did you have to do in exchange for that?" Mena asked.

"I have diabetes and I carry syringes with me for my insulin treatments," Stella said.

Mena felt her stomach sour.

Stella continued, "The man gave me a syringe to smuggle into the court-house. Once I was inside, I had to tape the syringe under the table in Ante-room F."

"That's how Priscilla got the syringe," Mena said, stunned by this revelation.

Kendrick said, "Stella is going to be facing some serious charges for this. I need to figure out the best way to help her through it—"

"Who gave you the fifty thousand dollars?" Mena demanded.

Stella looked up at Mena. "He said his name was Adam Russell."

Chapter Thirty-Nine

Mena returned to the penthouse, easing the door closed behind her. The stone floor was cool on her bare feet as she stepped out of her flats. The room was dark. The night sky devoid of stars stretched ahead through the floor to ceiling windows. She'd spent the last couple of hours with Kendrick and Stella, discussing the next steps they needed to take to introduce the new evidence to the police. Adam hadn't bothered to hide who he was from Stella when he approached her with the unsavory deal. He knew she was desperate and would keep her mouth shut about who paid her.

Stella's confession and the burner phone Mena had gotten from Farouk Essa might not be enough to get Julian out of trouble. With Uma and Adam still missing, there were too many ways the evidence could be misinterpreted. There was no guarantee the cops could prove that the number texted on the phone belonged to Adam Russell, either.

Kendrick's concern for Stella had annoyed Mena. He was delaying bringing the evidence to the station until tomorrow, to give Stella time to hire a good attorney. Mena didn't understand why the burner phone had to wait. She'd given him a critical piece of the puzzle, and he wasn't acting on it fast enough. She'd insisted Kendrick take it to be evaluated tonight, but he'd resisted and asked her to trust him.

She wondered if giving the burner phone to Kendrick was the best move?

Should she have taken her chances with Detective Francois and given it to him instead?

No. Julian trusted Kendrick. He'd told her to take the information to Kendrick to handle. She might not have faith in Kendrick, but she always trusted and believed in Julian. This is what he'd want her to do.

Mena reached inside her purse for the burner phone Julian had given her and turned down the wide hallway that led to the master bedroom. She knew he was going after Adam Russell, hoping to force him to reveal Priscilla's plans to the police. Mena hoped she got a call from him soon. She stepped toward the open doorway, then paused. She hadn't been home in over twenty-four hours, having spent last night with Julian in the basement of the Genesis Gallery, but she hadn't left their bedroom in disarray.

She took another tentative step forward, leaning slightly to get a better angle of the room. Pillows and sheets were tossed across the floor. The mattress had been upended and leaned at an awkward angle against the wall. The glass lamps were shattered, littering the carpet with reflective shards. Moonlight poured into the room from the open draperies.

Had someone broken into their home?

The penthouse was quiet. The subtle hum of the bars and restaurants on King Street and Bishop Avenue could be heard faintly in the distance.

Mena eased into the closet, quickly turning the combination on the safe. Opening the door slowly, she grabbed one of the guns from the top shelf and closed the door. Julian's clothes had been tossed onto the floor. Jagged cuts ripped the fabric. With the weapon gripped firmly in her hands, she stepped into the oversized room. The photos of the two of them that had rested on the bedside table were cut into shreds. The glass of the frames resting nearby shattered against the floor.

Mena heard a low moan, a slight grunt. She approached the en suite bathroom. Stepping over the littered contents of Julian's life. She reached the bathroom door.

A scream bubbled within her, but she held it in.

Sitting on the edge of the jacuzzi tub, Michael leaned slightly against the wall. His trousers unzipped. His hand wrapped around the shaft of his penis, pumping furiously as sweat beaded on his upper lip. His eyes stared intently across the room. Mena followed his gaze. Pictures of her had been taped to the mirror.

Michael moaned louder, grunting as he continued to masturbate until Mena saw the cloudy semen spurt across the bathroom floor. Michael exhaled softly, slowing his movements as he closed his eyes.

"What the hell are you doing?" Mena pointed the gun at Michael.

Michael's eyes opened slowly and rested on her face. He didn't seem the least bit surprised to see her or concerned about the weapon in her hand.

"Waiting for you to come home to me."

"I could shoot you. You broke into my house!" Mena screamed. "It would be self-defense."

"You could, but you won't. How would Julian feel when he finds out the man you killed was your husband? Think he would forgive you? I don't." Michael said. His hand moved slightly against his penis as it swelled. "I dream about making love to you every night. This penthouse should be ours, Mena. I should be the man fucking you in that bed. Not Julian fucking Montgomery. He doesn't deserve to take my place. No one does."

"Get out of my house. I'm not going to ruin my life by shooting you. But I will call the cops if you don't get out of here," Mena said.

Michael smiled. The same smile she'd seen years ago that had stolen her heart. Now it made her sick with regret.

"Not yet, my love. I finally put all the pieces together of what happened last weekend. One minute, I'm walking you to your casita after an amazing dinner," Michael said, his hand moving up and down his penis. "The next I'm waking up alone in my apartment in New York City. How does that happen, Mena?"

Mena lowered the gun slightly. A chill ran down her spine.

"You like watching me get off on you, don't you? You remember what it feels like to make love to me. How it feels to have my big dick ramming into your pussy, making you scream. You can have that again. I know I fucked you better than Julian ever could—"

"You're disgusting."

"No! You're disgusting! You lying, cheating bitch!" Michael roared, standing up. "You were supposed to give me another chance. I trusted you and you fucking lied to my face! You put a goddamn drug in my drink. You had some PC-5 thug drag me back to New York. I know what you did!"

Mena recoiled, taking a step backward. "You need to leave. Now. I will shoot you if you try to hurt me, Michael. I swear."

"Hurt you?" A pained look crossed Michael's face. "I'd never hurt you, Mena. I love you. I love you more than anyone has ever loved you. No one will love you more than me. Don't you get that?"

The look in Michael's eyes was of pure derangement as he rushed toward her.

Mena screamed as he lunged, knocking the gun across the room. Stumbling over the furniture and clothes crowded on the floor, she raced out of the bedroom toward the living room.

"Come back here, Mena!" Michael screamed.

Her feet slapped against the stone floor as she ran faster, trying to reach the front door to scream for help. She was almost there. Gripping the doorknob, she felt Michael's body slam into her. Pressing her against the door. His erection throbbed against her back as his hot breath blazed across her neck. His lips pressed against her bare shoulder, tongue sliding down her skin as his hands gripped her hips.

"No, Michael," Mena whispered. "Please ... don't."

Chapter Forty

Julian lowered the binoculars as a breeze whistled through the dense foliage of the jungle.

Standing on the private terrace of the Heliconia Hotel, Adam Russell took another gulp of the tumbler of dark liquor. The bottle of Bishop's rum teetered on the edge of the balcony, well within his reach. The Palmchat Islands' most wanted man had eluded law enforcement by hiding out in a sex hotel that catered to female clientele. The hotel was known for carrying out the sexual fantasies of women and was advertised strictly by word of mouth. The location was remote on the island of St. Mateo. Entering Fort Knox was easier than getting onto the hotel grounds. It was a known operation of the PC-5, making Adam's choice of a hiding place that more secure.

The rustling of the leaves grew louder as Julian lowered himself from the perch of a rubber tree. Uma had kept her word, giving him the exact location of Russell in exchange for returning her key. Not that Julian had lost interest in finding out what the key opened. The pictures he'd emailed to his computer program were being analyzed. He should have a good idea of what the key opened in a matter of hours. Once he'd confirmed that following the trail of the key was worthwhile, a plastic version of the key could be printed from the 3-D printer on his yacht. He hoped Russell would give him all that he needed, but he'd be fooling himself if he thought it would be that easy.

Approaching the hotel, Julian assessed the easiest entry point to Russell's room. Not surprisingly, there was no video surveillance on the property. Nothing that could reveal the powerful women who indulged in their services or any PC-5 business that may occur there. Russell grabbed the bottle of Bishop's rum, tipping it toward his glass. A trickle of fluid barely coated the bottom. Russell glanced at the sky with bleary eyes, then turned and walked into the hotel room.

Julian pushed through the brush and crossed the narrow grassy knoll toward the side of the hotel building. His steps were whisper quiet as he approached the trellis covered in bougainvillea attached to the wall near the balcony. He gripped the wood, wincing at the thorns piercing his skin as he rose higher to the second level. The leap was about five feet from his position on the trellis to the balcony. A rush of adrenaline coursed through his body as he was reminded of all the training he'd done as a Navy SEAL. The pure exhilaration of facing danger head on rippled through him. Crouching slightly, Julian pushed off the trellis twisting his body in the air. His fingers landed with a loud thud against the railing.

Julian hoisted himself over the balcony and stood, meeting the eyes of Adam Russell.

"Can't say I'm surprised to see you," Russell slurred, as he took a step back. "Want a drink? I was just opening another bottle."

Disappearing inside, Russell walked toward the bar a few feet from the French doors. Julian followed him.

"Make mine a double," Julian said.

Russell poured rum into two glass tumblers, nearly to the top, then slid one toward Julian. He raised the glass in the air. "Slainte."

Julian took a sip of the smooth liquor, allowing the warmth to trail down his throat into his stomach.

"The minute I heard you'd been *abducted* from Tiverton, I knew you'd come after me. I don't know how you pulled it off, though. Cops and PIIB are still confused about what happened to you," Russell said. Crossing from behind the bar, he walked to a group of couches arranged across from each other and sat on one side. "Have a seat."

Julian joined Russell. "Just like they're confused about what happened to you."

"Touche."

"I met your new girlfriend." Julian swirled the liquor around in his glass, then took another sip.

Russell chuckled. "Women. Can't trust them, can we? I'm sure Mena's keeping some secret from you too. Just a matter of time before she does something that comes back to bite you in the ass."

Julian was quiet. The images of Mena in the photographs with the unidentified man flooded his mind. What if he'd been wrong about them? What if they had nothing to do with Priscilla Dumay's revenge? Then who the hell was that guy and why was Mena with him?

"We struck a deal that worked for her. Not so much for you," Julian said.

"Any deal Uma made with you will work out to be in my best interest. Care to share the details?"

"No. I'm here to find out what Dumay is planning for me and Mena. She wants the world to believe that I tried to kill her in the courthouse. Both of you went through a lot of trouble to make it look believable. Did a good job too, since I was sent to Tiverton and assigned to the same unit where Zak Webber was serving his time. Was that her endgame? Get me sent to Tiverton so Zak could kill me?"

Russell tapped his nose and pointed his finger at Julian. "Navy trained you well. You almost got it right."

"What part am I missing?"

"The part I haven't quite figured out yet. Priscilla insisted that she wouldn't be convicted of the crimes against her. She had no plans of going to prison. She planned to convince the jury she was innocent, but she didn't give me details on that part."

"Let me guess, Quentin is handling that?"

"Maybe," Adam responded, taking another gulp of the rum. "My role was to set you up for premeditated attempted murder. I bribed the guards assigned to Priscilla to give her enough time alone to lure you to the anteroom. I bribed the court reporter to smuggle the vial of poison into the courthouse. And Quentin took care of getting Priscilla the burner phone to call you."

"Stella Young, the court reporter, was working for you?" Julian took a sip of rum, anger rolling within him as he listened to Russell's cavalier explanation of how he plotted with Dumay to ruin his fucking life.

"She was in a bind, left a woman with some bad medical problems from a car accident and was being sued. I gave her the money to settle, and she did what I asked. It was a mutually beneficial one-time transaction."

"Then you faked phone calls to make it look like Mena asked Uma to bribe the guards," Julian said.

"Laying a trap requires layers upon layers of intersecting evidence. You're too smart to be obvious, that would have been a red flag for the cops. So, I had to think like you, be covert like I'd expect you to do if you'd planned this yourself. Involving Mena was necessary to make your guilt look more plausible."

"Dumay isn't focused on Mena, then?"

"I didn't say that. She wants to hurt Mena, but not kill her."

"She's planning to kidnap Mena again." Julian said, remembering his conversation with Dumay in the anteroom.

"Yes, but only after Zak killed you or you were convicted. She wasn't making another move on Mena until you were out of the picture. That's why after she found out what you did in Central Sulawesi, she was desperate to get her hands on that laptop."

Julian cringed, draining the rest of the rum, then slammed the glass on the coffee table. "If Dumay wants me gone, why didn't she just deliver the laptop to NCIS. That would have been easier than setting up this ruse."

"Because she doesn't have the laptop," Adam said, placing the empty glass on the coffee table separating them. "I do."

Julian raised an eyebrow. "You have my laptop from Central Sulawesi?"

"Serial number 490C224 issued to Chief Petty Officer Julian Montgomery. I'll admit, you're good. You damn near wiped out all the evidence of what you'd done. Almost. Took a team of hackers months to find one little thread that got missed. Those uncorrupted parts of the hard drive and a conversation I had with Enrique Rivera Ortiz helped pull all the pieces together."

Tension clawed at Julian's neck. "What do you plan to do with it?"

"Make you a deal."

"I'm listening."

"Priscilla and I are in what you'd call a standoff. I have evidence that could bury her and she could bury me, literally. That makes our arrangements tenuous at best. I can't afford to refuse her requests, and she can't afford to push me too far. But I'm tired of this see-saw with her. I want out. You can help make that happen."

"Uma mentioned that Priscilla was threatening your life," Julian said. "What's that about?"

"She had a kill switch implanted in my heart. If a surgeon tries to remove it, the device self-detonates and I die instantly. Priscilla can control it remotely from anywhere on earth. I'm not sure about this, but I'd guess Quentin has control over it too, when Priscilla is unavailable. It doesn't matter if I flee with Uma and hide away in a place where they can't find me. With one tap on a computer, they can send a signal to blow up my heart."

"You're fucking kidding."

"How do you think all those surrogates started mysteriously dying before they could testify against her? All from heart complications. Priscilla is smart. She didn't engage the switch on them at the same time. She waited, staggered the murders so that doctors treating them would conclude they were having heart failure from the stress of being locked up."

"Guess that means if Priscilla needs you to break out of PIIB custody to kidnap Mena or frame me, you can't really say no. Seems like she has all the control," Julian said.

"That's where you're wrong. I've been stockpiling evidence of all of Priscilla's crimes for years. Microscopic body cameras were hidden in the buttons of my shirts and trousers where I recorded all of our interactions. The files are in safe deposit boxes controlled by different people around the world. They all know that if I don't check in with them every twenty-four hours, they are to send the evidence to Interpol. Priscilla knows this, which is why she can't push me too far. I do her dirty work, she pays me millions and we keep doing this awful dance."

"Does that mean you have proof of her asking you to frame me?"

"Cell phone video that will get you cleared in a matter of minutes," Adam said.

"And you'll give me that proof and the laptop if I do what exactly?"

"Corrupt the program that activates the kill switch in my heart and kill Priscilla, in that order," Adam said.

"That easy, huh?"

"You're the right man for the job. I'll even sweeten the deal. You'll get the evidence to clear your name from these pending charges now. After you've taken out Priscilla and corrupted the program so it can no longer trigger the kill switch, I'll give you the laptop. Do we have a deal?" Adam leaned over with his hand extended.

Julian stared back at the man, then said. "Yeah, we have a deal."

The door to the hotel room burst open, banging against the wall. Trampled stomps of police officers and PIIB agents dressed in SWAT gear poured into the room, guns raised.

"Hands up! On the floor! Get on the floor now!"

Chapter Forty-One

Leaning over the balcony railing, Mena held the warm mug in her hands. The smell of the strong coffee with more than a dash of Bishop's rum soothed her before she even took a sip.

Lucy Hargrove, the residential manager at Harmony Towers, placed a hand gently against her shoulder. Mena glanced back at the pretty woman with red hair in a low fade. The logo for the iconic television show, "I Love Lucy" was tattooed on the side of her head.

"You sure you're okay?" Lucy asked. "You're trembling."

"I'm fine. Just a bit distracted," Mena mumbled, then took a sip of the coffee. Lucy's timing had been perfect. After her neighbor had called down to the front desk complaining about screams and noises coming from the penthouse, Lucy had arrived with a security guard pounding on her door. Mena's body had trembled with each knock, her body pressed against the other side.

"Mena, if you don't open up, I'm coming inside. I have our security guard with me," Lucy had yelled from the other side of the door.

Michael had released her from his grip, allowing her to breathe again. She turned and glared at him as he slowly zipped his trousers and tucked his shirt inside his pants. His face adopted a passive look, professional and calm as he ran a hand over his hair and motioned for Mena to open the door.

Mena hadn't hesitated to swing the door open wide. Lucy looked shocked to see another man in the penthouse she shared with Julian.

"I apologize for the commotion. Mena's been really upset with Julian missing. I'm sure you understand. I'm Dr. Marsh, an old ... friend. I wanted to make sure she was doing okay under the circumstances," Michael had explained to Lucy and the security guard.

"It's late. You should probably get going," Mena said, urging Michael out of the door.

"We'll finish catching up another time," Michael said. The words lingered like a threat between them. "I'll be in touch soon."

Mena nearly collapsed once Michael was out of the penthouse and escorted to the elevator by the security guard. Lucy had been kind enough to make her some coffee and stick around.

Lucy said, "You probably need to get some rest, Mena. It's been almost a week since Julian was abducted from prison. You've been so strong all this time, but I can understand if you lost it tonight. Ms. Vincent was concerned when she heard noise coming from here."

Mena made a mental note to thank Janelle Vincent, the daughter of King Street Lounge owner Bimbo Vincent and owner of Penthouse Suite B. If she hadn't sounded the alarm, Mena shuddered to think what Michael would have done to her.

"I'll stop by and apologize to her in the morning. Thanks for coming to check on me," Mena said.

"My pleasure. I always thought you and Julian were a lovely couple. From the moment I met the two of you when you came to look at the apartment Ella used to live in, I knew you were good people, as they say. I don't know what happened in the courthouse with Julian and that woman, but I don't believe for one minute that he tried to kill her," Lucy said.

Mena nodded. "Thanks. That means a lot, considering what most of the islanders think about him now. The articles in the *Palmchat Gazette* only make it worse, calling him a fallen hero."

"It's horrible. I swear that paper has gotten so much worse since it was taken over by the Bronson's. It was a much better paper when it was owned locally," Lucy agreed.

"I think I will try to get some rest now," Mena said, walking back into the penthouse. Lucy followed her inside. Mena pressed the button to close the automated accordion doors.

"I can stick around for the night, if you'd like. You have plenty of space here—"

"No, it's okay." Mena led Lucy to the door, then opened it. She couldn't explain to Lucy the disaster in the master bedroom that she would spend most of the night cleaning up.

"Call me if you need anything," Lucy said as she exited.

Mena shut the door behind her and shivered. She couldn't believe what had happened with Michael. He'd become obsessed with her. He'd broken into her home and tried to destroy all of Julian's belongings. Any hope she had of convincing him to give her a divorce had vanished. He would never let her go without being forced to. And there was only one person who could make that happen.

Julian.

Mena had to come clean and tell Julian the truth. She'd kept it from him for too long, thinking she could handle this situation on her own. Michael had been delusional and dangerous tonight. If Lucy hadn't shown up with the guard, Mena knew that Michael would have raped her.

She hated to put more pressure on Julian with everything he was up against fighting Priscilla Dumay, but she was completely out of options. She had a chance to tell him the truth when he'd proposed to her on the secluded beach in St. Killian. In hindsight, she should have told him how much she wanted to be his wife, but that a legal glitch caused her to still be married to Michael. It seemed so reasonable now, but back then, she'd panicked. All she could think about was losing Julian because of Michael. She'd thought getting a divorce would be simple. She was wrong. Months later, she was still lying to Julian and Michael was getting closer and closer to revealing the truth to the world.

What would Julian do when she told him the truth? He would be angry and upset at her for the lies she'd told. The one thing she knew without any doubt was how important trust was to Julian. He'd trusted her with his deepest, darkest secret. A secret that could land him in prison for the rest of his life. Yet she hadn't done the same. She'd kept her secret hidden, choosing not to trust in him or his love to help her deal with it. That fact would be a devastating blow to their relationship. One that could end them for good.

Mena was out of choices. If she didn't tell Julian, Michael would. If she did and Julian hated her for her lies, then it wouldn't matter that she was still legally married. But there was a chance that Julian would still love her and support her. That he would help her fight Michael and get the divorce so she could marry Julian.

The buzz of her cell phone startled her. Grabbing it from the counter, she saw the Palmchat Islands Alert scrolling across the screen.

Dread seeped through her as she read the text: *Escaped inmate Julian Montgomery has been spotted in St. Mateo. He is considered armed and dangerous. Stay inside until the inmate is apprehended.*

Chapter Forty-Two

Julian moved before his brain even registered his actions. Legs pumping, he sprinted toward the open French doors of the balcony. Pressing his hands against the smooth stone, he propelled his body upward, straddling the balustrade. A quick glance back.

Law enforcement clad in combat gear. Jackets brandishing the letters SWAT. Guns raised, the cops screamed at him to freeze. Do not move.

Do.

Not.

Move.

Julian exhaled, swinging his other leg over the edge, then free fell to the ground as a round of bullets whizzed overhead. Sparks from the gunshots ricocheted off nearby trees. Bracing himself for impact, he allowed his body to relax. The impact was harder than he'd expected, but he'd trained for longer falls than a two-story drop. His body rolled over and over until he came to a stop near the edge of the jungle.

Without another thought, he burst forth through the wide leaves and plunged into the dark abyss of the St. Mateo jungle. Ducking, he kept low. Legs churned through the brush, scratching and clawing at his skin. Zigzagging, he was losing ground, running blind hoping the full moon would penetrate the dense foliage to give him a chance to figure out which direction he should run. The earth was thick and muddy beneath his feet, sucking his combat boots deeper into its depths.

Slowing him down.

Precious seconds needed.

If he was going to get away.

Trampled footsteps and shouts permeated the air behind him. The manhunt to capture him. By any means necessary. Beams of light bounced off the trees and foliage from the SWAT Team's flashlights. Quick moments of illumination, enough for Julian to adjust his trajectory. A plan forming in his mind. A way to escape.

On a mission, he would have prepared for the worst-case scenario. Taken the time to study the terrain. Planned a tactical escape route, or two or three, of least likely detection. SEALs always trained to failure. Anticipated anything and everything that could go wrong. He hadn't had that luxury.

All he had were his instincts.

A decade of SEAL missions capturing terrorists at his disposal.

But more importantly, years of dirtboarding down these mountains towering over the Valley of Waterfalls with Broman etched into his mind.

Ripping through the trees, he banged against brush and thorns as he increased his speed.

The heady, fragrant scent of flowers clung in the air, suffocating and thick.

Adrenaline boosted into overdrive as the terrain grew steep and rocky.

The footsteps were fainter, fanning out to cover more of the jungle, but still committed to tracking him. The loud barks of dogs joining the chorus of chaos closing in on him.

The jungle shifted vertically, heading up the mountain. A quick glance to his left and he saw a path down the cliff side toward the creek below.

He took the road less traveled. Grabbing rocks and branches, he hauled himself up the mountain. Hands stinging from the scrapes and scratches, bounding higher until the sounds were faint behind him. The night air was brisk and clean. He gulped breaths, took a swipe at the sweat pouring down his face and into his eyes, then maneuvered toward a wide tree growing horizontally from a crevice in the mountain rock.

Hidden from view, Julian rested against the tree, his back flat against its trunk.

Ahead, a ridge loomed with darkened crevices.

Caves hollowed out by nature, and time dotted along the mountainside.

A branch snapped.

Julian froze.

Heavy breathing and rocks skittering.

Close.

Too close.

Someone not fooled by his ascent.

Focusing, he zeroed in on the sounds.

Crunching footsteps scrambling up the mountain. Rocks popping, tumbling down as the cop continued his pursuit.

Fifteen feet below, thirty-degree angle from where Julian sat and gaining ground.

He didn't have much time.

Choosing the closest crevice, Julian prayed it was a deep cave and crawled along the brush, slow and steady. Silent.

Ahead, a darkened depression behind a slight ridge.

Hands pressed into the muck of the earth, he felt the sting of mosquitoes and ants feasting on his skin.

He wasn't far.

The man behind him had slowed, likely contemplating what Julian's next move would be before choosing a direction.

Reaching the edge of the ridge, Julian grabbed the ledge and hoisted his body over, dangling into the mouth of a cave. His fingers straining from the weight of his body, he calculated the fall was longer than the drop from the terrace of the Heliconia Hotel. Bracing himself, he let go.

Slamming into the side of the cave, he tucked into a roll, flipping over and over.

Head banging against rocks, he tried to slow his descent, but the angle of the inner cave made that damn near impossible. Tucking his arms to his chest, he leaned into the roll until his body came to a stop.

Laying on his back, he glanced up at the narrow opening of the cave.

Waiting. Listening.

A dark form peered in the gap, staring down at him.

Fuck!

Julian scrambled to his feet.

He scanned the dark void, rushing toward a tunnel near the back, unsure of where it would lead.

A loud thud resounded in the cavity.

Julian turned, watching the cop tumble down the side into the cave.

Veering toward one side of the tunnel to obscure any view of his movements, Julian hurried through the tight space. It grew narrower, lower as he continued on, forcing him to crouch as he looked for a way out. Some kind of escape.

He couldn't get captured now. Not when he was so close to getting the evidence he needed from Russell to clear his name. Russell likely surrendered to the SWAT Team knowing how valuable he was to them. He wouldn't be hauled off to Tiverton but placed in another cushy witness protection home where he'd bide his time until he escaped again.

Julian didn't have the same luxury.

If he was captured, he'd be back in Tiverton, in solitary, with a list of additional crimes tacked onto his charges. In prison, the deal he'd struck with Adam Russell would be moot. Any hope he had of thwarting Dumay's revenge, of getting back to his life with Mena, would be diminished to a sliver of a pipe dream.

He would not let that happen.

Loud pounding steps resonated behind him.

The cop had found the tunnel.

Julian pressed onward, his hands slapping against wet rock. The soft sound of water trickling through the cave grew louder. Quads burning, he recognized the shift of the terrain increasing in altitude.

Up ahead, a soft shaft of moonlight broke through, reflecting into the cave.

Julian quickened his pace, ducked and scrambled on his hands and knees to squeeze through the tight orifice, before dropping into a flat ledge below. A torrent of water about two feet deep rushed across his legs, soaking his clothes. The pounding of a waterfall roared in his ears. He looked left toward the sound. The dense water shown silver under the moonlight as it tumbled past an opening in the mountain.

To his right, a ragged crack stretched from the ceiling to the basin floor, revealing a picturesque view of the Valley of the Waterfalls. A lush area surrounded by mountains dotted with waterfalls. Adventurous tourists rafted the river below to get spectacular pictures of the UNESCO World Heritage Site.

Julian eased closer toward the waterfall. He didn't know how high he'd climbed. How far it would be to the river below. His options were limited. Risky. Dangerous.

A loud splash erupted behind him. Steps pounded in the water, coming nearer.

Julian took another step toward the waterfall, so close that he could reach a finger out and touch the raging waters.

"There's no way out."

He knew that voice.

"There's always a way out," Julian responded, turning to face his good friend, Detective Kendrick Caillouet.

"Come on, Julian. Turn yourself in," Kendrick pleaded.

Chuckling, Julian leaned against the cave wall. His friend looked exhausted, covered with mud. The police issued Sig Sauer pistol dangling at his side.

"I have to clear my name," Julian said.

"Listen to me. More evidence has come in proving that Adam Russell was involved. We have him in custody and once we interrogate him, we'll be able to figure out how Dumay set you up. You are so close to being free. Stop running and turn yourself in." Kendrick took a step toward him.

Julian stepped backward, closer to the edge.

"Think about Mena. She's going crazy worried about you."

Pang pierced his heart at hearing her name. Everything he was doing was to protect the life that he wanted to share with her. The odds were stacked against him. Adam was right about Dumay having the upper hand. She'd spun a web that had them all trapped, and he had to get himself out before she devoured them whole. Working with the cops or the PIIB wouldn't give him his freedom. He knew Mena would worry, but he also knew she trusted him. Believed in him. She would understand what he had to do.

"The only way I'm getting my life back is if you let me go," Julian said. "I'm close to having real definitive proof of everything Dumay set in motion—"

"Good! Then let me help you. Share what you know with me and I promise, you won't have to be in Tiverton for much longer. Julian, you need to do this the right way." Kendrick placed his gun in the holster and raised his hands in the air, walking closer to Julian. "Come on, my friend. Come with me."

"I can't." Julian turned and looked at the water rushing down from the mouth of the cave.

Closing his eyes, he stepped off the ledge and plunged into the waterfall.

Chapter Forty-Three

A vision of Mena filled his mind. The deep dark skin he caressed as he made love to her in every room, nook and cranny of the penthouse they shared. The look in her eyes when she moaned his name, gripping his back, and grinding against his erection. The way she whispered, I love you, in his ear after they climaxed. The safe place she'd created for him. Freedom to live again when he thought his life was over. The guilt he could live with now, encouraged to put the past behind him to build a future with her. The woman he'd die for. The woman he'd do anything to live for.

Rushing water slammed against Julian's head, neck and back as he plummeted through the waterfall, arms and legs flailing. What should have been a quick descent seemed to pass in slow motion. Water pushed into his nose, burning his sinuses. He resisted the involuntary reflex to cough or breathe, protecting his lungs from filling with water. Pain like sledgehammers pummeled relentlessly as his body was tossed like a rag doll under the torrent of the waterfall. He tried to open his eyes, but the force of the water against his face pressed his eyelids closed.

The roar of water grew in intensity, then ceased.

Free falling through the air, his body tumbled and twisted. Julian dared to open one eye. Stalactites hung like jagged upside down mountains, crowding the roof of a cave. Jungle vines, thick as ropes, snaked through the rocks that sped by as he fell faster, propelled by the flood of water rushing into the cave. He'd slipped into another crevice of the mountain instead of falling into the river below.

Leaning his head slightly, he saw the end drawing near. The edge of the rocky surface disappeared into a dark void. Panicking wasn't an option. Fire blazed through his muscles. His head crashed against the rocky wall, stunning him. The pain exploded within his head. His mind reeled.

Inhaling a deep breath of air, Julian clenched his eyes shut. He plunged into the water. A rushing roar filled his ears. Sinking fast and deep,

He'd trained for situations like this. Arms bound, feet bound, caught in equipment at the bottom of the training pool in Coronado, with only minutes to free himself and get to safety. He knew the dangers of panicking. Hyperventilating. Fear. Any of those take hold and you were dead. He kept his mind blank, forcing his eyes open as the surface of the water grew further and further away.

He visualized Mena's face. Smiling at him. He couldn't die in the bottom of this obscure cenote. He had to get back to Mena, one way or another. He had to force his body to move.

Air bubbles seeped through his lips as he hit the bottom of the cenote floor. Seaweed and coral tangled around his body. His head throbbed, dulling his senses and reflexes. Trash floated through the water, plastic bottles and jugs brushed against his skin. Julian had to hold his breath for as long as possible. He had two minutes, maybe three, before his body would force all the air from his lungs, desperate to breathe again.

Concentrating through the searing pain, he focused on his feet, trying to propel himself up through the dark murky water. His efforts were rewarded with excruciating pain in his leg, tangled and caught in something on the cenote floor. He fought to move his hands, barely able to make out their form in the water. The silence was deafening, calling to him as a watery resting place for his body.

No fucking way his life was ending like this.

Julian closed his eyes. Mena's face floated to the surface of his mind. Her body was partially submerged in the ocean. He saw her laughing as she splashed through the sea, daring him to catch her. Racing to their favorite spot to watch the sunrise on the jetty at Saffron Beach. She was drifting away, increasing the space between them. Turning, she frowned, scolding him for taking too long.

"We're going to miss the sunrise," Mena's voice burst through his ears. "Come on."

Julian reached for her. The searing pain subsided. His eyes flew open, staring into the cloudy waters of the cenote at the shadow of his hand, moving in the water toward the vines snaking around his leg.

Ignoring the pain, Julian jerked and yanked at the branches until his leg was free. His lungs felt like they were about to burst.

He didn't have much time.

Shifting his position, he crouched low against the ocean floor, then pushed his thigh muscles with every force within him. His body burst upward through the water. Air bubbles seeping from his mouth, unable to be contained as he craved fresh air.

He still couldn't see the surface of the water. The cenote was deeper than he'd thought. Fifty feet. Maybe more. Propelling his arms up and down, he tried to increase his speed, but his lungs were out of air. He needed to breathe.

Panic gripped him as he rose higher, but nowhere close to breaking the surface. Pumping his thighs harder, Julian struggled to swim upward, desperate to break the surface. The urge to open his mouth and breathe was almost uncontrollable. He couldn't hold his breath for much longer, but the surface of the water seemed out of reach. He could see the opening to the cave. He wasn't going to make it. His mouth opened. The water was salty, gritty as he involuntarily swallowed, then gagged and coughed. Body seizing, Julian floated lower as his world went black.

Chapter Forty-Four

Mena steered the rental car along the winding road.

The news radio host's voice blared through the speakers: *Cell phone video of campers in the Valley of Waterfalls show what appears to be the fugitive, Julian Montgomery, tumbling head over foot down a waterfall and plunging into a river below. The waterfall, known as The Lonely Sister, is over three hundred feet tall and passes over several caves and tunnels of the mountain. It is unclear how far Montgomery fell. St. Mateo and St. Basil Police SWAT Teams as well as the PIIB are scouring the area for the missing Tiverton inmate. All residents of St. Mateo are urged to remain indoors until the criminal is apprehended.*

The story hadn't changed since Mena left St. Basil earlier that morning. The thought of Julian being captured and remanded back to Tiverton filled her with dread. But the truth was much worse. How the hell had he fallen from a waterfall?

She kept telling herself that Julian was a frogman, for God's sake. He'd trained for worse conditions. If anyone knew how to survive that fate and escape capture by the police, it was an ex-Navy SEAL. Julian had to be alive. He had to be hiding out, biding his time until the cops stopped looking for him. He would call her when it was safe.

Mena glanced at the burner phone resting on the passenger seat of the car. It had been silent since the moment the first Palmchat Islands alert had blasted across every cell phone on the island. Omar and Regina had offered to sit with her as she waited for news on Julian, but she didn't want them around in case Julian contacted her. He could need her help. She didn't want to make her best friends accessories to harboring a fugitive. She would do it all on her own. If Julian needed her, she was going to do whatever he asked. He'd risked his life over and over for her in Kenya. Driven only by his love for her. It was time for her to do the same for him.

Easing the car off the highway and onto the scenic road, Mena looked up in amazement as the Valley of Waterfalls appeared. The mountains stretched toward the sky on each side of the valley, enchanting as the sunrise began its ascent. Breathtaking was the only word that came to mind. Waterfalls cascaded through cave openings across the terrain, giving the mountains the appearance of weeping at the sheer beauty of its own existence. Mena wished she was visiting the iconic site under better circumstances.

Steering the compact car around a sharp bend, Mena slowed the vehicle. Up ahead, red, blue and white flashing lights danced across the road. A barricade blocked cars from passing and the traffic was being diverted. Mena pulled out of the lane onto the shoulder and put the car in park.

Exiting the vehicle, she slipped the burner phone into her pocket and walked slowly toward the officer directing the traffic. Behind him, cops clustered in groups in front of the jungle, pointing up at a waterfall and then gesturing toward a path that led to the rushing waters of the Pourciau River.

Mena stared up at the massive waterfall. Was that where Julian had fallen from? A shudder rocked her body as reality sunk in. Mena paused and pressed her hand against the coarse rocks next to the road. She almost couldn't catch her breath thinking of Julian falling from so high. She tried to tell herself not to worry.

Julian could handle this.

Couldn't he?

A memory of Julian lying unconscious on the front porch of the blue house in Giriftu as the rebel gang pulled her away filled her mind.

Julian being beaten in the red desert, then handcuffed to the military vehicle by Tubeec's men.

His body collapsing to the ground outside the Gulfstream as she pounded on the window, screaming his name.

As strong as Julian was, he wasn't invincible.

He could be—

"Ma'am, you can't be out here. Please return to your vehicle. No visitors are allowed into the Valley of Waterfalls today," the cop said, curt and firm.

A cop behind the man shouted, "Get teams heading west along the upper bank and another team to scour the area from here to the Three Amigas waterfalls. If he survived, we're going to find him!"

A group of five officers, dressed in SWAT gear and carrying rifles, headed into the jungle toward the mountain. Another group of a dozen or more officers poured out of the jungle, heading down toward the riverbank.

"Ma'am. Return to your car now!"

Mena stumbled, then turned toward the river as voices raised over the roiling waters. Emerging from a copse of dense trees, she watched Kendrick wave away two officers who approached him. Soaking wet, Kendrick looked haunted as he gazed back up at the mountain in disbelief.

Rushing past the traffic cop, Mena ran over to Kendrick. "What happened? Did you find Julian?"

"Mena? What are you doing here?" Kendrick asked.

"Do you know where he fell? Have you found him?"

Kendrick shook his head. A deep frown settled between his eyes. Mena forced herself to breathe.

"I tried to get him to turn himself in, he just ..."

"He just ... what? What! Tell me what happened to him!" Mena said.

"He wouldn't listen to reason. He didn't trust that I could help him out of this mess. I could have helped him." Kendrick's eyes were vacant as he spoke. "I should have just let him go. Why didn't I just let him go?"

"What are you saying?" Mena asked. "What happened up there?"

"He jumped."

"Jumped?"

"Off the mountain into the waterfall. He jumped instead of turning himself in."

Mena took a step back, her head lifting to stare up at the mountains. The stunning waterfalls flowed freely from the various caves on the surface down hundreds of feet to the river.

"He jumped from the waterfall on purpose?" Mena asked, confused.

"He said he had to clear his name. He couldn't turn himself in and he jumped. I don't think anyone could survive a fall like that ... not even him."

Chapter Forty-Five

The trails on the Valley of Waterfalls were busier today, now that the police had moved their search for Julian downstream and reopened the hiking trails near the Heliconia Hotel. Mena looked through the binoculars. She could barely make out the Palmchat Islands Coast Guard dive team exiting the water, four men in wetsuits with oxygen masks walking out of the river.

Julian wasn't with them. It had been a week since he'd jumped over the waterfall and he was still missing. Rumors were gaining traction that even if he'd survived the fall into the rough waters of the Pourciau River, he'd probably drowned, caught in a riptide common in this area. Others surmised that he may have made it to shore, but died from injuries sustained or from lack of food and water in the jungle.

Mena refused to even consider any possibility that ended with Julian dead. She knew he was still out there ... alive. Wouldn't she know it if he were dead? Feel it somewhere in the core of the love that connected them? Like a light dimming within her that had lost connection to its source.

She kept reminding herself that Julian was a highly trained special operative. An ex-Navy SEAL. The elite group had to have prepared him for situations like this. He could be waiting until the cops and SWAT teams gave up the search for him. But why hadn't he called her to let her know he was okay. She kept the burner phone with her at all times. It lay silent.

"How much longer are you planning to stay here?" Beaujean asked, interrupting her thoughts.

Mena glanced at the sun, still high in the sky even as the afternoon waned. "Not much longer. I was going to walk down to the corner store to get some snacks and then head back to the house."

"I mean in St. Mateo," Beaujean said, his tone blunt.

The police had restricted tourists and visitors to the area, but anyone owning a home along the banks of the river, as Beaujean did, was allowed to enter. His offer to allow her to stay at his riverfront home, which was more like a fortified mansion, had been a godsend when she'd needed it most. Mena had been surprised to wake and find him in the kitchen waiting for her this morning. He hadn't called or indicated that he'd be coming by to check on her.

"I don't know. I can't leave yet, but I understand if you want me to find other accommodations. I'm sure you didn't expect for me to be here this long."

"You should come back to St. Basil. Omar and Regina are worried sick about you. There's plenty of work to keep you busy and take your mind off the waiting."

"I've talked to them and my mom and dad almost every day. They understand why I can't leave yet. Not until there's some news about where Julian is. I can't even think about work. That's probably not what you want to hear," Mena said, annoyed by his insistence that she get back to normal.

"No. It isn't. But your team is managing without you, although none of them are as skilled and experienced with laser conservation as you are. There's a backlog building that needs your special attention—"

"Beaujean, I don't care about that. Julian is missing ... unless," Mena paused, turning to stare at her boss. He'd summoned her to his home before to reassure her after the presumed abduction of Julian from Tiverton. "Do you know where Julian is? Do you know that he's okay?"

"Not this time. I don't know anything more than you." Beaujean said, plucking a heliconia flower from an overgrown bush along the hiking trail. "There's nothing you can do for Julian here. It's just waiting for the cops to find him or for him to emerge on his own. You sure you don't want to go to St. Basil?"

"I can't explain it, but I feel like he's still here ... in St. Mateo. I need to stay a little longer for my own peace of mind," Mena said.

"Intuition can be a powerful motivator. It can also mislead you from the obvious truth." Beaujean's words were slow, hesitant, as he looked at her intently.

"Julian isn't dead. I know he isn't," Mena insisted. "I'll pack my things and be out of your home this afternoon. I'm sure I can find another cabin nearby available for rent."

"I'm not kicking you out. You can stay at my place as long as you need," Beaujean said, dismissing her offer. "I've been where you are, Mena. I knew in my gut without any doubt that I'd be able to pick my life back up from the moment it had been snatched away from me. I'd have to do a bit of damage control for some mistakes I'd made back then, but I would be able to get everything back that I had. But I was wrong. My instincts were wrong. Everything I thought I could have when I woke from that coma no longer existed. I hope your reality turns out different from mine."

Turning slowly, he left her alone and headed back up the trail.

Crossing over the hiking trail, Mena detoured down a beaten path that led to the convenience store near the road. A steady stream of cars passed as locals with vacation homes in the area finished their hikes for the day. Mena would give anything to be here on vacation with Julian. Not wondering where he was. Or if he was still alive. She didn't know how she'd survive if Julian was gone.

At a break in the traffic, she walked across the street to the store and pushed the door open.

"Good afternoon, what can I get for you?" The clerk behind the counter grabbed her thick dark tresses and twisted her hair into a bun on top of her head.

"Junk food?" Mena asked, glancing around the store at the rows of health food, salads, juices and water.

The woman gave her a wink, then dropped below the counter. After several seconds she stood back up, holding a couple of packages of chocolate chip cookies. "This is the best I can do."

"I'll take it," Mena said.

"Haven't seen you around before. Are you a new owner of one of the properties?" the clerk asked.

"No. My boss owns the house up on the ledge across the street and is letting me stay there for a while."

"I know the house you're talking about. It's stunning." the clerk said, ringing up the two packages of cookies. "Would you like some water or pop with that?"

"Water would be great, thank you." Mena leaned against the counter and stared out the windows of the storefront. A group of coast guard divers, holding heavy equipment on their backs, hiked along the side of the road, heading toward the river.

"You picked a bad time for a vacation. Its tense here with all the cops and PIIB agents scurrying around looking for that missing inmate. But they've shifted focus now."

"Shifted focus in what way?"

"That group of guys that passed by are part of the search and recovery unit of the island coast guards. They were in here this morning talking about how they found evidence that the inmate had drowned, and his body was probably floating in one of the underground caves that the river flows over. Divers are being sent in to find his body."

Chapter Forty-Six

The failure to recover the body of missing inmate, Julian Montgomery, over the past two weeks has perplexed local law enforcement in St. Mateo and the Palmchat Islands Investigative Bureau. An anonymous source within the PIIB indicated that the agency has not ruled out the option that the ex-U.S. Navy SEAL could have survived the fall from The Lonely Sister Waterfall in St. Mateo and is alluding capture.

"Is this true?" Mena asked, reaching across the table cluttered with the remnants of the buffet breakfast to hand the tablet back to Linda Montgomery.

The retired Naval Intelligence Officer reached a thin hand toward the electronic device and placed it in the oversized purse resting on her lap.

The latest article in the *Palmchat Gazette* gave Mena a bit of hope. More than she'd been able to muster as the days stretched with no sign of Julian. The burner phone he'd given her remained frustratingly silent.

"No," Linda replied, then sighed heavily as she signaled for the server. The polite man dressed in crisp white scurried toward the table, slipped the credit card from Linda's hand and rushed back toward the kitchen. The Reuben Hotel in the heart of St. Mateo's resort district was abnormally sparse this morning. With the search for the missing Tiverton inmate winding down, tourists were striking out to enjoy the attractions of the island without fear of running into an armed and dangerous man.

Staring into the intense cornflower blue eyes of the commanding woman, Mena saw none of Julian in her. Fair skinned, blond hair, thin and lithe—features in stark contrast to the man she loved.

Linda continued, "The reporter's source within the agency either wasn't being truthful or wasn't privy to the views of the lead investigators on Julian's case. Every person I spoke to said the search would soon be abandoned. No one at the agency believes Julian survived the fall. Some suspect that once the tides shift, his body will wash up from one of the underground caves and float to shore."

Mena looked away, disheartened by how matter-of-fact Linda relayed the possible death of Julian. Not once had Linda shown any emotion about her missing son, treating her trip to St. Mateo as a routine intelligence fact-find mission. Every discussion about Julian being arrested and escaping Tiverton had been performed with military precision—the facts without conjecture.

The only time Linda had softened when talking about Julian was after Mena had gotten her to open up about some of her son's embarrassing childhood mishaps and his antics with Broman. Linda hadn't been able to hide the fact that her son was her pride and joy as she shared stories Julian would likely cringe to hear retold. The memories had lightened Mena's spirits, distracting her from Julian's disappearance.

"But what do you really think?" Mena pressed.

"I think it's better if Julian isn't found ... for whatever reason. The truth is the recent evidence hasn't cleared him. The cops found a partial fingerprint of Priscilla Dumay's on the burner phone you helped to get from one of those correctional officers, but they still haven't been able to crack the encryption on the device to see what evidence could be on it. Farouk Essa was bluffing when he said he read texts between Dumay and Russell. He couldn't even get into the phone. Uma Fischer has disappeared from her rental home in the Tango Lowlands. The court reporter identified Russell as the person who bribed her into taking the syringe into the courthouse, but we don't know on who's orders because Russell isn't talking. Julian is in more trouble than before. The cops believe he staged the prison break. There is no way out for him."

The server returned, apologizing for interrupting their conversation as he handed the receipt and credit card back to Linda. She signed quickly, then reached for her large luggage resting against the wall near the table.

Mena pushed away from the table and stood, knocking a glass of water to the floor. Fumbling with the napkin to wipe up the spill, Mena said, "So, it's better that Julian is dead than alive to spend the rest of his life in prison. That's what you're saying? You don't care that your son could be dead."

Linda stared at the ceiling and took a long, drawn breath. Exhaling slowly, she turned her attention back to Mena. "I really like you. I love that you touched my son in a way that I never thought I would see. His love for you is unconditional. There is nothing he wouldn't do to protect you. Even if that means leaving you."

"Leaving me? What are you talking about?"

"Julian *can't* come back. There is no future for the two of you. Not anymore. If he is found alive, he will spend the rest of his life locked up in a maximum-security prison ... without *you*. That's a torture my son couldn't survive. You need to accept this."

Mena approached Linda, lowering her voice. "Octavia still believes she can get him acquitted. He has other options. He doesn't need to go on the run. Adam Russell is the better suspect. Octavia can prove reasonable doubt in court."

"Adam Russell didn't attack Priscilla Dumay in the courthouse in front of a St. Basil police detective and two prison correctional officers. The cops saw Julian kneeling over her body with the syringe. That domino pushed down all the rest and landed him in trouble. For every inch of him that is good and unselfish, there is that other reckless, take no prisoners, side that always rears its ugly head. He has no one to blame but himself."

"He didn't try to kill Priscilla. She set him up."

"That may be true. This time he was innocent. But I can't say that's always been the case for him in the past. Is it irony or karma? When you love a man like my son, it comes with heartbreaking risks, Mena. Julian would never be a safe choice. This was inevitable. It's time for you to go back to St. Basil and close this chapter of your life."

Linda grabbed the suitcase handle and walked out of the restaurant into the hotel lobby. Mena lingered behind, unnerved by her assessment of Julian and their relationship. Mena didn't care if loving Julian came with danger and unpredictability. She knew in her heart he was the perfect man for her. The one she'd never realized she wanted or even needed. Glancing down at the charm bracelet hanging from her wrist, she fingered the key charm, turning it over between her fingers as she caught up with Julian's mom.

"When we were in Kenya and I got kidnapped, Julian never gave up looking for me. No matter how hopeless it seemed, he would have kept looking until he found me. How can you ask me not to do the same for him? Especially if there is even the slightest chance he survived that fall."

"Because he would want you to go on with your life. If my son isn't dead at the bottom of that river, then he's chosen to live a life on the run. He will need to avoid capture for the rest of his life. That's not the kind of life he wants for you. He wouldn't ask you to walk away from your parents, your brothers, your best friends, sacrifice the great life you have to live one of constant danger with him. To be a criminal for him. He won't do that to you."

With each of Linda's words, a suffocating pain enveloped Mena's heart, threatening to crush her. She couldn't deny the truth as much as she wanted to. If Julian no longer thought he could beat the charges, would he turn away and not look back?

Mena knew the answer. Sadness welled within her.

A bellhop greeted Linda, grabbing her bag and placed it into the waiting taxi headed to the airport. She turned toward Mena and extended her arms. Mena stepped forward, welcoming the hug from Julian's mother.

Linda whispered into her ear. "Go back to St. Basil. Go back to your life."

Releasing Mena, Linda gave her a small smile, then turned and walked to the cab. Mena watched as the woman settled into the backseat and was whisked away from the hotel.

Standing alone in the portico, one thought resonated over and over in her mind.

Julian is alive out there somewhere, and I have to find him.

Chapter Forty-Seven

"Wangari, it's Mena. I'm sorry to call you so late, but it's an emergency. I need to get in touch with Sunny Tate, your dad's head of security. I wouldn't be calling if it wasn't extremely important. Can you please call me back with a number where I can reach her or ask her to call me?" Mena said, then repeated her phone number into the voice mailbox of Wangari's cell phone. Ending the call, she steered the rental car up the steep road leading to the riverfront home where she'd been staying for the past couple of weeks.

After Linda left for the airport, Mena had been summoned to yet another questioning by the St. Mateo police. They knew she was staying in the area, but so far, Mena had kept her location a secret with Beaujean's help. The questions had been the same. Detective Francois badgered her about whether she'd seen or heard from Julian. It pained her to know that her answers were the truth.

She had no clue where Julian was.

She hadn't heard from Julian in weeks.

She didn't know if he was alive or dead.

The sun had set hours ago before Mena was allowed to leave.

Mena thought about Linda's theory. She wasn't dismissing the prediction of Julian's behavior, but Linda didn't know the man her son had transformed into. The man Mena had fallen in love with. Julian wouldn't go on the run without making sure Mena was safe. He still knew Priscilla Dumay was a threat, not just to him, but to her as well. To Mena, that meant Julian hadn't gone far. Not yet.

Sunny Tate had already used her security team to bust him out of Tiverton. Maybe Julian had called her for help after he survived jumping into the waterfall. If anyone could help him get away, wouldn't it be the team he worked with in Kenya?

All Mena needed to do was have one conversation with the woman. She was sure she'd be able to get the truth out of her. If that didn't work, Mena could always lure Julian the best way she knew how—use herself as bait. Hadn't Julian risked his life, time and again, to save her. Mena bristled at the thought of tricking Julian out of hiding, but what other option did she have?

Steering the car along the curb in front of the home, Mena exited the vehicle and bounded up the steps to the front door. Mena paused, resting her hand against the ornate glass. A sob rumbled from deep within her and escaped her lips. Her eyes stung from the unshed tears. Crying wouldn't solve anything.

The only thing that brought her peace was being in the Valley of Waterfalls. The place Julian had last been seen. The trek she made each day fueled her, and oddly, comforted her.

Truthfully, going back to St. Basil, to the penthouse suite they shared in Harmony Towers filled with all of Julian's things and all of their memories was a torture of its own. Courage to face living without Julian would have to come from some place deep inside of her. A place she hadn't found yet.

Linda was right. Julian wouldn't expect her to save him, nor would he want her pressing pause on her life while he ran from the police. She could do nothing to help him, but that didn't mean she couldn't be of use to Octavia in clearing Julian's name. If she helped the attorney prove Julian was innocent, then he could stop hiding and come home to her.

Resolve strengthening, Mena knew that was her best move. She was going back to St. Basil and would work tirelessly to make sure that Julian was cleared of any wrongdoing. Once Julian knew the charges against him had been dropped, there would be nothing stopping him from coming back. Slipping the key into the door, Mena turned the knob and stepped inside.

The air of the lodge was charged and tense. Mena stood poised in the doorway, eyes darting around the open foyer and into the picturesque living room that overlooked the Valley of the Waterfalls. Someone was in here.

Slipping her hand into her purse, she wrapped her palm around the Beretta and lifted it slowly. The gun was heavy in her hands as she stepped inside the lodge and nudged the front door closed with her foot.

Water puddles pooled along the wooden floor, leading into the sunken living room. Mena approached slowly until a figure appeared, standing near the wide windows. She raised the gun higher, pointed toward the intruder.

"Who are you?" Mena asked.

Turning slowly, the lamps illuminated the water-soaked face of Sunny Tate. She was drenched, dressed in a diving wetsuit. Her hair slick next to her face. But her eyes arrested Mena. Puffy and red, swollen from shed tears.

"Never thought we'd meet like this," Sunny said, wringing her hands.

"I just called Wangari trying to reach you," Mena said, lowering the gun back into her purse.

"You should sit."

"Why?"

"Please, Mena. What I have to tell you is going to be hard enough."

Mena approached the high-backed chair near the windows and sat on the edge. Resting on the side table next to the chair was a burner phone coated in algae and seaweed. The small device sat next to a ripped black, long-sleeved combat shirt. The shirt Julian had put on before he'd kissed her goodbye in the basement of the Genesis Gallery.

Recoiling from the items, Mena stood. She had to put distance between herself and those ... things.

Sunny said, "It didn't make sense that there was no sign of Julian in the Pourciau River. That is, until my team discovered about a dozen caves behind the waterfall where Julian jumped. The coast guard searched a few of them, but the others are treacherous to reach. Too risky to search, especially since the likelihood of surviving a fall into one of them was really slim. So, we mapped the rest of them. After the coast guard moved further down the river, we explored a different cave each night hoping to find Julian."

"But you didn't?"

"No. We didn't find his ... body. We entered a cave tonight and saw this shirt floating on the surface of the water. We dove in, trying to get to the bottom to see if we could find Julian, but all we found was that burner phone. One of a half dozen I left behind for him at the basement in the Genesis Gallery. We kept diving to find him, but the cenote was dark and too deep. It was impossible to determine if his body was down there without risking our own lives."

Mena shook her head. "Well, that's okay because his body isn't in the bottom of some damn cenote cave. He had to have gotten out of there some kind of way."

"We found blood on rocks leading down into the cave. Julian's blood. Our tests confirmed it. When he jumped, the force of the waterfall slammed him into that cave. He must have hit his head hard and tumbled unconscious into the cenote. If he hadn't been knocked out from the fall, I know he could have gotten out of there."

"What are you saying?" Mena felt the roar of blood rushing in her ears. Her sight blurred as her body swayed.

Sunny dragged a hand down her face. "What you have to understand is that Julian and I were trained to weigh all options and every threat. But no matter how much you plan, train and prepare, there will always be something that you didn't account for. Something that could end your life. I believe Julian knew all the risks when he jumped from that mountain and that he would never regret his choice."

Sunny lifted a clear waterproofed bag from the floor near her feet and slowly unzipped it. Reaching inside, she pulled out an envelope.

Mena stared at the rectangle, fixated on the cream-colored Genesis Gallery stationery.

"I came to let you know that we're heading back to Kenya tonight. And to give you this," Sunny said.

"What is that?"

"A letter from Julian. When my team got him safely to the basement of the Genesis Gallery, he asked to see me before we headed back to Africa. He wanted my help to plan a special night for the two of you. Champagne, food, flowers. Ambiance. And he wanted to give me this." Sunny extended the envelope toward Mena. "He wanted you to have this in the event that—"

"Sunny, listen to me. We don't know that he didn't survive. His body hasn't been found, which means he could..." Mena's voice crumbled as sobs choked in her throat. "He could still be out there."

"Take this," Sunny whispered, a single tear rolling down her face, as she forced the envelope into Mena's hands. "These are Julian's last words to you, and only for your eyes. You'll want to have this with you in the days and weeks and years ahead to remind yourself of what a beautiful and special love the two of you shared."

"No, I can't. I won't believe he's gone. No!"

Chapter Forty-Eight

The tangled branches clawed at Mena's skin as she zigzagged through the unmarked trails, forging deeper into the heart of the jungle. The ground was thick with tangled branches, fallen leaves and mud, clawing at her feet as she pushed further into the midst. Her body instinctively knew where to go. The place she'd gone almost every day since she learned the exact spot Julian had jumped from. Her fists curled around the envelope in her hand, crushing the paper in her grasp.

How could he do this to her? How could he leave her with nothing more than a letter? She couldn't imagine reading it. That would be like confirming he was gone. She couldn't do that.

Mena slowed to a stop and leaned against a banana tree.

The tears that had refused to fall over the past several weeks coursed down her cheeks. She stared at the crumpled white envelope in her hand, blurred and fuzzy through the cloak of her cries. Body slumping, she teetered on the verge of hyperventilating.

She never imagined losing Julian like this.

Not the permanence that came with death.

All her fears had been wasted on the damage her marriage to Michael would do to their relationship.

Julian was the hero. Escaping danger, thwarting threats and taking down the evil in the world, even when he didn't feel worthy to have that role. He wasn't supposed to die trying to prove his own innocence. What kind of cruel world would end his life in such a tragic way?

Mena leaned her head back against the rough bark, trying to peek through the canopy of tangled branches to see the darkened sky. Shadows lurked between the trees, cloaking the area in inky blackness. A tomb where her hopes and dreams for a wonderful life with the man she loved had come to be buried. Once and for all.

"This was not supposed to happen," Mena choked out the words between sobs. "You were supposed to find a way to survive. How could you fight off bullets and bombs, but let nature take you down? In this place ..."

Mena stepped away from the tree, twirling her arms in a circle. "You loved these mountains. This was the one place you should have been safe. And all you left me with was this stupid letter."

She stumbled backward. "A letter! Really, Julian? I deserved so much more than this."

Watching the crumpled paper fall to the ground, Mena took a step back from where it lay, glowing bright white against the tangled branches and mud of the jungle floor.

She took another step backward. Then another, increasing her pace.

She wouldn't read the letter.

More steps backward as the envelope grew distant.

Not ever.

Her foot slammed into a root, knocking her off balance.

Her eyes never left the envelope. It skittered across the ground as a breeze pierced through the dense foliage. Extending her arm to brace her fall, her hip slammed into the ground, sending a spasm of pain through her body. Her hand grasped the damp ground and something soft, clammy and cool.

Jerking her head toward her hand, she saw the outline of pale fingers protruding from the leaves. She lifted her hand and stared at the dirt.

Was that really a hand?

She moved closer, reaching a finger tentatively toward it. Brushing her fingertips across the fingers. The skin felt cool, but not cold. Swiping away leaves, a hand emerged. Mena slid her fingers further down, past the palm to feel for a pulse along the wrist. She felt a faint thump, slow and methodical, but definitely there.

Someone was underneath this brush.

Mena froze.

Not someone.

Julian.

It had to be him.

Scrambling closer to the hand, she began to frantically dig through the fallen leaves and mud, revealing more of the arm. She shifted her focus to where she believed his head could be submerged, brushing away the foliage faster until she saw his dark brown hair, plastered against his head with mud and dirt. Mena leaned over, brushing away the leaves from the rest of his face.

"Julian," Mena whispered into his ear, pressing her face next to his. She could feel his shallow breath against her skin. His face felt feverish. He was asleep or unconscious. Digging more frantically, she pushed away the rest of the dirt, leaves and debris from covering his body.

Mena raised his head in her hands. "Julian, baby, it's me. It's Mena. I need you to open your eyes. You're safe now, but I can't do this alone. I need your help. Wake up, please. Julian, can you hear me?"

Julian stirred in her arms, coughing slightly. Large welts covered his skin from where the insects had feasted on him, but he was still the most amazing and handsome man. She had to get him out of the jungle and back to the riverfront home. Lifting a man more than twice her size was not something she'd ever prepared for.

"Come on, Julian. Wake up! Wake up now!" Mena said, praying he would come to. Even if he could only move slowly, that was better than her trying to drag him back to the house, which she didn't have the strength to do.

His eyelids fluttered, then opened slowly.

Mena stared into the soulful brown eyes she'd fallen in love with so many months ago.

"Hey. Julian, can you hear me?" Mena said. Sweat beaded against his face as she caressed his skin. His eyes were glazed and unsteady. He trembled in her embrace. He was ill. She had to get him out of here, but she couldn't do that without his help.

"Julian," Mena said, pressing her forehead against his. "Please talk to me. Say something."

Julian opened his mouth, then paused, swallowing hard. He blinked several times, then she recognized a slight curve of his lips as if he was trying to smile.

Julian's voice was hoarse and raspy. "You found me."

Chapter Forty-Nine

Julian stirred in her arms, his face pressed against her chest. Over thirty hours had passed since she'd found him covered in leaves in the jungle near the Valley of Waterfalls. The trek back to the house, which usually only took her thirty minutes, had taken over three hours as Julian struggled to cover the distance. Several times, they'd had to stop and rest as his body retched the contents of his empty stomach, dark yellow bile mixed with dry heaves.

As they'd approached the edge of the jungle, Mena was thankful Beaujean had allowed her to stay at his riverfront house in a secluded area of the Valley of Waterfalls. Frantic and ill-equipped to help Julian, Mena had taken a risk and called her boss. After relaying the details of finding Julian in the jungle and the symptoms he was exhibiting, Beaujean had arranged for a delivery of antibiotics, fever reducers, and enough groceries to last a couple more weeks that were delivered by the next midday.

Julian had suffered for hours, fighting nausea and a blazing fever she'd thought would never break. She'd followed the instructions, giving him regular doses of the pills, which he struggled to swallow. He could barely keep down any food, but she'd persisted so he could get his strength up. Julian had been too weak to stand or move, lying listlessly as whatever he'd contracted in the jungle ravished him. Mena held him close to her as the heat from his body burned against her skin. She hoped he could feel her love, her strength, willing him to fight against the sickness and come back to her.

Her prayers were answered a few hours ago as Mena woke shortly past noon. She'd placed a hand on Julian's forehead and found it was cool to the touch. The tossing and turning and painful groans that had stricken her with fear had dissipated into a calm sleep.

She didn't know what he'd been through over the past two weeks. But none of that mattered now.

He was alive.

He was safe.

And she was going to do whatever it took to make sure he stayed that way.

She'd already decided that she was all-in with him, even if it meant turning her back on the life she knew. She didn't want any more secrets between them or anything to ever separate them again. Telling him the truth about being married would be hard, but nothing compared to what Julian had been through. He deserved to know the truth after he was free from the charges hanging over him.

Julian's strong arms squeezed her as he lifted his head from her chest. He rested his chin against her breasts.

"You feeling better?" Mena asked.

"Only because of you. You saved my life."

"I still owe you a couple more."

Julian chuckled then grimaced, resting his head back on her chest. "How long have you been here?"

"I came the morning after you went missing. Your standoff with the police was all over the news. I thought you might call the burner phone or need my help. I wanted to be close by, but you never called me," Mena said.

"I wanted to, but I lost my phone after I jumped into the waterfall and fell into a cenote. Banged my head pretty bad and almost drowned trying to get out of there. I blacked out for a moment, but it was your voice that urged me to come back. I pushed through the surface of the water and clung to the vines until I could climb out of the cave," Julian said.

"That sounds horrible. How long did it take you to get out of there?"

"Not sure, two days. Maybe three. I had a nasty bump on my head and was pretty disoriented. After I got out, I kept moving from cave to cave, stealing food from trash cans and trying to hide from the swarm of officers looking for me. A few days ago, I started getting sick. Really weak. Could barely move. Wasn't sure if something bit me or if it was something I ate. The only thing I could do was hide in the jungle. I covered myself with leaves and hoped I wouldn't be found."

"But I found you. I can't tell you how many people told me to go back to St. Basil. There was no way you survived the fall. That you'd drowned. That you'd gotten away and decided to go off the grid instead of risking being sent back to Tiverton. Every conversation was another dire conclusion about you. I could not get myself to believe any of that was true."

"Because you know I'd never leave you. The only reason I fought to stay alive was to make it back to you, Mena. This sounds selfish, but I'm glad you stayed and didn't give up on me," Julian said.

"I won't lie. I almost gave up after Sunny came by. She gave me the letter you wrote to me, you know, in case ..."

Julian wrapped an arm tighter around Mena's stomach, the fingers of his free hand stroking her skin with light caresses. "Did you read it?"

"It pissed me off that you'd even write me a letter like that. That you'd even consider there was a chance that you wouldn't come back to me. I was mad as hell and devastated at the same time. That's why I ran into the jungle. The paper was burning a hole in my hand and I just wanted to get rid of it. That's when I tripped over you."

"Broman wrote Dawn a letter. It took her a long time to read it, but it helped her to get closure about what happened to him. I just wanted to do the same for you." Julian's voice was low as he tried to explain himself.

"I'm not Dawn and you're not Broman. A letter would be a cruel way for you to say goodbye to me. I don't need your words on paper. I need you fighting like hell so I never have to receive a letter like that in the first place," Mena said.

"I'm sorry," Julian whispered.

"Promise me you won't ever leave me again."

"I wish I could, but I don't know what it's going to take to get out of this mess with Dumay. I could still go to prison if I'm not able to fulfill the deal I made with Adam Russell," Julian said.

"What kind of deal?"

"Dumay implanted a kill switch in Russell's heart. An undetectable pacemaker of sorts that she or her brother, Tufa, can control from anywhere and kill him on the spot. That's how they've been killing off the surrogates. These kill switches were implanted into them. Russell wants me to dismantle the remote operation of the kill switch and take out Dumay," Julian explained.

"And in return?"

"He's going to give me evidence that proves Dumay set me up so I can help him get free from her. Once that's done, he'll give me the laptop. Dumay never had it. Russell has had it all this time," Julian said.

"Let me get this straight. He wants you to commit cold-blooded murder, so he won't have to? And you agreed to this?"

Julian was quiet.

"You can't do that."

"You mean I can't put a bullet in the head of the woman responsible for kidnapping and terrorizing you during the past year? For you, for Ella, for the surrogates—she doesn't deserve to live and continue to hurt people. It won't be the first time I was deployed to eliminate a threat," Julian said.

"What if you get caught? Then you'll go to Tiverton because you'll be guilty."

"I was trained to take out enemy threats without leaving a trace. People may suspect, but they'll never be able to prove anything," Julian said.

"You're not a SEAL anymore! The government hasn't sent you on a mission. This will be premeditated murder, Julian. I can't lose you if the cops figure out what you did and throw you back in prison."

Julian inhaled sharply, rising from his position against her. Mena instantly missed the warmth of his body next to hers as he struggled to hold himself up on shaky arms. Julian stared at her for a long moment. Their eyes locked on each other, neither willing nor even able to look away.

"If you want me to walk away from the deal I made with Russell, I'll do it. For you. Just say the word."

Mena hesitated. Adam Russell had the key to Julian's freedom from more than one crime hanging over his head. She didn't want to deny Julian the chance to get the evidence they both knew he desperately needed, but she couldn't condone him killing Priscilla to free himself. Finally, Mena said, "There's got to be another option. Helping Adam without killing Priscilla. Why can't you do that?"

"That wasn't the deal, Mena. Russell claims I didn't corrupt all the files on the laptop. He had hackers working for months to find proof of what I did. If that falls into the Navy's hands, I'm looking at life in prison—"

"And you're looking at the death penalty if Adam double crosses you and turns you in after you kill Priscilla. What are you going to do then? You said he's going to give you the proof to clear your name of these charges first. Once that happens, renegotiate the deal with him. You can stop Prissy without committing murder. You have to protect yourself. Adam can't be trusted," Mena insisted.

Julian leaned back, his gaze searching hers. She could almost see his mind processing her suggestion, contemplating and assessing whether it was a possibility.

"Alright, I'll do that."

"Promise?" Mena asked.

"I promise," Julian said, lowering himself back down to her. She slipped her hands around him as he heaved breaths from the exertion.

Relieved, Mena asked, "What's our next move?"

"Uma had this key on a chain around her neck. It freaked her out when I got it. She was willing to trade anything to get it back."

"So, you traded the key for Adam's location. That key must unlock something important. Something like—"

"Evidence Russell has on Dumay, maybe?"

"And not just that. The evidence that proves Prissy framed you and the laptop could be in there too. We need that key," Mena said.

"I took a picture on the burner phone, but that's lost in the bottom of the cenote I fell into."

"No, actually it's not. Sunny and her team recovered it and brought it to me. I'm not sure if it still works, but it's worth a try," Mena said. Easing out of the bed, she ventured into the sunken living room and grabbed the burner phone. Returning to the bedroom, she plugged it in and was relieved to see the phone starting to charge.

"After the phone charges, I'll be able to send the photos to the computer on my yacht to print a 3-D copy of the key."

Mena said, "While you search for what the key could open, I can head back to your boat and pick up the copy of the key."

"Can't let you do that. The cops are probably watching it like a hawk and will think it's suspicious that you're even there. It's too dangerous." Julian said.

"I can pretend that I'm grieving and just wanted to be closer to you by spending time on the boat. It's reasonable behavior for a woman whose boyfriend is missing and presumed dead. Even the cops won't question that. Besides, you're in no condition to stop me."

"You don't think I'm strong enough?" Julian raised an eyebrow.

"You spent the last thirty hours passed out. Your fever just broke a few hours ago. You've spent the last two weeks surviving on trash and river water. You're in no condition to put up much of a fight when I leave," Mena said. There was no way she would let him refuse her help. He needed her whether he wanted to admit it or not.

"You really don't think I'm back up to full strength?" Julian asked, a sly sexiness playing across his face.

"Julian," Mena whispered, a sensual swirling heading straight toward her most sensitive spot.

"How about I prove you wrong?"

Chapter Fifty

"You're such a tease," Mena said, standing in the doorway of the massive master bathroom. Julian held her gaze. Her face, devoid of makeup, surrounded by thick, dark disheveled hair, was more beautiful than he'd ever seen her. His heart was about to burst with love.

Julian leaned against the travertine tile of the walk-in shower that could hold at least four people, maybe more. Vichy shower heads extended from the ceiling and more from the side walls, pelting his body with soothing water. He'd wanted nothing more than to make love to Mena, but the remnants of his illness—the stale taste of vomit in his mouth, the wretched smell of his body from being in the jungle for weeks—had halted any thoughts of romance. Temporarily.

His eyes flickered slightly as sleep tried to pull him back in. But his dick had other ideas, coming to life faster than he could control at the sight of her.

Julian extended an arm toward Mena. "Come join me."

He could feel her blushing, even if her deep brown skin hid the evidence of it.

"We really don't have time for that. The faster I can get the replica of the key from the boat and you identify what the key could open, the faster we can be back with each other permanently," Mena said as she laid clothes on the bathroom counter. "I grabbed some of Beaujean's clothes for you to wear. Might be a little tight."

She giggled. The sound tickled his ears, and he smiled. The distance between them was too far for his liking. But he knew she made good points.

"Seriously, Julian. If there's one thing Kenya taught me was that we never have as much time as we think. I don't want us to waste any more of it," Mena insisted. A slight frown crept between her eyebrows as she stepped into the bathroom and crossed her arms over her chest. The move caused her breasts to rise beneath the skimpy tank top she wore.

Making love to the woman he adored wasn't a waste of time. It was the only thing that mattered to him right now. He could sense her worry that the plan wouldn't work. Some kind of way they'd be thwarted and separated yet again. The strength it had taken for her to hold on and believe he'd survived despite mounting evidence to the contrary proved how special she really was. The idea that she could lose him was ludicrous. He would fight any enemy to his last breath to be with her. Nothing and no one would stand in his way.

"I still need to prove to you that I'm strong enough," Julian said, turning to give her a full view of his naked body.

"You have nothing to prove to me. I want you to get all of your strength back," Mena said.

"Please," Julian's word was low, almost drowned out by the patter of the water in the shower. Before he'd uttered the last syllable, Mena was walking toward him. She gave him a look that damn near melted his heart. The love and devotion behind those seductive eyes made him regret ever doubting her. The photograph of Mena and the unknown guy flashed in his mind, but he pushed it away. Whatever it looked like, he knew it wasn't. Not when she was here, with him, willing to meet his every need and desire. Julian would make any man regret even thinking about taking her from him. Mena was his.

Her touch was confident and possessive as she stroked her hands along his wet arms. He felt himself becoming stronger, the passion and desire he felt for her pushed past any weariness he felt.

He pulled her to him, delighting in the water drenching her. Her clothes grew soaking wet, revealing her amazing curves. Slipping a hand along her wet tank top, Julian glided it over her head. She caressed his chest as he stared at the water trickling over her round, ample breasts.

For the past two weeks, he'd dreamed of this moment every day. Pulling her body next to his, Julian slipped his hands beneath the soaked fabric of her yoga pants. His hands cupped her ass as a torrent of emotions raged through him. The muddled confusion of his mind from fighting off the infection combined with the sensory overload of feeling every part of Mena's body against his skin arrested him. For a moment, he was lost as to what to do next. An insatiable desire to cling to the woman he loved, the woman he wondered if he'd ever see again, battled the unbridled lust driving him to ravish her body with intense love making, raw, unfiltered, possessive and commanding.

Mena eased the yoga pants and her panties from her hips. She stepped out of them, kicking them toward a corner of the shower without disturbing the grip he had on her.

Water cascaded down their bodies as they stood still next to each other. Julian closed his eyes and inhaled her familiar scent of sandalwood and orange. He knew he loved Mena, but in this moment he was overwhelmed by how much she meant to him. How he would do anything to protect their future, even if it meant risking his own life or breaking a promise he'd made to her. He wanted to pause time and live in this moment forever. He'd always thought fighting for Mena and protecting her was his number one priority, and maybe it still was. But in these simple moments of peace and serenity, with her next to him, he wanted to push the entire world away and have her all to himself.

Julian shifted, moving his head toward Mena's perfect face, and smoothed her wet hair behind her ears. Her eyes locked onto his.

"I can't imagine my life without you, Mena," Julian said.

"I don't want you to imagine a life without me," Mena said, resting her hands on the sides of his face as the warm water coated their bodies. "I know my actions have been confusing to you. I promise you, once you get cleared of the charges, I will explain everything. It took me a long time to become comfortable with my feelings for you. I'm sorry about that. But you have to believe me, Julian. You—"

Mena slipped her arms around his neck and lifted her body on her tiptoes to get to his eye-level. "You, Julian, are the love of my life. I'm so thankful that we found each other."

Lifting her body easily in his arms, he gripped her tightly, enveloping her as he brushed his lips softly against hers. Mena breathed slowly into his mouth, before pressing her lips firmly against his, devouring him in a ravenous kiss. Her hard nipples pressed against his chest. His cock grew heavy at the feel of her hot, damp skin against his. He needed to be in her. Now.

Swiveling her body around, he pressed her back against the tiles of the shower as the water pelted their skin. Mena grabbed his shoulders, bracing herself as she wrapped her thighs around his hips. He was so close to entering her, but held off for a moment as he watched her hands drop. She took him in one hand, sliding along the length of him, as he increased in size from the raw intensity of the pleasure of her touch. Her thumb glided along the crown of his cock, flicking against the skin and making him harder, which he would've thought was impossible. Guiding him toward her, Julian twitched at her entrance then entered her slowly, inch by inch, amazed by the slick warmth of her. Her muscles tightened around him, gripping his dick and sending a spasm of erotic sensations rippling through his body.

"Fuck!" Julian moaned. "I love you so much."

"Show me," Mena panted, her heels pressed against his back, urging him deeper. Julian had no plans to disappoint her. Shifting his stance for better leverage, he thrust deeply. Increasing his speed, he focused only on her body, her breathing, her moans of his name echoing within the shower. In and out until the pace of his rocking within her synchronized with her body grinding against him.

Mena laced her fingers through his wet hair, pulling his face toward her. His mouth found hers and she blazed her tongue against his, sucking as if her life depended on it. Julian stumbled, almost losing focus from the raw passion of her kiss. Almost, but not quite.

Cock straining for release, Julian delayed his own pleasure. He pumped faster within Mena. Their bodies banging together with the force of each thrust. She bucked against him, spurred by his hips, ramming his dick inside her.

"Julian, yes, Julian, please, come on baby," Mena muttered through her moans.

Julian rose to the challenge, reducing her words to simpering, incoherent grunts until a loud, untamed animalistic moan erupted from her. Mena's body arched in his arms as she bucked and spasmed in an intense orgasm.

Julian thrust harder as Mena came apart in his arms, growing limp. Only then did he give one last thrust, detonating his own explosive orgasm. His muscles tensed as he went blind to everything but the touch and feel of her, then collapsed in slow motion from the wake of the earth-shattering intensity. Catching himself, he lowered their bodies gently to the travertine tile floor of the shower.

A sly smile spread across Mena's lips. The water had shifted to lukewarm, making goosebumps raise on her skin. Julian lifted an arm up toward the shower handle and eased it around until the water shut off. Then laid down next to Mena, cradling her as her soft ass rested perfectly in the curve of his crotch. Stroking a hand lazily against her round breasts, he whispered, "Let me know when you're ready for round two."

Mena's laugh was deep and sensual. "I can't even see straight and you're gearing up for round two? What am I going to do with you?"

"Anything you want," Julian said, lifting her head from the hard floor and slipping his arm underneath. "Whenever you want. However you want."

"You're all mine," Mena said, her voice raising at the end as if asking a question.

"Forever," Julian responded, then leaned down to kiss her closed eyelids—

A loud bang shattered through the house. The sound of the front door slammed against the wall. Footsteps, dozens of them, heavy and determined, reverberated against the wooden floors, carrying beyond the closed door of the master bathroom.

A disembodied voice emerged through a megaphone. "Police! Come out with your hands up. Now!"

Chapter Fifty-One

Racing out of the bathroom, she and Julian peered out the window of the master bedroom. Dozens of police officers swarmed the plush green lawn behind the house, trampling over the flower beds and securing every exit point.

Panic nearly took her breath away. They were trapped. Julian would be arrested before he got the evidence from Adam Russell. The evidence they believed Uma had hidden in whatever the key on her necklace opened. It wouldn't matter if they could get a 3-D plastic copy if Julian got caught now.

"Look at me." Julian put on the clothes she'd brought into the bathroom.

"This is all my fault. I should have insisted that we leave the moment you were feeling better," Mena said.

"Hey," Julian grabbed her hand and bring it to his lips. The gentleness of his kiss was bittersweet. Was that the last time she'd feel his lips on hers for weeks, or worse, months?

Julian continued. "I'm going to find a way out of here, but you've got to stall them for me. Think you can do that?"

"The house is surrounded," Mena said, swinging an arm toward the window. "Every St. Mateo police officer is out on the yard. How are you going to get out of this?"

Julian gave her a sly smile. "You trust me?"

"Why do you always ask me that?" Mena asked, pressing her hands on her hips.

"Answer the question," Julian demanded.

How could he smile and tease her right now?

"Of course I do," Mena said. "But—"

"Then all I need you to do is go out there and pretend to be my worried, grieving girlfriend. I'll take care of the rest."

"I don't know how you're going to pull this off."

Julian stepped closer to her. "Neither do I. But I'll figure something out when you're not in here distracting me."

Mena detected the worry in his tone. She didn't want to do anything else to add to his concerns.

Mena kissed him on the lips, then exited the room. She rushed down the meandering hallway and into the living room. Pausing, she stared at the police officers swarming around. To her left, near the front door, she saw Detective Desmond Francois nodding intently at another officer, who dispensed orders to the cops on how to search the premises. His eyes met hers. Mena scowled and tried to look confused.

Stomping over to where they stood, Mena said, "Detective Francois, what's going on? What are you doing here?"

Mena gripped the belt of the terry-cloth robe tighter around her.

"Guess you were in the shower when we knocked," Detective Francois quipped, taking a moment to allow his eyes to drift from her face down to her bare feet.

"Yes, I was. But that doesn't explain why you and these officers have barged in."

The other detective standing next to Detective Francois peered at her with suspicious eyes but didn't utter a word.

"How long have you been renting this place?" Detective Francois asked, ignoring her question.

"I'm not," Mena said. She watched as the other officers fanned out and headed down hallways that led to the kitchen and the two guest bedrooms.

"Well, I know you don't own the place, so if you're not renting it, then why are you here? Trespassing?" Detective Francois asked.

"From what I can tell, you and these officers are the ones trespassing. The owner of the home is well aware that I'm here," Mena said.

"That's right, your good pal Beaujean Ali. Nice to have a former PC-5 director as a friend, I guess."

"He's my boss. He understood how worried I was that Julian had been missing for weeks and was gracious enough to let me stay here. I wanted to be close to where Julian had disappeared," Mena explained.

"But you're not worried about Julian anymore, are you?" Detective Francois asked.

Mena's mouth opened, then closed. She had to be very careful. "Why are you here?"

The other detective spoke, his voice deep and commanding. "Ms. Nix, I'm Detective Richland Francois of the St. Mateo police department."

"Francois?" Mena asked.

Detective Des Francois said, "This is my big bro. He's real good at tracking down fugitives like your boyfriend."

Richland frowned, then he continued, "My office received two separate calls about a possible break-in of this home yesterday. Each of them provided footage from their video surveillance systems that depicted a man and a woman emerging from the jungle shortly after midnight two days ago and making their way toward this house. The man, a white male, was clearly laboring, struggling to walk and potentially injured. The woman, a black female, was assisting him. Any of this ring a bell?"

Heart pounding in her chest, Mena forced her voice to remain calm. "No, I didn't see anyone coming close to this house on Sunday, but I admit I was probably asleep at that time. No one knocked on the door asking for help or anything."

The detectives exchanged glances.

"Do yourself a favor and just tell us where Julian is hiding," Des said. "We know you found him. Probably played nursemaid to his injuries, hoping that he'd get strong enough to leave. Where is he?"

"Wait a minute," Mena said, pointing a finger toward Des. "You think Julian survived? You believe he's actually alive and somewhere near here?"

Detective Richland Francois shook his head, then walked away toward a group of officers huddling in the sunken living room.

"Your little act is cute. Trust me, you don't want to face charges for harboring a fugitive. This is not helping your boyfriend. You tell us where he is and I won't even mention you were here. How about that?" Des asked.

"I don't know where he is. All I keep hearing is that Julian died in the fall or drowned shortly after. But if you're here, that must mean there's some hope that Julian survived."

"If that's true, then why are you still here? Why didn't you go back to St. Basil days ago when we officially converted to a search and recovery?" Des narrowed his eyes.

Mena knew she was botching the attempt to convince the detective that she didn't know Julian was alive, but she didn't care. None of the officers had approached the hallway leading to the master bedroom yet. She hoped Julian had enough time to figure a way out without being detected by the police searching the house.

"Look what we found." Richland's voice boomed across the living room.

Mena turned and groaned inwardly.

Crossing the space, Richland held Julian's torn shirt in front of Des. Ripped and torn, the muddy and algae covered fabric was stiff. "I'm guessing if we test this, we'll find Julian's DNA on it."

"Yes, you will," Mena admitted.

"So, stop wasting time and tell us where Julian is hiding," Des interjected.

"I know his DNA will be on that shirt because his old Navy buddy, Sunny Tate, found it in a cave behind the waterfall. Julian worked with her security firm in Africa. When he went missing, they came to the Palmchat Islands to search for him, and this is what they found. Sunny came here two days ago to tell me they were stopping their search, and that shirt was the reason."

"What exactly did she say about this shirt?" Richland asked.

"To Sunny, that shirt was proof that Julian had drowned in the cave. She said there was a cenote inside that was deeper and murkier than they expected. Diving to the bottom was near impossible, and visibility was minimal. She thought Julian had drowned and his shirt had come dislodged and floated to the surface. Julian asked her to give me a letter if he ... if anything bad ever happened to him. So, that's why she was here and that's how I got that shirt."

Handing the shirt to one of the officers who placed it in a plastic bag, Richland asked, "Where's the letter?"

"What?"

"The letter you claim this woman gave to you. Where is it?" Richland demanded.

"I was upset, and I didn't want some goodbye letter from the man I loved. I didn't even know how to deal with my emotions so I just took off into the jungle and I left it there," Mena said, memories of Sunny's visit emerging in her mind. If Sunny hadn't brought her that letter, Mena never would have found Julian in the jungle.

"And you said that was two days ago?"

"Yes."

"About what time?"

"I don't remember. It was late, nighttime."

Richland cleared his throat. "So, you were in the jungle at night two days ago. That would put you there only a few hours before the cameras detected the white male and black female emerging from the jungle, wouldn't you say?"

Her mouth dry, Mena instinctively looked away. She'd said too much.

Des said, "Let's go."

Pushing past her, Des and Richland headed toward the hallway that led to the master bedroom.

Mena rushed behind them. "Wait a minute. Do you even have a search warrant to be here?"

"Spoken like a woman harboring a fugitive," Des said, then lifted a leg and kicked the bedroom door open.

The two detectives entered, guns raised. The room was empty. Window closed.

Mena stood in the doorway, sneaking a glance at the closed door to the bathroom. Des and Richland headed to opposite sides and searched the room. Drawers opened and closed. Pillows sailed across the room. Closets opened. Bed tilted on two legs to peer underneath. Her luggage unzipped and contents strewn across the floor.

Des lifted a prescription pill bottle and shook it toward her. "Antibiotics?"

"I wasn't feeling well—"

"You might want to stop talking before you incriminate yourself further," Richland warned, then lifted two empty cups from the bedside table.

"I'm guessing you like to bring two plates of food with two forks and two cups when you eat. Who knew a woman your size ate so much," Des said, as he held open a plastic bag for Richland to place the dishes inside.

It was just a matter of time before they found Julian hiding in the bathroom. She wouldn't let him go through this alone. If they were going to be busted, it would be together.

The police radio clipped to Richland's belt beeped. Slipping a hand over it, he said, "What did you find?"

A voice responded from the other end. "Nothing. House is clean. So are the grounds. No sign of Montgomery anywhere."

Richland pointed at the bathroom door.

Mena slumped against the door frame. It was about to be over for Julian. And for her.

Des raised his gun and reached for the doorknob. Twisting it slowly, he opened the door and stepped inside. Richland scrutinized her from the middle of the room as he snapped the plastic gloves from his hands.

Des stepped back into the room. A disgusted look creased his face. "It's empty."

Chapter Fifty-Two

Pulling the baseball cap down lower on his face, Julian climbed out of the underground tunnel and scanned the area. He recognized this part of the Valley of Waterfalls, near a secluded fishing town rarely visited by tourists. As Mena held off the cops, Julian had needed a miracle to escape the room before he was found. Hiding out in the vacation home of a member of the island cartel had more perks than he'd bargained for. Darting across the massive walk-in closet of the master bedroom, Julian had thought of hiding behind the air duct, which was covered with a wide three by three-foot metal plate. The location of the duct was perfect, partially obscured by a line of clothes near the front of the closet and more likely to be overlooked than if it was on the back wall.

Grabbing a butter knife from the dinner he'd inhaled only hours earlier, he'd loosened the screws and removed the plate only to find he wasn't staring into an air duct after all.

A tunnel was carved out of the dirt, the bottom lined with wooden boards. The area wasn't big enough to stand, but he could crawl comfortably within the space. The question was, where the hell did it lead to? Julian didn't take time to ponder the answer to that question as he scrambled inside. From the tunnel side, he could easily secure the metal plate back in place, making it nearly impossible for anyone to detect that it had been opened.

Moving quickly in the pitch black, cramped space, Julian covered what felt like miles until he hit a dead end. Reaching a hand against the dirt packed walls, his fingers detected wooden slats rising up one side in a makeshift ladder. Hoisting himself up, he blindly reached the top and pressed on a flat surface which gave way without much effort.

Julian glanced down at his dirt stained clothes. He'd swiped a hat before entering the tunnel, hoping the crude excuse for a disguise would buy him time until he figured out his next move. He hoped Mena was okay back at the house with the police. The last thing he wanted was to crawl his way to freedom while she stayed behind and was arrested for helping him escape.

A part of him wanted to go back through the tunnel and check on her, but that was the worst thing he could do. Most likely he'd get caught, and Mena would be furious at him for not trusting her. Slipping his hand in the jeans, he pulled out the algae covered burner phone. At least he still had a way to call her, but he couldn't do it too soon. The cops were likely watching her every move now and would be suspicious of any calls she received.

Slipping out of the jungle, Julian hustled across the small beach. His canvas tennis shoes sank in the soft damp sand as he approached one of the fishing boats. Several men busied themselves, untangling nets and preparing for the night fishing that brought in fresh seafood for the markets in the morning.

"Hey," Julian said, approaching a man in the boat closest to the jungle. "I got lost hiking and missed the last ferry. I need to get over to Tango Lowlands. Are you headed toward St. Felipe?"

"No, but Rollie is. Two boats over. He fishes close to St. Felipe and could drop you off," the man said without bothering to even look at him. One less person who could recognize him.

Julian stepped away and headed past another boat, stopping at the one where Rollie was working feverishly to spread his net across the interior of the tiny boat.

"Rollie?"

"That's me," Rollie said, pausing his work to glance up at him.

Julian checked his watch. Almost midnight. "Look, I'm low on cash. Got lost hiking and have had a shitty day. Just trying to get over to St. Felipe,

Tango Lowlands. Guy over there said you fish in the area and might help me out."

"How much money you got?" Rollie asked.

Julian shrugged. "Five bucks."

"That'll do," Rollie gave him a wide grin after Julian placed the bill in his hand. "Hope you can swim. I don't have life jackets if the seas get rough."

"Yeah, I'm pretty good at swimming," Julian said. He'd been the fastest swimmer in BUD/S, tackling all the water training and tests easily.

"Well come on now, I don't have all night," Rollie said, ushering him forward.

Julian stepped onto the small boat, then tugged the cap down further to hide his face. Seconds later, Rollie pulled the ripcord. The boat shook from the force of the motor as the old man eased it away from the beach and into the darkened waters. Sea spray pelted Julian's face. The waves slapped against the boat as the low hum of the motor filled the air. The overcast sky blocked the moonlight, bathing the boat and the sea in eerie darkness.

Thirty minutes later, Rollie eased the boat onto the coarse black sand beach of Tango Lowlands. Julian thanked the man, shaking his hand, then stepped out. Turning toward the towering palm trees that stood like a fortress, Julian jogged across the beach. He followed the single road that meandered through the secluded village of recluses. Skirting towards the eastern edge of the lowlands, Julian raced toward Uma Fischer's rental. He slowed as he approached the yellow house across from the horse stables.

Grabbing the burner phone, he accessed the note taking app, found Uma's number and texted.

I'm alive. Get word to your bf that our deal is still on.

Julian slumped down against a tree about fifty yards from the house and propped the phone on his leg, waiting for her reply.

As much as he hated to admit it, he and Russell had a lot in common. At the top of the list, an enemy that both of them wanted to be rid of. The pacemaker kill switch Dumay had placed in Russell without his knowledge was a testament to the woman's diabolical commitment to controlling her criminal empire. Russell was powerless to go against her. Dumay hoped the laptop from Central Sulawesi would give her the same control over Julian. But she hadn't anticipated Russell using it for his own plans.

Twenty minutes later, he got the response.

Will be in touch with instructions.

Minutes later, Uma emerged from the back of the house. She reached down and unlocked the chain that secured three bicycles to a tree in her yard. Mounting the ten speed, Uma took off down the road toward the steep mountain pass that led up and out of the Tango Lowlands.

Julian waited several moments before running over to grab one of the other bikes. Jumping on, he pedaled through the jungle, keeping enough distance to prevent Uma from realizing she was being followed.

Where the hell was she going?

Julian assumed Russell was still in PIIB custody. Had the bastard slipped away from them for a third time? Was she going to lead Julian right to him?

Julian slowed as Uma came to a stop at the bottom of the steep road. Time ticked by excruciatingly slow as Uma struggled up the forty-degree grade toward the top of the mountain. Julian glanced at the burner phone. Almost an hour had passed when Uma finally reached the top. He watched her disappear around the S-curve that led to the St. Felipe Outer Coastal Highway.

Switching the gear on his bike, Julian took a wide arc to build up speed and raced up the incline, covering the distance in about fifteen minutes. Uma biked along the deserted road headed toward the nearest town to Tango Lowlands—King Township. The town was home to the Original Hullabaloo Coffee Shop, had a convenience store and a farmer's market where Tango Lowlands residents sold their crops and fruit to tourists flooding the area each day.

He followed her at a safe distance until she arrived at the town. Pulling his bike to a stop along the side of the road, he watched as Uma clutched a box under her arm. Just past two in the morning, the town was quiet and still. A few streetlights illuminated the area, but most of the roads and businesses were dark. Julian emerged from the shadows and followed her.

Uma walked past a couple of shops hawking Hullabaloo and Felipe Brewery Company souvenirs until she reached the St. Felipe Post and Parcel. She pulled out a small flashlight and pointed it at the deadbolt lock on the door. Inserting a key inside, she turned the knob and disappeared into the post office. Four minutes passed, and she exited the door, empty handed, and locked it behind her. Uma darted across the street to where she'd laid her bike along the sidewalk and jumped back on, pedaling furiously back toward the road that led down to Tango Lowlands.

Julian glanced toward the pastel pink stone building. Uma had a key to the government-controlled post office in King Township. The key around her neck must open a P.O. box inside. What was in the box and why had his text prompted her to bring it here in the middle of the night? Could that be the evidence he needed to clear his name? Was that how she kept Russell's evidence safe by sneaking into the facility with a stolen key? He had to admit, it was a smart plan. No one who worked at the post office would ever see her entering or leaving the building, making it that much harder for Russell's enemies to find his stash.

As soon as he could get the replica key he'd sent to print on his 3-D printer, the sooner he could see exactly what Uma and Russell were hiding in that post office.

Slipping the burner phone from his pocket, he dialed the number he knew by heart.

The line answered after the first ring.

"Julian? Is that you?" Mena asked.

"Yeah," Julian smiled, thankful she'd been able to answer his call. "It's me."

Chapter Fifty-Three

There was nothing left for Julian to do but wait for Mena to arrive from St. Basil. They'd agreed to meet outside the Original Hullabaloo coffee shop at eight in the morning when the first tour buses arrived to sample the Palm-chat Islands' most famous brew. The crowds would provide ample cover and distraction for their meeting. As the dawn broke, Julian had peered inside the window of the post office and saw a wall of small P.O. boxes, none large enough to fit the box Uma had taken inside. But near the back wall was a line of four large mailboxes above the smaller ones. Once he had the replica of Uma's key, he'd enter the post office and try to figure out which one the key opened.

Julian glanced at his watch. It was half-past nine. Mena should have been here by now. The coffee shop had opened at seven for locals and tourists who came to try flavors that could only be obtained at the original shop. Julian had joined the crowd, ordering a blonde double espresso shot and a Hulla-baloo t-shirt to change out of the dirt caked shirt he'd been in all night. He hadn't slept and felt sluggish. The strong coffee had given him the boost he needed. The clean shirt reduced the likelihood of stares, allowing him to blend in with the other tourists.

An hour later, the tour buses arrived, bringing hoards up the mountains to meet with the tour guides dressed in the signature Turquoise t-shirts emblazoned with the Hullabaloo Coffee logo. Each guide led a group of twenty through pathways in the mountains across the street to see the coffee bushes before returning thirty minutes later for the tasting tour. He'd watched three rounds of tours start and end, and still Mena hadn't arrived.

Every thirty minutes, he'd changed locations, adjusting the baseball cap in various positions to alter his look. He didn't want any of the workers to get spooked by seeing him hang around for longer than any of the other tourists. He checked the burner.

No messages from Mena. She hadn't returned any of his calls or texts.

And she was almost two hours late.

Had she run into some complication? Maybe the printer had jammed, and the key didn't print?

He never should have let her go alone.

As soon as he knew what the key likely opened, he should have told her to wait in St. Basil for him. He could have gotten the key himself while she was safely at home in their penthouse at Harmony Towers. What was he thinking, putting her in that position? He'd avoided being caught for weeks. What was a couple more days?

Unease snaked along his spine as he bolted from his chair.

He couldn't wait any longer. He needed to get back to St. Basil and find out what the hell had happened to Mena.

A hand pressed against his back. He smelled the fragrant scent of sandalwood and orange wafting around him. Relief flooded through his body.

"Sorry, I was late. Didn't mean to worry you," Mena said.

Julian spun around, grabbing her in a tight embrace. "What happened? Are you okay?"

Mena nodded as she pressed the key in his hand. "Go. I don't want you to lose anymore time."

"You sure you're okay?" Julian searched her face. Mena looked pensive, frazzled, but beautiful as usual. She was right. He didn't have time to question her about what had held her up. Getting the contents of the mailbox was top priority. He'd get details from her later.

"Julian. Go," Mena insisted. Her coral sundress blew in the wind.

Julian gave her a quick kiss on the lips, then walked casually toward the St. Felipe Post and Parcel. Fingering the plastic key in his hand, he saw the imprint of the number four.

"Good morning, sir!" a man greeted him as he entered.

"Good morning," Julian said, as he walked past the counter toward the four oversized mailboxes at the back of the room. A few tourists milled about, picking up post cards and chatting away about mailing souvenirs to their friends.

Staring ahead, each box had a single number stamped in the center. Julian stretched the key toward box 4, pressing it into the keyhole. The plastic was stiff. Julian applied more force, and the key turned, opening the steel door. Reaching a hand inside, he pulled out a series of boxes.

"Hullaballoo Tea," Julian murmured under his breath as he opened one. Just as he suspected. There was a lot more than tea in the box. The first one contained a thumb drive. Russell said he had evidence on a cell phone that would clear his name. The cell phone had to be in one of these boxes. Opening two more, he found more thumb drives hidden in between the tea bags, but no cell phone until he pulled out the fifth box. A phone was tucked along the long edge, packed in tightly with about twenty tea bags. Slipping it from the box, he pressed the on button, relieved that the battery was still charged.

He tapped the screen and saw only one video file. Pressing the button to lower the volume, he pressed play. Dumay appeared. An almost full body shot as she moved around a dingy holding room at what Julian guessed was Tiverton Prison. From the angle of the camera, he suspected Russell was sitting down in a chair across from her.

"I still don't understand how you plan to get Julian to attack you. He's smarter than that," Russell's voice was heard.

"That's what the burner phone is for. Once you get that smuggled into the court-house, I'll call Julian and let him know we have something that he is desperate to get back. He won't be able to resist coming to me, even if it is to see if I'm bluffing. Once he comes to the room, I'll throw lazirprene in his face. Not too much. Can't have him para-lyzed when the cops come in or it will look like someone attacked both of us."

"I don't know. Seems like a long shot to me."

"I don't do long-shots. My plan is foolproof. Julian will be on the floor, unable to move. I'll place the syringe in his hand to get his fingerprints on it and then inject myself."

"You trust Tubeec Hirad? What if whatever compound he concocted in that vial actually kills you?" Russell asked.

"Then I'll see you in hell. If I die, you'll be dead within the hour and you and I both know I can make that happen. That little ticking time bomb I put in your chest will go kaboom," Dumay said.

"What do you need me to do?" Russell asked.

"Find a way to get that syringe in the courthouse and get rid of my guards. I'll take care of the rest."

Julian pressed end on the video and slipped the phone in his pocket. He'd had doubts the mailbox would have what he needed, but watching the video changed everything. He'd found the smoking gun that would free him.

Julian turned.

The tourists who had been pouring over postcards were being escorted out of the door. Julian stared at the tall, commanding man approaching him. He wore a dark jacket with St. Basil Police Department etched across the chest. Six other police officers flanked him, assault rifles pointed at Julian's face.

"This was too easy. Getting your girlfriend to betray you. You falling for the setup," the cop said, flashing a badge in his face. Detective Desmond Francois.

Julian eased the boxes to the floor and raised his hands in the air.

Detective Francois said, "Julian Montgomery, you're under arrest."

Chapter Fifty-Four

Feet and ankles shackled in heavy prison cuffs, Julian shuffled down the wide hallway separating the near empty jail cells inside the St. Basil Municipal Jail.

"Round three of questioning by the detectives?" Julian called out to the guard. "Or am I being transferred back to Tiverton?"

The past seventy-two hours had been filled with almost nonstop interrogation by Detective Francois. Octavia had been swift and direct with her instructions on which questions he could answer and which the detectives would have to be left wondering.

Julian had protected those he cared about. Denying any knowledge of how he was abducted from Tiverton was easy since TIDES hadn't let him in on that little secret. Weaving a story to carve them out of his days after being free had been tricky. He'd kept Beaujean Ali and the Genesis Gallery out of his new story as well.

"Above my pay grade, Montgomery. I'm throwing you in the holding room and someone else will let you know what's going on," the guard said, remotely accessing the lock on the thick, steel door. He pulled Julian forward as the door slid open and pushed him onto the other side.

Stepping inside the dim holding room, Julian glanced at the four walls, similar to the rooms he'd been in over the past three days as he was hammered with questions for hours on end.

The detective had taunted him about Mena's betrayal that led to his capture. Pointing out how she'd quickly cracked under pressure and agreed to lead the cops to him. He was in custody and he had the love of his life to thank for losing his freedom.

Julian hadn't flinched. He was stoic as he waited for the monologue to end and the questions to resume. Each time Octavia had tried to find out what happened to the evidence from the post office box, the detective evaded her questions. At one point, he'd slipped up and acknowledged that while Adam Russell was still in PIIB custody, the man was stonewalling the federal agents, providing nothing to help or hurt Julian's case.

Julian held his hands out, waiting for the guard to lock him down to the table.

"They said no lock this time." The door slid closed behind the guard, resounding with a loud echo as the lock was re-engaged.

Julian took a deep breath. Drumming his fingers across the table, his mind wandered to Mena.

She'd looked stunning the last time he saw her, dressed in the coral sundress she'd purchased on one of their impromptu trips to St. Killian before Dumay's trial had begun. He remembered how she'd playfully teased him with a mini fashion show as she tried on dress after dress in the exclusive boutique near Avalon Estates. Julian had swelled with love for her, pleased that the five-figure price tag on the piece no longer bothered him. The payday from Timothy Irungu meant he could spoil the woman he loved with the finer things in life.

She'd left with quite a haul that day, but the coral sundress had been his favorite. The warm color made a striking contrast to her deep brown skin, giving her a carefree and exquisite air.

Even though she'd worked with the cops to set him up, he wanted to see her. He yearned to be near her, to talk to her, to tell her—

The door opened slowly.

Julian leaned back in the chair, guarding himself for another onslaught from Detective Francois.

Except, it wasn't either of the detectives walking through the door.

Mena eased past the guard, then stopped, standing near the middle of the room. Her eyes locked onto his. Guilt and shame clouded her beautiful face.

"Hey, don't cry," Julian called out to her. "Mena, come here."

She shook her head. "I shouldn't be here. Not after I betrayed you."

Julian stood quickly and tried to rush toward her. Stumbling over his feet, still shackled at the ankles, he tumbled to the floor.

"Julian, are you okay?" Mena rushed to his side, kneeling next to him.

Laughing, he reached a hand toward her. "Come here, Mena."

"How can you laugh right now? How can you even stand to look at me after what I did to you?" Mena asked.

"Because you did exactly what I would have wanted you to do in that situation. Your life is not worth protecting mine. I never wanted to put you in danger or get you arrested for helping me. You made the right choice," Julian insisted.

Mena slipped an arm around his shoulders as he braced himself and stood. Towering over her, he slipped his arms around her waist and kissed the top of her head.

"You have to know how sorry I am for setting you up. I never meant to hurt you like that," Mena said, looking up at him. His heart broke as tears filled her eyes.

"You think that made me stop loving you? It didn't. You were and you will always be the fierce, brave and courageous love of my life. Mena, you did what you needed to do to survive. I'm proud of you for making that choice. Do you know how much I would have hated to know that you were sitting in a jail cell trying to protect me? You don't belong in a place like this."

"Neither do you. I think there's news about your case. I got a call from Octavia this morning telling me to meet her here at four p.m. Do you have any idea what it could be?"

A soft knock floated from behind. Julian lifted his head to see Octavia Constant entering the room.

Mena turned in his arms to face the lawyer.

"Don't look so scared. It's all good news." Octavia said.

Julian held his breath, waiting to hear what she would say.

"The police were able to authenticate the video recording on the cell phone they found in your possession when they apprehended you. Adam Russell corroborated the footage. The detectives and the D.A. all agree that it is Priscilla Dumay and Adam Russell discussing the plot to set you up at the courthouse. The detectives couldn't uncover any evidence that you'd escaped Tiverton and have closed the investigation as an abduction by an unknown party, likely hired by Priscilla Dumay. In addition, the post office box that you led them to had more damning evidence against Dumay that has the PIIB in high spirits. I wasn't privy to those details and frankly, I didn't think you'd care about that. What's most important is what I'm going to tell you next. All the charges have been dropped against you, Julian. You're a free man."

Mena shrieked, turning toward him. Her smile brightened the entire room as she flung her arms around his neck. "Did you hear that? This nightmare is over!"

Julian lifted her in his arms and kissed her deeply, relieved that he'd stopped Dumay once again.

Chapter Fifty-Five

"You sure you don't mind waiting here for me?" Julian asked, caressing Mena's arms. "A hospital really isn't the best place for you to kick off our vacation."

They wasted no time setting sail after Julian was released from police custody. He wanted the last month of his life to be a distant memory. Living as a recluse for three years before he met Mena had dulled his skills, his ability to see threats and dismantle them before they could do damage. He had underestimated Priscilla Dumay, and that had almost been his downfall. Now he was ready to go on the offensive. He'd need to sharpen his skills, get back the precision he'd lost before he could hold up his end of the deal with Adam Russell.

But not until he got some TLC from Mena.

"Excuse me if it's going to take a while before I feel comfortable being away from you. I know you want to check in on Broman before we sail down to Trinidad. I'm perfectly fine waiting here until your visit is over," Mena said, giving him a playful wink. "I have a bag of snacks and my e-reader with some salacious erotica to get me in the mood. Take your time. I'm not going anywhere."

"Erotica?" Julian raised an eyebrow.

"Where do you think I get all my ideas from?" Mena rubbed her hand down his chest, stopping just short of the belt on his jeans.

"I can't wait to see what you have in store for me next," Julian said. He leaned down and kissed her, brushing his lips seductively across hers.

"Then stop wasting time and go see Broman."

Julian gave her a salute, then turned and walked down the wide hallway toward Broman's new room on the exclusive private floor. Dawn had told him that Broman had been relocated to be with the rest of the patients undergoing the same protocol, some of whom had demanded an extra layer of secrecy and security to participate. Julian figured some forgotten celebrity or politician could be a patient now, dictating the change.

Approaching the door, Julian paused and stared at the name on the gold plaque—B. Garrison. What would Broman think about everything he'd gone through over the past month? Trying to save his own ass, he walked right into Dumay's trap. Would Broman want him to man up and accept the consequences for his actions all those years ago? Or would he understand that he'd changed and maybe even deserved the happiness he had now with Mena?

Julian couldn't be sure. The one thing he did know was that if Broman came out of the coma, he would let his best friend decide his fate. Dumay couldn't be allowed to continue to wreak havoc on the lives of innocent people or to avoid the consequences of her crimes. Despite the terrible things Russell had done under her direction, the man couldn't be blamed for trying to stay alive. The kill switch was a diabolical move and one that Dumay had used not just on Russell, but on the surrogates. By finding the controls and dismantling them, he could save Russell and the rest of the surrogates. Getting the laptop back was more like the cherry on top.

Pulling the door open, Julian stepped inside and stared at the empty bed. The sheets were scrunched toward the bottom, but there was no sign of Broman. Had he awoken from the coma?

"You just missed him," a woman's voice came from behind.

Julian turned and looked at the nurse entering the room. "Is he okay?"

"Julian, right?"

"Yeah, that's me."

"Dawn said you'd be showing up. Broman had a bit of a setback, regressed on the progress he'd been making. Dr. Marsh wanted to take him for some extensive tests. Dawn is with him, but it's not worth waiting. He'll be gone for the next several hours."

"So, the protocol has made him worse, not better?" Julian asked, tension clawing at the back of his neck.

"No, I don't want to give that impression. He was improving at a nice pace and he's lost some of that improvement. But overall, he's still exhibiting better brain function and response to stimuli than he was when he first got here," the nurse explained.

"It's a matter of adjusting the protocol once they figure out why his results declined. Kind of two steps forward, one step back."

"Exactly."

Julian thanked the nurse for the information and headed out of the hospital room. Walking down the wide hallway, he glanced at the names outside the doors, wondering if they were all patients undergoing the same protocol as Broman. Too many people whose lives had been stolen as they lay trapped in a coma. He hoped they all made it out—

Julian paused at one door, staring at the name on the plaque.

P. Dumay

Maybe all except one.

Glancing around, Julian expected a guard to be posted at the entrance to her hospital room, but the area was empty except for a few nurses huddled at the nurses' station. They were pointing at something on the computer screen, engaged in a heated discussion.

Against his better judgment, Julian pushed the door inward and stepped inside, closing it behind him. Across the room, Priscilla Dumay lay still in the bed. Her dark tresses spread out on the peach colored sheets. The room had a warm, cozy feel. Small tables rested on each side of the bed, with lamps emitting a soft light. A sofa was tucked away in the corner of the room, near the window. A soft throw blanket hung from the armrest.

Everything that Dumay had expected to happen while she was in the coma had been stopped. The urge to let the bitch know was too strong for Julian to resist. He grew closer to the bed. Dumay's chest rose and fell as medical equipment hissed and beeped in the room. If he wanted to put an end to her, this was a good opportunity.

Or was that what she wanted?

Another chance to destroy his life because he couldn't exercise self-control. As the saying went, fool me once shame on you. Fool me twice ...

Julian stopped near the edge of the bed. "You thought you had it all planned perfectly, didn't you? You would ruin my life and make sure I ended up in prison, get Zak to kill me while you ... what? Spent the rest of your days in a medical facility pretending to be incapacitated after emerging from the coma? What was your end game?"

Dragging a hand down the back of his head, Julian took a quick glance over his shoulder, then turned back toward the bed.

"Guess what? Your plan didn't work. I'm still a free man. I'm still going to be the one to make sure you pay for your crimes. I'm going to be the one to make sure you suffer the loss of your freedom for trying to hurt Mena. You thought I fucked up your life before. Just wait until what I do next."

Julian walked closer to her. He stared down at the serene face with eyes closed. His heart skipped a beat. He reached a hand toward her face. That face—

"Fuck!" Julian said.

Without a doubt, the woman in this bed was ... not ... Priscilla Dumay.

Chapter Fifty-Six

Mena spun around in the empty hallway. How had she gotten so turned around? The directions to the private waiting area from the nurse had seemed simple before Mena turned into a maze of intersecting and haphazard halls. Retracing her steps was pointless. She needed to find someone to lead her back to where she'd been trying to go in the first place.

An elevator dinged behind her.

Mena turned toward the sound, hoping whoever was exiting would be a Good Samaritan and help her out. A man in a white lab coat exited and turned down the hallway, heading away from her. Mena hurried toward him.

"Excuse me, sir. I'm lost. Could you help me find the waiting room on this floor?" Mena asked, trying to temper her embarrassment.

The man turned around to face her, his eyes registering the same shock that shot through her body. Mena's hands flew to her mouth, stifling the scream that almost escaped.

She frowned. "Michael? What the hell are you doing here?"

"I ... um ...," Michael stammered, then regained his composure. "I work here."

"Work? Here? No, you can't. You work in New York City. You live in New York City. There's no way you can work in the Aerie Islands," Mena said, her voice hitting a higher octave.

"Why don't we talk about this in my office?" Michael said, as two other medical professionals turned the corner and headed in their direction.

"Fine," Mena said, following him toward an office on the left side of the hallway. Walking inside, Mena glanced at the desk and two chairs crammed into the tight space. She walked toward the far wall and watched as Michael closed the door.

His eyes downcast, Michael stuffed his hands in the pockets of his lab coat. "I owe you an apology. My behavior the last time we were together was beyond deplorable. I never want to make you feel afraid—"

"Cut the crap, Michael. Explain to me why you are in the Aerie Islands. When did you take a job here and for God's sake, why would you?" Mena demanded.

Michael exhaled and walked behind his desk, easing down into the leather chair. His eyes bore into hers as he said, "Because I wanted to be close to you."

"What happened to your practice in New York?" Mena noticed the wedding band on his finger. The same one she'd placed there when they'd gotten married years ago.

"I resigned, sold the apartment on Central Park West and moved here. Mena, you must hate me right now because of what happened at your penthouse. But I swear to you, I'm going to do everything I can to make it up to you. To get your forgiveness. I will prove to you that I would never hurt you. I love you."

"You don't know what it means to love someone, Michael. I don't know how many ways I can say this to you. We are over. Divorce papers or not, I'm never going to be in a relationship with you again," Mena said.

"Don't say that."

"What is it going to take for you to get that through your head?"

"So, you told Julian about us? That you're still my wife?"

Mena looked away. She planned to tell Julian the truth tonight, while they sailed to Trinidad. On the open seas, neither of them would be able to leave and would be forced to deal with the bombshell she had dropped. Mena hoped he would understand after she explained to him what happened and why it took her so long to tell him the truth.

"I haven't told him yet, but I'm going to. This secret is not something you can hold over my head any longer. Julian and I will fight you, together," Mena said.

Michael scoffed. "You think it's going to be that easy? He's just going to forgive and forget. The two of you sailing away on your happily ever after. You're delusional if you think that brute is going to understand that you belong to me."

"I do not belong to you!" Mena screamed. "You mean nothing to me, Michael. Your claim on me is only on paper. You don't have my heart or my love."

"Maybe not right now, but I'll still be here after Julian can't find a way to forgive you. All the love you have for him won't be enough for him to get past your lies. Trust me. I know how it feels to be in that situation. I'll be able to help you through that pain," Michael said.

"I can't deal with you anymore," Mena turned and marched toward the door. A hand gripped her arm, yanking her backward. She turned and stared up into Michael's hazel eyes.

"Do not walk away from me," Michael whispered, snaking his arm around her waist. "You are my wife. Mine! I will not let another man have you. Ever. Do you understand me? I have ways to make sure that Julian walks away from you for good."

"Let go of me. Julian loves me more than you ever could. Will he be upset? Of course, but not enough to end our relationship," Mena said, pushing away from Michael.

"Does he love you more than Broman? I'm sure if it came down to his best friend getting his life back and his love for you, he'd choose Broman every time. I could make him choose," Michael said.

"How do you know about Broman?"

Michael sneered. "I make it my business to know everything about my patients, including how they ended up in a coma. A devastating story, really. One even Broman's wife doesn't know. Julian Montgomery, in the jungles of Central Sulawesi, tried to play the hero and hunt down a terrorist. But he never stopped to consider that he was leading the terrorist to the SEAL team location instead. Four SEALs died because of Julian. His best friend in a coma for years. Julian owes that man his life back. I can give it to Broman, but Julian will have to do something for me."

Mena slapped Michael. Her hand stinging from the force of the blow. "You bastard!"

Michael grabbed her shoulders. "I told you I would do anything to get you back."

Mena twisted in his grasp.

"What the hell is going on here?"

Mena's heart stopped as she recognized Julian's voice from behind her. No. This could not be happening.

Michael released his grip and stepped away from her.

She took a deep breath.

"Mena, why are you in here with Broman's doctor?" Julian asked, his tone suspicious as his eyes darted between them.

Mena opened her mouth to speak, but no words came out. Behind Julian were two police officers.

One of the officers pushed past Julian and addressed Michael. "Dr. Marsh, the woman in the hospital room assigned to Priscilla Dumay is actually not Priscilla Dumay. Did you have her moved to a different room?"

Michael shook his head, frowning slightly. "No, Priscilla should still be in her room. What do you mean that's not her?"

"I'm going to need you to come with me and bring all of your medical records for Priscilla Dumay with you," the officer said.

"Sure thing," Michael said, grabbing a tablet from the desk and heading toward the door.

Julian stepped in front of Michael, stopping him from passing. "What the fuck was going on in here? Why were you in here alone with Mena?"

Michael pushed past Julian, then turned and said, "I have every right to be in a room alone with my wife!"

Epilogue

Tension crawled through Julian's muscles as he grabbed clothes from the chest in the closet and shoved them into the duffel bag. His phone beeped. Julian pulled it from the back pocket of his pants and glanced at the confirmation text from the airline. His flight was on time and would depart in three hours.

Not nearly soon enough.

The walls were closing in, suffocating and oppressive, threatening to crush him. He battled his memories, flashes of that day in the Aerie Islands. His anger hadn't subsided. In two days, the inferno blazing within him had intensified. He had to get away before he did something he regretted.

Something he wouldn't be able to take back.

If he decided he wanted to take it back.

Grabbing a couple pair of shoes, he pushed them into the overstuffed bag and wrestled with the zipper.

The scent of sandalwood and oranges wafted into the closet, haunting him. He could feel her watching him. But he couldn't look at her. Not yet. Every time he stared in Mena's face now, he saw another man's wife. A woman who belonged to someone other than him. She'd stood before God, her family and friends, and pledged to love that man until death did them part. And they were still married. Even now. Even when she insisted that he and not that fucker was the man she wanted to spend the rest of her life with.

"How long will you be gone?" Mena asked, her voice low and soft.

Julian didn't want to look at her puffy face, swollen from crying through the night. He didn't want to be reminded that Mena was still the legally and lawfully wedded wife of Dr. Michael Marsh. The motherfucker in the pictures with Mena he'd received when he was in Tiverton. Broman's doctor. The man who had his best friend's life in his hands was the same man who had taken Mena away from him.

Buzzed from finishing two bottles of vodka as he slept on the balcony last night, Julian was numb. His heart had been ripped from his chest. He couldn't remember how it felt to love Mena. How it felt to risk everything, his freedom, his life, for her.

"Don't know," Julian muttered, slinging the duffel bag over his shoulder. He turned and faced Mena as she stood in the doorway of the closet, blocking him from leaving. For the first time, she looked like a stranger to him. Too much he hadn't known about her. Too much she hadn't trusted him enough to share.

"What about us?" Mena asked.

"What about us," Julian deadpanned, dropping the duffel bag onto the floor.

"I thought maybe we should talk more about everything," Mena said, stumbling over her words.

They'd talked enough. He knew every detail about Mena's marriage to the polygamist, Dr. Michael Marsh. She'd told him every excruciating detail from the moment she'd first met the bastard in Miami to the day his other wife showed up on her doorstep. The shock of finding out Michael had three other wives had destroyed her. She'd thought her marriage was void because of the other women. Coming to St. Basil had been like pushing the reset button on her life, putting everything behind her. But she'd been wrong. It wasn't behind her.

Julian's brain processed and understood what happened. But his heart had been decimated. She'd kept so much from him, never trusting him with her deepest and darkest moments. How could she say she loved him, but not truly have shared herself with him? Who the fuck had he fallen in love with? Did he even know?

He'd bared all of his sins, laid them before her so she'd know exactly who he was asking her to take a chance on. To fall in love with.

Mena hadn't reciprocated. What else was she hiding from him? Things that she hadn't been forced to admit.

"There's nothing more to say, Mena. This isn't a complicated situation. Legally, you're still ..." Julian paused, struck by how hard it was for him to say the words out loud. He took a deep breath and continued, "married to Dr. Michael Marsh. Now, I know why you turned down my marriage proposal."

"You have to know that I wanted to say yes. There's nothing more that I want in this world than to be your wife."

"But you can't be my wife. Not when you're still his wife."

Mena looked away, waving a hand absently under her running nose.

The floodgates he had tried to suppress opened, and he knew he couldn't close them now. "Why didn't you tell me?"

Mena's body shook with a fresh wave of tears.

"Mena! What the fuck did you think I was going to do?" Julian screamed, unable to stop himself.

"What was I supposed to say? Oh, by the way, Julian. I know you proposed, and you just bought this gorgeous penthouse to prove to me how much you love me, but we need to move to Florida for six months so I can get a divorce from my husband who I thought I was free from?" Mena rambled.

A disgusted laugh erupted from his throat. "Yeah. You know you could've said it just like that. Would've been fucking better than finding out from that bastard!"

"I was going to tell you myself that night—"

"I don't even understand you. I thought I did, but this proves that I don't. We really don't know each other, do we?"

"We know the things that matter most. I panicked and tried to get rid of Michael before that stupid marriage wrecked what we have. I know it was a mistake. I wish I had been honest."

"You really thought *that* would wreck us? Really? Don't you know *me* by now? Haven't I proved to you how much I fucking love you! What sense does this make? Doesn't matter that I risked my goddamn life to protect you, to save you from ruthless terrorists across two damn continents. That's not enough for you to believe in me," Julian paused and took a deep breath. Yelling at Mena wasn't helping.

The sound of her whimpered cries stretched toward him, but he didn't even feel the pull to comfort her. His anger was too strong, blinding him.

Mena pleaded with him. "I made a horrible mistake. I'm so sorry."

"Don't be sorry. Fix it," Julian said, grabbing the duffel bag. He had to get going before he missed the boarding window for his flight.

"What do you mean?"

"I mean, get the fucking divorce. Go back to fucking Florida or whatever the fuck you have to do and end your marriage to Michael Marsh. I don't know how long I'm going to be gone, but when I get back, I want to know that part of your life is over."

Mena dragged a hand down her face. She nodded as she stared back at him. He saw a flash of the woman he loved. He ached to touch her, but he couldn't.

Silence stretched between them until Mena said. "I don't want you to go."

"I know," Julian said. He believed she regretted lying to him, but right now he couldn't see past his own pain to forgive her.

"If I could go back and change how I handled all of this, I would. I would've told you the truth the moment I found out. I hate how much I hurt you. I hate seeing the disappointment in your eyes. The hurt. The betrayal."

Julian closed the space between them. His face so close to hers, he could feel her breath caressing his skin. "What else do you see?"

Mena stared into his eyes, her breath hitching in her throat as she moved to touch his face but stopped herself.

This was the test. If they were going to survive, she'd have to answer him. She'd have to truly see him. "Say it. Tell me what else you see in my eyes."

Mena whispered one word. "Love."

His muscles relaxed as he slipped past Mena and walked into the massive bedroom they shared. Turning back to her, Julian said, "Try not to forget that while I'm gone."

Thank you for reading! I hope you loved the continuation of the soul mates love story of Julian and Mena. Julian took extreme risks to prove his innocence, thwarting Priscilla's plans of revenge. But his happiness was brief when Michael revealed that he was Mena's husband!

If you enjoyed THE FALLEN HERO, then I know you'll love the last book in the series, THE UNEXPECTED HERO.

Julian's world was ripped apart when he found out Mena was married to another man.

Mena and Julian face the biggest test of their relationship as Julian struggles to forgive her for not trusting him with the truth.

Lurking in the shadows, Priscilla Dumay hasn't given up on getting revenge as she plans diabolical attacks on every person that dared to cross her.

Can Julian and Mena finally stop Priscilla before she destroys their love and their lives?

CLICK HERE TO READ THE UNEXPECTED HERO TODAY!

https://bit.ly/theunexpectedhero

If you enjoyed my novel, I'd appreciate your help in spreading the word, including telling a friend. Reviews help readers find books! I would love it if you left a review of THE FALLEN HERO on Amazon, BookBub or your favorite book site.

Angel Vane has been entertaining readers with her brand of crime thrillers for women. Now you can get one of her novellas for FREE, you just need to go to the link and tell her where to send it:

GET MY FREE SHORT STORY NOW
https://BookHip.com/PJQDTT

Also by Angel Vane

HERO IN PARADISE SERIES

Ex-Navy Seal Julian Montgomery fights off threats to the new life he's trying to build with art conservator Mena Nix. A gripping romantic suspense series with diabolical enemies, unpredictable twists and steamy romance!

THE HIDDEN THREAT (Prequel Novella)

THE ACCIDENTAL HERO

THE RELENTLESS HERO

THE FALLEN HERO

THE UNEXPECTED HERO

STAND-ALONE NOVELS

Stand-alone romantic mystery novels all set in the fictional Palmchat Islands.

THE UNWORTHY WIFE

THE SILENT ENEMY

About the Author

Angel Vane has a dramatic personality, is prone to exaggeration and is in perpetual pursuit of her creative muse. She loves writing, reading, traveling, spa days and soap operas. Angel resides in Tomball, Texas.

For more information:
angelvaneauthor@gmail.com

About the Publisher

BonzaiMoon Books is a family-run, artisanal publishing company created in the summer of 2014. We publish works of fiction in various genres. Our passion and focus is working with authors who write the books you want to read, and giving those authors the opportunity to have more direct input in the publishing of their work.

For more information:
www.bonzaimoonbooks.com
info@bonzaimoonbooks.com

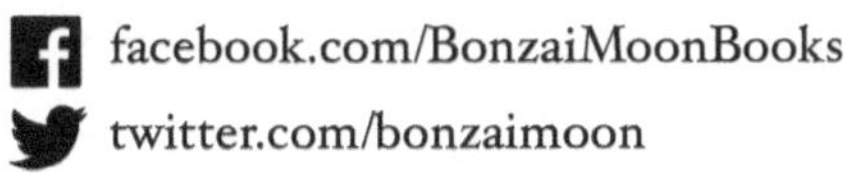
facebook.com/BonzaiMoonBooks
twitter.com/bonzaimoon